0712 $6 95

Additional Praise for *Werewolves in Their Youth*

"Werewolves in Their Youth bears the mark of the master craftsman. Chabon casts his net into the sea of language and brings it up brimming. Glittering, perfect, living sentences unskein across the page, but that's not all: This fisher of words also fillets out the insights lurking beneath the play of syllables....This man's gift is supernatural."
—Susan Balee, *Philadelphia Inquirer*

"Masterful...Michael Chabon possesses such intimacy with language that his psychologically acute metaphoric descriptions bloom in the mind with as much prismatic dazzle as the fireworks ignited by psychedelics.... [A] knockout volume...A structural marvel...Chabon is a luminous and thrilling writer: funny, imaginative, insightful, and madly in love with our wild and timid species."
—Donna Seaman, *Chicago Tribune*

"Engaging...His writing just gets better with time.... As wicked pleasures go, this delicious, disturbing, and masterful collection is a killer."
—Autumn Stephens, *San Francisco Chronicle*

"Clever and sharply crafted verbal confections."
—*Entertainment Weekly*

"The stories are often delightful, always disturbing, and oddly memorable."
—Barbara Fisher, *Boston Globe*

"Genuine Fitzgerald territory—that place where young married couples dance separately with strangers, where former football heroes stare down the dwindling time clock of youth, where the houses mock their inhabitants, and every party is a disaster waiting to happen. And like Fitzgerald's sentences, Chabon's can be as perfect and self-contained as plovers' eggs."
—*Salon*

"Disturbing and glib, outrageous, sad, and poetic at turns, Michael Chabon's stories embrace the major heartbreaks and minor debacles that congeal into, well, life."
—Chris Solomon, *Seattle Times*

"The nine stories in *Werewolves* weave luminous prose with wrenching imagery.... Chabon wields his wit and insight like a scalpel, flensing away the surface details of troubled lives to show the cancerous core."
—*Denver Post*

ALSO BY MICHAEL CHABON

The Mysteries of Pittsburgh
A Model World and Other Stories
Wonder Boys

Werewolves

in Their Youth

Stories

MICHAEL CHABON

Picador
New York

Picador® is a U.S. registered trademark and is used by St. Martin's Press under license from Pan Books Limited.

For information on Picador Reading Group Guides, as well as ordering, please contact the Trade Marketing department at St. Martin's Press.
Phone: 1-800-221-7945 extension 763
Fax: 212-677-7456
E-mail: trademarketing@stmartins.com

The stories in this work originally appeared in *Esquire, GQ, Harper's, The New Yorker,* and *Playboy.* "Spikes" was originally published in *Save Our Strength.*

ISBN 0-312-25438-5

First published in the United States by Random House

10 9 8 7

To Ayelet

Contents

Werewolves in Their Youth

Werewolves in Their Youth

I HAD known him as a bulldozer, as a samurai, as an android programmed to kill, as Plastic Man and Titanium Man and Matter-Eater Lad, as a Buick Electra, as a Peterbilt truck, and even, for a week, as the Mackinac Bridge, but it was as a werewolf that Timothy Stokes finally went too far. I wasn't there when it happened. I was down in the ravine at the edge of the schoolyard, founding a capital for an empire of ants. "Now, of course, this right here, this lovely structure, is the Temple of El-bok," I explained to the ants, adopting the tone my mother employed to ease newly-weds through the emptied-out rooms of the depressed housing market in which she spent her days. I pointed to a pyramid of red clay at the center of a plaza paved with the crazy cross-hatching of my handprints. "And this, natu-rally, is the Palace of the Ant Emperor. But, ha ha, you knew that, of course. Okay, and over *here*"—I pointed to a sort of circular corral I'd formed by poking a row of sharp-ened twigs into the ground—"all of this is for keeping your ant *slaves*. Isn't that nice? And over here's where you milk your little aphids." On the heights above my city stood the mound of an ordinary antville. All around me the cold red earth was stitched with a black embroidery of ants. By dint of forced transport and at the cost of not a few severed abdomens and thoraxes I succeeded in getting some of the ants to follow the Imperial Formic Highway, a broad groove in the clay running out the main gates of the city, up the steep slope of the ravine, and thence out into the tremendousness of the world. With my store of snapped-off ant body parts I pearled the black eyes of El-bok the Pitiless, an ant-shaped idol molded into the apex of the pyramid. I had just begun to describe, to myself and to the ants, the complicated rites sacred to the god whose worship I was imposing on them when I heard the first screams from the playground.

"Oh, no," I said, rising to my feet. "Timothy Stokes." The girls screamed at Timothy the same way every time he came after them—in unison and with a trill that sounded almost like delight, as if they were watching the family cat trot past with something bloody in its jaws. I scrambled up the side of the ravine and emerged as Timo-thy, shoulders hunched, arms outstretched, growled real-istically and declared that he was hungry for the throats of puny humans. Timothy said this or something like it every time he turned into a werewolf, and I would not have been too concerned if, in the course of his last trans-formation, he hadn't actually gone and bitten Virginia Pease on the neck. It was common knowledge around school that Virginia's parents had since written a letter to the principal, and that the next time Timothy Stokes hurt somebody he was going to be expelled. Timothy was, in our teacher Mrs. Gladfelter's words, one strike away from an out, and there was a widespread if unarticulated hope among his classmates, their parents, and all of the teachers at Copland Fork Elementary that one day soon he would provide the authorities with the excuse they needed to pack him off to Special School. I stood there awhile, above my little city, rolling a particle of ant between my fingers, watching Timothy pursue a snarling, lupine course along the hopscotch crosses. I knew that someone ought to do something to calm him down, but I was the only person in our school who could have any reason to want to save Timothy Stokes from expulsion, and I hated him with all my heart.

"I have been cursed for three hundred years!" he declaimed. He was wearing his standard uniform of white dungarees and a plain white undershirt, even though it was a chilly afternoon in October and all the rest of us had long since been bundled up for autumn in corduroy and down. Among the odd traits of the alien race from which Timothy Stokes was popularly supposed to have sprung was an apparent imperviousness to cold; in the midst of a February snowstorm he would show up on your doorstep, replying to your mother's questions only when she addressed him as Untivak, full of plans to build igloos and drink seal blood and chew raw blubber, wearing only the usual white jeans and T-shirt, plus a pair of giant black hip boots that must have belonged to his father—an undiscussed victim of the war in Vietnam. Timothy had just turned eleven, but he was already as tall as Mrs. Gladfelter and his bodily strength was famous; earlier that year, in the course of a two-week period during which Timothy believed himself to be an electromagnetic crane, we had on several occasions seen him swing an iron manhole cover straight up over his head.

"I have been cursed to stalk the night through all eternity," he went on, his voice orotund, carrying all across the playground. When it came to such favorite subjects as lycanthropy and rotary-wing aircraft, he used big words, and had facts and figures accurately memorized, and sounded like the Brainiac some took him for, but I knew he was not as intelligent as his serious manner and heavy black spectacles led people to believe. His grades were always among the lowest in the class. "I have been searching for prey as lovely as *you!*"

He lunged toward the nearest wall of the cage of girls around him. The girls peeled away from him as though sprayed with a hose, bumped shoulders, clung shrieking to each other's sleeves. Some of them were singing the song we sang about Timothy Stokes,

> Timothy Stokes,
> Timothy Stokes,
> You're going to the home
> for crazy folks,

and the one singing the loudest was Virginia Pease herself, in her furry black coat and her bright red tights. She was standing screened by Sheila and Siobhan Fahey, her best friends, dangling one skinny red leg toward Timothy and then jerking it away again when Timothy swiped at it with one of his werewolf paws. Virginia had blond hair, and she was the only girl in the fifth grade with pierced ears *and* painted fingernails, and Timothy Stokes was in love with her. I knew this because the Stokeses lived next door to us and I was privy to all kinds of secrets about Timothy that I had absolutely no desire to know. I forbade myself, with an almost religious severity, to show Timothy any kindness or regard. I would never let him sit beside me, at lunch or in class, and if he tried to talk to me on the playground I ignored him; it was bad enough that I had to live next door to him.

It was toward Virginia that Timothy now advanced, a rattling growl in his throat. She drew back behind her girl-friends, and their screaming now grew less melodious, less purely formal. Timothy crouched down on all fours. He rolled his wild white eyes and took a last look around him. That was when he saw me, halfway across the yellow distance of the soccer field. He was looking at me, I thought, as though he hoped I might have something I wanted to tell him. Instantly I dropped flat on my belly, my heart pounding the way it did when I was spotted trying to spy on a baseball game or a birthday party. I slid down into the ravine backward, doing considerable damage to the ramparts of my city, flattening one wing of the imperial palace. All through the ten minutes of growling and alarums that followed I lay there, without moving. I lay with my cheek in the dirt. At first I could hear the girls shouting for Mrs. Gladfelter, and then I heard Mrs. Gladfelter herself, sounding very angry, and then I thought I could hear the voice of Mr. Albert, the P.E. teacher, who always stepped in to break up fights when it was too late, and some bully had already knocked the glasses from your face and sent your books spinning away across the floor of the gym. Then the bell sounded the end of recess, and everything got very quiet, but I just stayed there in the ravine, at the gates of the city of the ants.

As I tried to repair the damage I had done to its walls, I told myself that I didn't feel sorry at all for stupid old Timothy Stokes, but then I would remember the confused look in his eyes as I had abandoned him to his fate, to all the unimaginable things that would be done to him in the fabulous corridors of the Special School. I kept recalling something that I had heard Timothy's mother say to mine, just a couple of days earlier. I should explain that at this point in my childhood I had acquired the shameful habit of eavesdropping on the conversations of adults, particularly my parents, and, worse, of snooping in their drawers—a pastime or compulsion that in recent months had led me to discover nude photographs of my mother taken with my father's Polaroid; school documents and physicians' reports detailing my own learning disability, juvenile obesity, hyperactivity, and loneliness; and, most recently, a letter from my mother's attorney cheerily explaining that if my father persisted in his current pattern of violent behavior he could be restrained from coming anywhere near my mother ever again—a development for which I had on certain bad evenings prayed to God with desperation, but which, now that it had become an actual possibility, struck me as the most miraculous of all the awful wonders set loose upon the world in the course of the past year. There had been no mention in the lawyer's letter of whether my father would be allowed to come near *me*. At any rate, I had been hanging over the banister of the hall stairs the other morning, listening in, when Mrs. Stokes—her name was Althea—came over to retrieve a two-hundred-dollar pair of Zeiss binoculars Timothy had given me the day before in exchange for three tattered Mister Miracle comic books and a 1794 one-dollar coin that he believed to be genuine but that I knew perfectly well to have been a premium my father received several years before on subscribing to *American Heritage*.

"You know," Althea Stokes had told my mother, in that big, sad donkey voice of hers, "your little Paul is Timothy's only friend."

I DECIDED to spend the afternoon in the ravine. The sun started down behind the embankment, and the moon, rising early, emerged from the rooftops of the houses somebody was putting up in front of the school—brand-new split-level houses my mother and her company were having a hard time selling. The moon, I noticed, was not quite full. As I worked to rebuild the ghost town I had made, I felt keenly that my failure to help Timothy was really only the latest chapter in a lifelong history of inadequacy and powerlessness. The very last line of that letter I'd found among my mother's papers was "I think we should be able to have this thing wrapped up by November fifteenth." If this was true, then I had less than one month in which to effect a reconciliation between my parents—a goal that, apart from wishing for, I had done nothing at all to bring about. Now it appeared that my father would not even be *allowed* to come home anymore. My fingers grew stiff and caked with clay, and my nose ran, and I cried for a while and then stopped crying, and still it seemed that my absence from the classroom went unnoticed. I was feeling pretty sorry for myself. After a while I gave up on my city building and just lay there on my back, gazing up at the moon. I didn't hear the scrape of footsteps until they were just above my head.

"Paul?" said Mrs. Gladfelter, leaning over the lip of the ravine, hands against her thighs. "Paul Kovel, what on earth are you doing out here?"

"Nothing," I said. "I didn't hear the bell."

"Paul," she said. "Now, listen to me. Paul, I need your help."

"With what?" I didn't think she looked angry, but her face was upside down and it was hard to tell.

"Well, with Timothy, Paul. I guess he's just very wound up right now. You know. Well, he's pretending he's a werewolf today, and even though that's fine, and we all know how Timothy is sometimes, we have serious things to discuss with him, and we'd like him to stop pretending for just a little while."

"But what if he isn't pretending, Mrs. Gladfelter?" I said. "What if he really is a werewolf?"

"Well, maybe he is, Paul, but if you would just come inside and talk to him for a little bit, I think we might be able to persuade him to change back into Timothy. You're his friend, Paul. I asked him if he'd like to talk to you, and he said yes."

"I'm *not* his friend, Mrs. Gladfelter. I swear to God. I can't do anything."

"Couldn't you try?"

I shook my head. I hoped that I didn't start crying again.

"Paul, Timothy is in trouble." All at once her voice grew sharp. "He needs your help, and I need your help, too. Now if you come right this minute, and get up out of that dirt, then I'll forget that you didn't come in from recess. If you don't come back inside, I'll have to speak to your mother." She held out her hand. "Now, come on, Paul. Please."

And so I took her hand, and let her pull me out of the ravine and across the deserted playground, aware that in doing so I was merely proving the unspoken corollary that my mother had left hanging, the other morning, in the air between her and Mrs. Stokes. There was a song about me, too, I'm afraid—a popular little number that went

> What's that smell-o?
> Paul Kovel-o
> He's a big fat hippo Jell-O
> He's a snoop
> He smells like poop
> He smells like tomato beef
> Alphabet soup

because at some point in my career I had acquired the reputation, inexplicable to me, for exuding an odor of Campbell's tomato soup—a reputation that no amount of bathing or studied avoidance of all the brands and varieties of canned soup ever rid me of. As if this were not bad enough, I had to go around with a thick wad of electrician's tape on the hinge of my eyeglasses and a huge Western-style tooled-leather belt stuffed one and a half times around the loops of my trousers. It had been my father's belt, and bore his name, Melvin, stamped along its length, in big yellow capital letters set amid bright green cacti, like a cheery frontier invitation for all to come and yank my underpants up into my crack. I sat alone at lunch under an invisible and mysterious hood of tomato smell— a scent dangerously similar to the acrid tang of vomit— walked myself home from school, and figured in all the dramas, ceremonials, and epic struggles of my classmates only in the unlikely but mythologically requisite role of King of the Retards. Timothy Stokes, I knew, as I followed Mrs. Gladfelter down the long, silent hallway to the office, hating him more and more with each step, was *my* only friend.

He was sitting in a corner of the office, trapped in an orange vinyl armchair. There was a roman numeral three scratched into his left cheek and his brilliant white shirt and trousers were patterned with a camouflage of grass and dirt and asphalt. His chest swelled and then subsided deeply, swelled and subsided. Mr. Buterbaugh, the principal, was standing over him, arms folded across his chest. He was watching Timothy, looking amazed and skeptical and somehow offended. Mrs. Maloney, the school secretary, who a dozen times a month typed the cruel words "tomato soup" onto the cafeteria menus that my mother cruelly affixed with a magnet to our refrigerator, rose from behind her desk when we came in, and gathered up her purse and sweater.

"I finally reached Timothy's mother, Mrs. Gladfelter," she said. "She was at work, but she said she would be here as soon as she could." She lowered her voice. "And we called Dr. Schachter, too. His office said he'd call back." She cleared her throat. "So I'm going to take my break now."

At two o'clock every day, I knew, Mrs. Maloney sneaked around to the windowless side of the school building and stood behind the power transformer, smoking an Eve cigarette. I turned, with a sinking heart, and looked at the clock over the door to Mr. Buterbaugh's office. I hadn't missed the whole afternoon, after all, lying there in the ditch for what had seemed to me like many hours. There was still another ninety minutes to be gotten through.

"Well, now, Timothy." Mrs. Gladfelter took me by the shoulders and maneuvered me around her. "Look who I found," she said.

"Hey, Timothy," I said.

Timothy didn't look up. Mrs. Gladfelter gave me a gentle push toward him, in the small of my back.

"Why don't you sit down, Paul?"

"No." I stiffened, and pushed the other way.

"Please sit down, Paul," said Mr. Buterbaugh, showing me his teeth. Although his last name forced him to adopt a somewhat remote and disciplinarian manner with the other kids at Copland, Mr. Buterbaugh always took pains with me. He made me swap high fives with him and kept up with my grades. At first I had attributed his kindness to the fact that he was a little heavy and had probably been a fat kid, too, but then I kept hearing from my mother about how she had run into Bob Buterbaugh at this singles' bar or that party and he had said the nicest things about me. I stopped pushing against Mrs. Gladfelter and let myself be steered toward the row of orange chairs. "That's the way. Sit down and wait with Timothy until his mother gets here."

"Mr. B. and I will be sitting right inside his office, Paul."

"No!" I didn't want to be left alone with Timothy, not because I was afraid of him but because I was afraid that somebody would come into the office and see us sitting there, two matching rejects in matching orange chairs.

"That's enough now, Paul," said Mr. Buterbaugh, his friendly smile looking more false than usual. I could see that he was very angry. "Sit down."

"It's all *right*," said Mrs. Gladfelter. "You see what you can do about helping Timothy turn back into Timothy. We're just going to give you a little privacy." She followed Mr. Buterbaugh into his office and then poked her head back around the door. "I'm going to leave this door open, in case you need us. All right?"

"This much," I said, holding my hands six inches apart.

There were three chairs next to Timothy's. I took the farthest, and showed him my back, so that anyone passing by the windows of the office would not be able to conclude that he and I were engaged in any sort of conversation at all.

"Are you expelled?" I said. There was no reply. "Are you, Timothy?" Again he said nothing, and I couldn't stop myself from turning around to look at him. "Timothy, are you expelled?"

"I'm not Timothy, Professor," said Timothy, gravely but not without a certain air of satisfaction. He didn't look at me. "I'm afraid your precious antidote didn't work."

"Come on, Timothy," I said. "Cut it out. The moon's not even full today."

Now he turned the werewolf glint of his regard toward me. "Where were you?" he said. "I was looking for you."

"I was in the ditch."

"With the ants?"

I nodded.

"I heard you talking to them before."

"So?"

"So, are you Ant-Man?"

"No, dummy."

"Why not?"

"Because, I'm not anybody. You're not anybody, either."

We fell silent for a while and just sat there, not looking at each other, kicking at the legs of our chairs. I could hear Mrs. Gladfelter and Mr. Buterbaugh talking softly in his office; Mr. Buterbaugh called her Elizabeth. The telephone rang. A light flashed twice on Mrs. Maloney's phone, then held steady.

"Thanks for calling back, Joel," I heard Mr. Buterbaugh say. "Yes, I'm afraid so."

"I went to see Dr. Schachter a couple times," I said. "He had Micronauts and the Fembots."

"He has Stretch Armstrong, too."

"I know."

"Why did *you* go see him? Did your mother make you?"

"Yeah," I said.

"How come?"

"I don't know. She said I was having problems. With my anger, or I don't know." Actually, she had said—and at first Dr. Schachter had concurred—that I needed to learn to "manage" my anger. This was a diagnosis that I never understood, since it seemed to me that I had no problems at all managing my anger. It was my judgment that I managed it much better than my parents managed theirs, and even Dr. Schachter had to agree with that. In fact, the last time I saw him, he suggested that I try to stop managing my anger quite so well. "I don't know," I said to Timothy. "I guess I was mad about my dad and things."

"He had to go to jail."

"Just for one night."

"How come?"

"He had too much to drink," I said, with a disingenuous shrug. My father was not much of a drinker, and when he crashed the party my mother had thrown last weekend to celebrate the closing of her first really big sale, he broke a window, knocked over a chafing dish, which set fire to a batik picture of Jerusalem, and raised a bloody blue plum under my mother's right eye. People had tended to blame the unaccustomed effects of the fifth of Gilbey's that was later found in the glove compartment of his car. Only my mother and I knew that he was secretly a madman.

"Did you visit him in jail?"

"No, stupid. God! You're such a retard! You *belong* in Special School, Timothy. I hope they make you eat special food and wear a special helmet or something." I heard the distant slam of the school's front door, and then a pair of hard shoes knocking along the hall. "Here comes your retard mother," I said.

"What *kind* of special helmet?" said Timothy. It was

never very easy to hurt his feelings. "Ant-Man wears a helmet."

Mrs. Stokes entered the office. She was a tall, thin woman, much older than my mother, with long gray hair and red, veiny hands. She wore clogs with white knee-socks, and in the evenings after dinner she went onto her deck and smoked a pipe. Every morning she made Timothy pancakes for his breakfast, which sounded okay until you found out that she put things in them like carrots and leftover pieces of corn.

"Oh, hello, Paul," she said, in her Eeyore voice.

"Mrs. Stokes," said Mrs. Gladfelter, coming out of the principal's office. She smiled. "It's been kind of a long afternoon for Timothy, I'm afraid."

"How is Virginia?" said Mrs. Stokes. She still hadn't looked at Timothy.

"Oh, she'll be fine," Mr. Buterbaugh said. "Just a little shaken up. We sent her home early. Of course," he added, "her parents are going to want to speak to you."

"Of course," said Mrs. Stokes. I saw that she was still wearing her white apron and her photo name tag from her job. She worked at the bone factory out in the Huxley Industrial Park, where they made plastic skulls and skeletons for medical schools. It was her job to string together all the delicate beadwork of the hands and feet. "I'm ready to do whatever you think would be best for Timothy."

"I'm not Timothy," said Timothy.

"Oh, please, Timmy, stop this nonsense for once."

"I'm cursed." He leaned over and brought his face very close to mine. "Tell them about the curse, Professor."

I looked at Timothy, and for the first time saw that a thin, dark down of wolfish hair had grown upon his cheek. Then I looked at Mr. Buterbaugh, and found that he was watching me with an air of earnest expectancy, as though he honestly thought there might be an eternal black-magical curse on Timothy and was more than willing to listen to anything I might have to say on the subject. I shrugged.

"Are you going to make him go to Special School?" I said.

"All right, Paul, thank you," said Mrs. Gladfelter. "You may go back to class now. We're watching a movie with Mrs. Hampt's class this afternoon."

Mrs. Maloney had reappeared in the doorway, her cheeks flushed, her lipstick fresh, smelling of cigarette.

"I'll see that he gets there," she said—uncharitably, I thought.

"See you later, Timothy," I said. He didn't answer me; he had started to growl again. As I followed Mrs. Maloney out of the office I looked back and saw Mr. Buterbaugh and Mrs. Gladfelter and poor old Mrs. Stokes standing in a hopeless circle around Timothy. I thought for a second, and then I turned back toward them and raised an imaginary rifle to my shoulder.

"This is a dart gun," I announced. Everyone looked at me, but I was talking to Timothy now. I was almost but not quite embarrassed. "It's filled with darts of my special antidote, and I made it stronger than it used to be, and it's going to work this time. And also, um, there's a tranquil-izer mixed in."

Timothy looked up, and bared his teeth at me, and I took aim right between his eyes. I jerked my hands twice, and went *fwup! fwup!* Timothy's head snapped back, and his eyelids fluttered. He shook himself all over. He swallowed, once. Then he held his hands out before him, as if wondering at their hairless pallor.

"It seems to have worked," he said, his voice cool and reasonable and fine. Anyone could see he was still playing his endless game, but all the grown-ups, Mr. Buterbaugh in particular, looked very pleased with both of us.

"Thank you very much, Paul." Mr. Buterbaugh gave

me a pat on the head. "Remember to say hello to your mother for me."

"I'm not Paul," I said, and everybody laughed but Timothy Stokes.

WHEN I got home from school my mother was down in the basement, at my father's workbench, dressed in the paint-spattered blue jeans and hooded sweatshirt she put on whenever it was time to do dirty work. She had pulled her hair back into a tight ponytail. Normally I would have been glad to see her home from work already and dressed this way. One of the sources of friction between us, and among the various angers that I had supposedly been attempting to manage, was my dislike of the way she looked as she went off to work in the morning, in her plaid suit jackets, her tan stockings, her blouses with their little silk bow ties, her cabasset of hairsprayed hair. In the days before she went back to work my mother had been a genuine hippie—bushy-headed, legs unshaven, dressed in vast dresses with Indian patterns; she was there to fix bowls of hot whole-grain cereal in the morning and to give me a snack of dried pineapple and milk in the kitchen when I came home. Now, every morning, I fixed myself a breakfast of cornflakes and coffee, and when I got home I generally turned on the television and ate the box of Yodels that I purchased at High's every day on my way back from school. But my pleasure at the sight of her in her old, ruined jeans, patched with a scrap of a genuine Mao jacket she had bought as a student at McGill, was diminished when I saw that she was dressed this way so that she could stand at my father's workbench and toss all the delicate furniture of his home laboratory into an assortment of battered liquor cartons.

"But, Mom," I said, watching as she backhanded into a box an entire S-shaped rack of stoppered test tubes. The glass, in shattering, made a festive tinkle, as of little bells, and the dank basement air was quickly suffused with a harsh chemical stink of bananas and mold and burnt matches. "Those are his experiments."

"I know it," said my mother, looking grave, her voice filled with vandalistic glee. My father was a research chemist for the Food and Drug Administration. He was a small man with a scraggly gray beard and thick spectacles. He wore plaid sports jackets with patches on the elbows, carried his pens in a plastic pocket liner, and went to services every Saturday morning. He held a national ranking in chess (173) and a Canadian patent for a culture medium still widely used in that country, where he had been born and raised. "And he worked very hard on them all." She hefted the heavy black binder in which my father kept his lab notes and dropped it into a box that had once contained bottles of Captain Morgan rum; there was a leering picture of a pirate on the side. "For years." The laboratory notebook landed with a crunch of glass, breaking the throats of a dozen Erlenmeyer flasks beneath it. "I've asked him many, many times to come over here and pick up his things, Paulie. You know that. He's had his chance."

"I know." On his departure from our house, my father had taken only a plaid valise full of summer clothing and my grandfather's Russian chess set, whose black pieces had once been fingered by Alexander Alekhine.

"It's been months now, Paulie," my mother said. "I've got to conclude that he just doesn't want any of his stuff."

"I know," I said.

She surveyed the wreckage of my father's home laboratory—a little ruefully now, I thought—and then looked at me. "I guess it must seem to you like I'm being kind of mean," she said. "Eh?"

I didn't say anything. She held out her hand to me. I grabbed it and tugged her to her feet. She lifted the Captain Morgan carton and stacked it atop a Smirnoff carton filled with commercially prepared reagents in their bottles and jars; there was a further crunch of glass as the upper box settled into the lower. She hoisted the stacked boxes to her hip and jogged them once to get a better grip. One carton remained on the floor beside the workbench. We both looked at it.

"I'll come back for that one," my mother said, after a pause. She turned, and started slowly up the stairs.

For a minute I stood there with my hands jammed into my pockets, staring down into the box at my father's cru-cible tongs, at his coils of clear plastic tubing, at his stir-rers, pipettes, and stopcocks wrapped like taffy in stiff white paper. I knelt down and wrapped my arms around the carton and lowered my face into it and inhaled a clean, rubbery smell like that of a new Band-Aid. Then I lifted the carton and carried it upstairs, through the laundry room, and out into the garage, trying to fight off an unsettling feeling that I was throwing my father away. The rear hatch of our Datsun was raised, and the backseats had been folded forward.

"Thank you, sweetie," said my mother, gently, as I handed her the last carton. "Now I just have to load up a few more things, and then I'm going to run all this stuff over to Mr. Kappelman's office." Mr. Kappelman was my father's lawyer; my mother's lawyer was a woman she called Deirdre. "You can just stay here, okay? You don't have to help me anymore."

"There's no room for me anyway," I said.

Most of the space in the car was already taken up by packed liquor boxes. I could see the fuzzy sleeve of my father's green angora sweater poking out of one carton, and, through the finger holes in the side of another, I could make out the cracked black spines of his college chemistry texts. Stuffed into the spaces among the boxes and into odd nooks of the car's interior were my father's bicycle helmet, his clarinet case, his bust of Paul Morphy, his brass wall barometer, his shoeshine kit, his vaporizer,

the panama hat he liked to wear at the beach, the beige
plastic bedpan that had come home from the hospital with
him after his deviated-septum operation and now held all
his razors and combs and the panoply of gleaming instruments he employed to trim the hair that grew from the
various features of his face, a grocery bag full of his shoe
trees, the Montreal Junior Chess Championship trophy he
had won in 1953, his tie rack, his earmuffs, and one Earth
shoe. There was barely enough room left in the car for
the three boxes my mother and I had dragged up from the
basement. I helped her squeeze them into place, audibly
doing more damage to their rank-smelling contents, and
then my mother put her hands on the edge of the hatch
and got ready to slam it.

She said, "Stand clear." I flinched. I guess I must have
shut my eyes; after a second or two I realized that she
hadn't closed the door yet, and when I looked at her again
her eyes were scanning my face, darting very quickly back
and forth, the way they did when she thought I might
have a fever.

"Paul," she said, "how was school today?"

"Fine."

"How's your asthma?"

"Good."

She took her hands off the lip of the hatch and crouched
down in front of me. Her face, I saw, was still buried
under the thick layer of beige frosting that she applied to it
every morning.

"Paul," she said. "What's the matter, honey?"

"Nothing," I said, turning from her unrecognizable
face. "I'll be right back." I started away from her.

"Paul—" She took hold of my arm.

"I have to go to the *bath*room!" I said, twisting free of
her. "You look ugly," I added as I ran back into the house.

I went to the telephone and dialed my father's number
at work. The departmental secretary said that he was

down the hall. I said that I would wait. I carried the phone over to the couch, where I had thrown my parka, and took my daily box of Yodels from its hiding place inside the torn orange lining. By the time my father took me off hold I had eaten three of them. This didn't require all that much time, to be honest.

"Dr. Kovel," said my father as he came clattering onto the line.

"Dad?"

"Paul. Where are you?"

"Dad, I'm at home. Guess what, Dad? I got expelled from school today."

"What? What's this?"

"Yeah, um, I got really mad, and I thought I was a werewolf, and I, um, I bit this girl, you know—Virginia Pease? On the neck. I didn't break the skin, though," I added. "And so they expelled me. Can you come over?"

"Paul, I'm at work."

"I know."

"What is all this?" His breath blew heavy through the line and made an irritated rattle in the receiver at my ear. "All right, listen, I'll be there as soon as I can get away, eh?" Now his voice grew thick, as though on the other end of the line, while he held the receiver in the middle of his blank little office in Rockville, Maryland, his face had gone red with embarrassment. "Is your mother there?"

I told him to hold on, and went back out to the garage.

"Mom," I said, "Dad's on the phone." I said these words in a voice so normal and cheerful that it hurt my heart to hear them. "He wants to talk to you." I smiled the conspiratorial little smile I had so often seen her use on her clients as she hinted that the seller just might be willing to come down. "I think he wants to apologize."

"Did you *call* him?"

"Oh, uh, yeah. Yes. I had to," I said, remembering my

story. "Because I got expelled from school. I have to go to Special School now. Starting tomorrow, probably."

My mother put down the hoe she had been trying to squeeze into the back of her car and went, rather unwillingly, I thought, to the phone. Before she stepped into the house she looked back at me with a doubtful smile. I looked away. I stood there, behind her car, gazing in at all my father's belongings. My mother had said that she planned to take them over to his lawyer's office, but I didn't believe her. I believed that she meant to take them to the dump. I hesitated for an instant, then reached in for my father's laboratory notebook. He had always been more than willing to show me parts of it, whenever I asked him to; and naturally I had taken many furtive looks at its innermost pages when he wasn't around. But I had never really comprehended its contents, nor the tenor of the experiments he'd been performing down there in our basement over the years, although I had a general sense of disappointment about them, as I did about his whole interest, professional and avocational, in the chemistry of mildews and molds. Yet even if there was nothing of interest in his notes—a likelihood that I still could not fully accept—I nonetheless felt a sudden urge to possess the notebook itself. Perhaps someday I would be able to decipher its cryptic formulae and crabbed script, and thence derive all manner of marvelous pastes of invisibility and mind-control dusts, unheard-of vitamins and deadly fungal poisons and powders that repelled gravity. I reached for the notebook and then decided also to take two of the boxes of laboratory equipment. I knew who would keep them safe for me; I hoped, as I never had before, that he would still want to be my friend.

I peered around the side of the garage, to make sure that my mother wasn't watching from the front windows, then ran as quickly as I could toward the stand of young maples and pricker bushes that separated us from the

Stokeses. The boxes were very heavy, and the shards of glass within them jingled like change. It was dinnertime, and nearly dark, but none of the lights were on in Timothy's house. I supposed that he had been taken to see Dr. Schachter, and all at once I worried that he would never come home again, that they would just send Timothy straight off to Special School that day. Some people claimed that the little yellow van that sometimes passed us when we were on our way to school in the morning, its windows filled with the blank, cheerful faces of strange boys none of us knew, was the daily bus to Special School; but other people said that you had to go live there forever, like reform school or prison, and get visits from your parents on the weekends.

My mother was calling me. "Pau-aul!" she cried. She was one of those women who have a hard time raising their voices; it always came out sounding hoarse and friendless whenever she called me home. "*Pau*-lie!"

I hid in the brambles and studied the dark face of Timothy's house, trying to decide what to do with my father's things. My arms were growing tired, and I needed to go to the bathroom, and for now, I decided, I would leave the boxes at the basement door. I would come back later to ask Timothy, who on occasion appeared in the avatar of the faithful robot from *Lost in Space,* to guard them for me. Timothy slept in the basement of the Stokeses' house, under a wall hung from floor to ceiling with his vast arsenal of toy swords and firearms, in a room strewn with dismembered telephones and the bones of imitation skeletons. I tiptoed around the side of the Stokeses' house and into their weedy backyard. The moon was high and brilliant in the sky by now, and I thought that, after all, it was pretty nearly full. I approached the basement door, keeping an uneasy eye on the shadows in the trees, and the shadows under the Stokeses' deck, and the shadows gathered on the swings of the creaking jungle gym. Since my last visit, I saw, Timothy had marked the entrance to his labyrinth with two neat pyramids of plastic skulls. My mother's raspy voice fell silent, and there was only the sound of cars out on the country road, and the ghostly squeak of the swing set and the forlorn crooning of a blind Dalmatian that lived at the bottom of our street. Carelessly I dropped the boxes on the step, between the grinning pyramids, and ran back through the trees toward my house, heart pounding, tearing my clothes on the teeth of the underbrush, certain that something quick and terrible was following me every step of the way.

"I'm home!" I said, coming into the brightness and warmth of our hall. "Here I am."

"There you are," said my mother, though she didn't look all that happy to see me. She laid a heavy hand on my shoulder. It smelled of butyric acid and dextrorotatory sucrose and also very faintly of Canoe. "I just got off the phone with Bob Buterbaugh, Paul. He told me what really happened at school today." She had yanked her hair free of its ponytail and now it shot out in ragged arcs around her head, tangled like the vanes of a wrecked umbrella. "Do you want to explain yourself to me? Why did you lie?"

"Is Dad coming over?"

"Well, yes, he is, Paul—"

"Great."

"—because he feels that he really needs to see you, tonight. But the two of you will have to sit outside in the car and talk, or go somewhere else. I'm not going to let him in the house."

I was astonished. "Why not?"

"Because, Paul, your dad—you know as well as I do— he's become, well, you know how he's been lately. I don't have to tell you." As if she were angry, she folded her arms, and clenched her jaw. But I could see that she was trying to keep herself from crying. "I have to set some limits."

"You mean he can't come over to our house anymore? Ever again?"

There were tears in her eyes. "Ever again," she said. Once more she crouched before me, and I let her take me in her arms, but I did not return her embrace. In the picture window at the end of the hall I watched her reflection hugging mine. I didn't want to be comforted on the impending loss of my father. I wanted him not to be lost, and it seemed to me that it would be her fault if he was.

"He said he's going to collect his things. So I guess it's a good thing I didn't get rid of them, eh?" She gave me a poke in the ribs. "He must want them after all. Hey," she said. "What is it? What's the matter?" She followed my gaze toward the picture window, where our embracing reflections looked back at us with startled expressions.

"Nothing," I said. A light had just come on in the Stokeses' house. "I—I have to go over to Timothy's. I left something there."

"What?"

"My Luger," I said, remembering a toy I had lent to Timothy sometime last summer. "The pink one that squirts."

"Well, it's time to eat," said my mother. "You can go after."

"But what if Dad comes?"

"Well, what if he does? You can go over to Timothy's tomorrow. He's probably not allowed to see anyone anyway."

IN FIVE minutes I bolted my dinner—one of those bizarre conglomerations of bottled tomato sauces, casseroles-in-boxes, and leftover Chinese lunches that were then the national dishes of our disordered and temporizing homeland—and ran out the front door into the night. I was sure that Timothy had found the cartons by now. What if he thought I had meant them for a present and refused to give them back? My father was going to be angry enough about my mother's treatment of his chemistry things, but it would be worse when he found out that most of them, including his notebook, were missing. I sprinted across our yard as quickly as I could, considering my asthma, and went crashing through the maple trees toward the Stokeses' house. There was a burst of red light as a thin branch slapped against my left eye, and I cried out, and covered my face, and ran headlong into Timothy Stokes. My chin struck his chest and I sat down hard.

He smiled, and knelt beside me. "Are you all right, Professor?" he said. He was wearing the same pair of white jeans and stained T-shirt, under an unbuttoned jacket that was too large for him and that bore over the breast pocket his own last name, printed in block letters on a strip of cloth. He pulled a flashlight from his pocket and switched it on. The beam threw eerie shadows across his cheeks and forehead, and his little brown eyes were alight behind his glasses. I saw at once that the antidote I'd administered to him that afternoon had worn off, and he showed no sign of having been subjected to any weird therapies or electroshock helmets. His face looked as solemn and stupid as ever. He wore a rifle strapped across his back and a plastic commando knife in his boot, and three Sgt. Fury and His Howling Commandos hand grenades poked through the web belt of his canteen, and in his right hand he was carrying, as though it were another weapon, the thick, black, case-bound notebook.

"That's my father's," I said. "You can't have it."

"I already photographed all of its contents with my spy camera," he explained. "I have every page on microfilm. Plus I ran an extensive computer analysis on them." He lowered his voice. "Your father is a very dangerous man.

Look here." He opened the notebook and shone the flashlight on a page where my father had written, "Myco. K. P889, L. 443, Tr. 23," and then a date from three years earlier. The rest of the page was an illegible mishmash of numbers and abbreviations, some of them connected by sharp forceful arrows. The entry went on for several pages in the same fashion, cramped by haste and marginalia. I had seen plenty like it before, and I had no doubt that it described a process that could be used to get rid of something that grew between the tiles of your bathroom, or on the skin of your pears.

"Did you see?" said Timothy.

"See what?" I said.

"Your father is Ant-Man," he said gravely. "I've suspected it for a long time." He unhooked the canteen from his belt. It was covered in green canvas and it sloshed as he waved it around. "This is the antidote."

He clamped the notebook under one arm and with his freed hand unscrewed the cap. I inclined my face slightly toward the mouth of the canteen, extended my fingers, and wafted the air above it toward my nostrils, delicately, as my father had shown me. I detected no odor this way, however. So he stuck it right under my nose.

"It smells like Coke," I said. "You put salt in it." Timothy didn't say anything, but I thought I saw disappointment flicker across his flashlit face. "What would happen if I drank it?" I added quickly, not wanting to let him down. There was something about the way Timothy played his game, the thoroughness with which he imagined, that never failed to entrance me.

"That's what I'd like to know," said Timothy. "What if it said in this book, here, that your father has been giving you the secret formula to drink, like one drop at a time in your cereal, ever since you were a little baby? And what if that's why you can talk to ants, too?"

"What if," I said. I had always felt sorry for Ant-Man, a

superhero whose powers condemned him to the disappointing comradeship of bugs. "Timothy, what happened
to you today? What did they say? Are you expelled?"

"Shh," said Timothy. The notebook went flapping to
the ground as he reached for me, and drew me to him,
and covered my mouth with his hand. His voice fell to a
harsh whisper. "Someone's coming."

I heard the sound of a car climbing the hill. A pair of
headlights splashed light across the front of my house. I
yanked my head free of his grasp.

"It's my dad!" I said. "Timothy, I need to get his stuff
back—now!"

"Quiet." Timothy loosened his hold on me and brought
the canteen up to my lips. I took a step away from him.
"Quick," he said. "Swallow this antidote. We don't have
time to test it. You'll just have to take the risk." He patted
the dull black barrel of his rifle. "I've already loaded this
baby with antidote darts."

From the distant front porch of our house I could hear
our front door squeal on its hinges, and then the separate voices of my parents, saying hello. I tried to make
sense of their murmurings, but we were too far away.
After a while there was another long squeal of hinges, and
the door slammed shut, and then our house creaked and
resounded with the passage of feet along its hallway.

"Oh, my God," I said. "I think she let him go inside."

"Come on," said Timothy. "Drink this."

"I'm not drinking that stuff," I said.

"All right, then," he said. "*I'll* drink it." He threw back
his head and took a long swallow. Then he handed the
canteen to me, and I drank down the rest of the antidote.
It was sweet and sharp tasting, and bitter through and
through. I felt pretty sure that it was just Coca-Cola
mixed with good old sodium chloride, but then, after I
got it down, I realized there must have been something
else mixed into it—something that burned.

"Take this," he said, handing me the plastic commando knife. He said that it was in case something went wrong; the rifle was only for delivering the antidote. He said, "Stay down."

He led me out of the trees, across our moonlit back-yard, and up the short, grassy slope that rose to the back of our house—a silvery gray shape loping along in a sort of crouched-over commando half-trot. The sleeves of my parka whispered against my sides as I ran. I belched up a fiery blast of his formula, and then laughed a tipsy little laugh. Timothy stepped up onto our patio and unslung the rifle from his shoulder. A radiant cloud of light from our living room came pouring out through the sliding-glass door, illuminating the trees and the lawn chairs and the grill, and the crown of Timothy's close-cropped head as he knelt down, raised the rifle, and waited for me to catch up to him. When I got there he was peering in, his face looking blank and amazed behind the luminous disks of his spectacles, his breath coming regular and heavy.

"Can you feel it?" I said, kneeling beside him. "Is it working?"

He didn't say anything. I looked. My father and my mother were sitting on the sofa. He was holding her in his arms. Her face was red and streaked with tears, and her mouth was fastened against his. Her sweatshirt was hiked up around her throat, and one of her breasts hung loose and shaking and astonishingly white. The other breast my father held, roughly, in his hairy hand, as if he were trying to crush it.

"What are they doing?" Timothy whispered. He set the rifle down on the patio. "Are those your parents?"

I tried to think of something to say. I was dizzy with surprise, and the formula we had swallowed was making me feel like I was going to be sick. I sat there for a minute or so beside Timothy, watching the struggle of those two people, who had been transformed forever by a real and powerful curse, the very least of whose magical effects was me. I felt as though I had been spying on them for my entire life, to no profit at all. After a moment I had to look away. Timothy's gun was lying on the ground beside me. I reached for it, and held it in my grip, and found that it weighed far more than I had expected. Its breechblock was steely and cool.

"Timothy, is this real?" I said, but I knew he would never be able to answer me.

I stood up, my head spinning, and stumbled off the patio, onto the frost-bright grass. Timothy lingered for a moment longer, then came hurtling away from the window, passing me on our way into the woods. Under the maple trees we threw up whatever it was that he had given us to drink. He seemed to lose some of his enthusiasm for our game after that, and when I told him to go home and leave me alone he did.

LATER ON that night, my father and I fetched his notebook from the pile of dead leaves in the woods where Timothy had dropped it, and went over together to the Stokeses' house to retrieve all the pieces of his shattered laboratory. My father's arm lay heavy around my neck. I told Althea Stokes about the rifle, and Timothy was forced to produce it and surrender it to her. It had been, she said, his father's. I helped my father carry the cartons out to his car, and then in silence we and my mother removed all of his other belongings, one by one, from her hatchback, and loaded them into the trunk of our big old Chevrolet Impala. Then my father drove away.

The next morning at eight, a little yellow bus full of unknown boys pulled up in front of the Stokeses' house, and sounded its angry horn, and Timothy went out to meet it.

House Hunting

THE HOUSE was all wrong for them. An ivy-covered Nor-
man country manor with an eccentric roofline, a fat,
pointed tower, and latticed mullions in the downstairs
windows, it sat perched on the northwest shoulder of
Lake Washington, a few blocks to the east of the house
in which Christy had grown up. The neighborhood was
subject to regular invasion by armies of gardeners, land-
scape contractors, and installers of genuine Umbrian granite paving stone, but nevertheless it was obvious the house
had been got up to be sold. The blue paint on the shutters
looked slick and wet, fresh black mulch churned around
the pansies by the driveway, and the immense front lawn
had been polished to a hard shine. The listing agent's sign
was a discreet red-and-white escutcheon, on a black iron
stake, that read simply, "Herman Silk," with a telephone
number, in an elegant sans serif type.

"This?" Daniel Diamond said, his heart sinking in a
kind of giddy fizz within him. Although they had all the
windows open, Mr. Hogue's car was choked with the
smell of his cologne, a harsh extract of wintergreen and

brine which the realtor had been emitting more fiercely, like flop sweat, the nearer they got to the house. It was aggravating Daniel's allergies, and he wished he'd thought to pop a Claritin before leaving the apartment that morning. "This is the one?"

"That's the one," Hogue said, sounding weary, as though he had spent the entire day dragging them around town in his ancient Mercedes sedan, showing them one perfectly good house after another, each of which they had rejected with the most arbitrary and picayune of rationales. In fact, it was only ten o'clock in the morning, and this was the very first place he'd brought them to see. Bob Hogue was a leathery man of indefinite middle age, wearing a green polo shirt, tan chinos, and a madras blazer in the palette favored by manufacturers of the cellophane grass that goes into Easter baskets. His rectilinear wrinkles, his crew cut, his chin like a couple of knuckles, his nose lettered with minute red script, gave him the look of a jet pilot gone to seed. "What's the matter with it? Not good enough for you?"

Daniel and his wife, Christy Kite, looked at each other across the back of Christy's seat—Christy could never ride in the rear of any vehicle without experiencing acute motion sickness.

"Well, it's awfully big, Mr. Hogue," she said, tentatively, leaning to look past the realtor at the house. Christy had gone to college in Palo Alto, where she studied French and led cheers for a football team that lost all the big games. She had the Stanford graduate's aggressive nice manners, and the eyes of a cheerleader atop a struggling pyramid of girls. She had been the Apple Queen of Roosevelt High. From her mother, she had learned to try very hard to arrange everything in life with the flawlessness of a photograph in a house-and-garden magazine, and then to take it just as hard when the black plums went uneaten in the red McCoy bowl and filled the kitchen with a stink of garbage, or when the dazzling white masses of Shasta daisies in the backyard were eaten by aphids.

"Yeah, I don't know, Mr. Hogue," Daniel said. "I think—"

"Oh, but it is beautiful," Christy said. She furrowed her brow and narrowed her eyes. She poked her tongue gamely from a corner of her mouth. She was trying her hardest, Daniel could see, to imagine living in that house with him. House hunting, like all their efforts to improve things between them—the counseling, the long walks, the watching of a movie called *Spanking Brittany Blue*—had been her idea. But after a moment her face went slack, and her eyes sought Daniel's, and in them he saw, for the first time since their wedding the summer before last, the luster of real despair, as if she feared they would find no home for their marriage, not in Seattle or anywhere in the world. Then she shrugged and reached up to retie her scarf, a sheer white piece of Italian silk patterned with lemons and limes. She opened her door, and started to get out of the car.

"Just a minute, you," Hogue said, taking her arm. She fell back into the car at once, and favored Hogue with her calmest and most obliging Apple Queen smile, but Daniel could see her nostrils flaring like a rabbit's. "Don't be in such a rush," Hogue went on irritably. "You're always running off half-cocked." He leaned over to open the glove compartment and rummaged around inside it until he found a package of Pall Malls. He pushed in the cigarette lighter and tapped one end of a wrinkled cigarette against the dashboard. "You can't rush into a thing like this. It could turn out to be a terrible mistake."

At once, like people trapped in an empty bus station with a fanatical pamphleteer, Daniel and Christy agreed with Hogue.

"We're careful people," Christy said. Carefully, she

averted her face from Hogue's gaze, and gave her husband
a brief grimace of not quite mock alarm.

"Careful people with limited resources," Daniel said.
He hadn't decided whether to tell Christy that, two days
earlier, her father had taken him to lunch at the University Club and offered to make a present of any reasonably
priced house they might choose. After the war, Mr. Kite
had founded an industrial advertising agency, landed the
accounts of several major suppliers to Boeing, and then, at
the age of sixty-two, sold his company for enough money
to buy a condominium on the ninth hole at Salishan and
a little cabaña down on the beach at Cabo San Lucas.
Daniel, a graduate student in astronomy at U.W., where
Christy taught psychology, didn't have any money of his
own. Neither, for that matter, did his father, who, in the
years of Mr. Kite's prosperity, had run two liquor stores, a
printshop, and a five-and-dime into the ground, and now
lived with Daniel's mother amid the coconut palms and
peeling white stucco of an internment camp for impover-
ished old people not far from Delray Beach. "Maybe we
ought to just—"

Christy cut him off with a sharp look. The lighter
popped out, and Hogue reached for it, and they watched
in uncomfortable silence as, hands shaking, he tried to light
his cigarette. After several seconds and a great deal of fear-
some wheezing, the few frayed strands of tobacco he had
succeeded in getting lit fell out of the end of the cigarette,
landed in his lap, and began to burn his chinos. He slapped
at his thigh, scowling all the while at the house, as if it, or
its occupants, were somehow responsible for his ignition.

"Maybe we ought to take a look at it, Mr. Hogue,"
Christy said.

Mr. Hogue looked back over at the house. He took a
deep breath.

"I guess we'd better," he said. He opened his door and
got out of the car, eyeing the house warily.

Daniel and Christy lingered a moment by the Mercedes, whispering.

"He looks like he's seen a ghost," Christy observed, buttoning the top button of her white cardigan. "He looks awful."

"Did he look better at our wedding?"

Daniel understood that Bob Hogue had been among the guests at their wedding, the summer before last, but his recollection of that remote afternoon had grown vague. In fact, the great event itself had, at the time, unfolded around him at a certain vague remove. He had felt not like the star attraction, along with Christy, of a moderately lavish civil ceremony held on the slope of a Laurelhurst lawn so much as like a tourist, lost in a foreign country, who had turned in to an unfamiliar street and found himself swallowed up in the clamor of a parade marking the feast day of some silken and barbarous religion. He remembered this Bob Hogue and his handsome wife, Monica, no better than he remembered Bill and Sylvia Bond, Roger and Evelyn Holsapple, Ralph and Betsy Lindstrom, or any of the three hundred other handsome old friends of his in-laws who had made up the bulk of the wedding guests. He knew that Hogue was a college chum and occasional golfing partner of his father-in-law's, and he was aware that an acrid ribbon of bad news was sent curling toward the ceiling of any room in which Bob Hogue's name was brought up, though he could never keep straight whether Hogue had married the lush, or fathered the Scientologist, or lost a piece of his left lung to cancer.

"To tell you the truth," Christy said, "I don't remember him at our wedding. I don't really know the Hogues very well. I just kind of remember how he looked when I was little."

"Well, no wonder he looks awful, then." He stepped back to admire her in her smart green Vittadini dress. Her bare legs were new-shaven, so smooth that they glinted in the sun, and through the gaps in her open-toed flats you could see a couple of slender toes, nails painted pink. "You, however, look very nice."

She smiled, and her pupils dilated, flooding her eyes with a darkness. "I liked what we did last night."

"So did I," Daniel said at once. Last night they had lain on top of their down comforter, with their heads at opposite ends of their bed, and massaged each other's feet with fragrant oil, by candlelight, while Al Green cooed to them in the background. This was an activity recommended to them by their couples therapist as a means of generating a nonthreatening sense of physical closeness between them. Daniel blushed now at this recollection, which he found painful and sad. To his great regret there was nothing even remotely erotic to him about feet, his wife's or anyone's. You might have permitted him to anoint the graceful foot of Semiramis or Hedy Lamarr, and he would not have popped a boner. He slid a hand up under the hem of Christy's dress and tried to skate his index and middle fingers up the smooth, hard surface of her right thigh, but she moved, and somehow Daniel's entire hand ended up thrust between her legs, as though he were attempting to hold open the doors of an elevator.

"Ouch," said Christy. "You don't have to be so rough."

"Sorry," said Daniel.

They started up the driveway after Mr. Hogue.

"Who's Herman Silk?" Daniel said, as they passed the discreet little sign.

"Who's Herman Silk?" Hogue wove a puzzling thread of bitterness into the question. "That's a good one." Daniel wondered if he should recognize the name from some local real-estate scandal or recent round of litigation in the neighborhood. He tried to keep track of such mainstays of Kite-family conversation, but it was hard, in particular since they were generally served up, in the Kite house, with liberal amounts of Canadian Club and soda. "That's very funny," said Hogue.

When they got to the front door, Mr. Hogue could not seem to work the combination of the lockbox there. He tried several different permutations of what he thought was the code and then, in a display of bafflement at once childish and elderly, reached into his pocket and attempted to stick one of his own keys in the lock.

"Funny," he muttered, as this hopeless stratagem in due course failed. "Herman Silk. Ha."

Christy looked at Daniel, her eyes filled with apology for having led them into this intensifying disaster. Daniel smiled and gave his shoulders an attenuated shrug, characteristic of him, that did not quite absolve her of blame.

"Uh, why don't you tell me the combination, Mr. Hogue?" Christy suggested, yanking the lockbox out of his hands. She, who was willing to lie for hours listening to Reverend Al while Daniel worked over her oiled foot like a desperate man trying to summon a djinn, was finally losing patience. Daniel's heart was stirred by a wan hope that very soon now they would have to give up on old Mr. Hogue, on buying a house, on Christy's entire project of addressing and finding solutions for their problem. Now that things were starting to go so wrong, he hoped they could just return to their apartment on Queen Anne Hill and resume ignoring their problem, the strategy he preferred.

Hogue fed Christy the combination one digit at a time, and she worked the tumblers. She gave a sharp tug on the lockbox. It held firm.

"Are you sure that's the right number?" she said.

"Of course it's the right number," Hogue snapped. All at once his face had turned as red as the wrapper of his Pall

Malls. One would have said that he was furious with Christy and Daniel, that he had had his fill of the unreasonable demands and the cruel hectoring to which they had subjected him over the last forty years. "Why are you always pestering me like that? Don't you know I'm doing my best?"

Daniel and Christy looked at each other. Christy bit her lip, and Daniel saw that she had been afraid something like this might happen. A sudden clear memory of Mr. Hogue at the wedding returned to him. There had been a series of toasts after dinner, and Mr. Hogue had risen to say a few words. His face had gone full of blood and he looked unsteady on his feet. The woman sitting beside him, Monica Hogue—slender, youthful, with red spectacles and a cute gray bob—had given his elbow a discreet tug. For a moment the air under the great white tent had grown still and sour, and the guests had looked down at their plates.

"Well, sure we do, Mr. Hogue," Christy said. "We know you've been doing a great job for us, and we really appreciate it. Don't we, Daniel?"

"Well, yeah. We really do."

The blood went out of Hogue's face.

"Excuse me," he said. "I—I'm sorry, you kids. I'm not feeling very well today." He ran a hand across the close-cropped top of his head. "Here. Let me see something. There used to be—" He backed down the steps and, half crouched, hands on his knees, scanned the ground under the long rhododendron hedges that flanked the door. He moved crabwise along the row of shrubbery until he disappeared around the corner of the house.

"I remember him now," said Daniel.

Christy laughed, through her nose, and then sadly shook her head.

"I hope he's all right."

"I think he just needs a drink."

"Hush, Daniel, please."

"Do you remember the toast he gave at the wedding?"

"Did he make a toast?"

"It was 'To our wives and lovers, may they never meet.' "

"I don't remember that."

"Pretty fucking appropriate wedding-toast material, I thought."

"Daniel."

"This is a waste."

"Daniel, please don't say that. We're going to work this all out."

"Christy," Daniel said. "Please don't say that."

"What else can I say?"

"Nothing," Daniel said. "I don't think you know how to say anything else."

"Found it!" Hogue came back around the house toward them, favoring the young couple with his realtor's smile—the smile of someone who knows that he has been discussed unfavorably in his absence. He was brandishing a medium-sized, mottled gray stone, and for a wild instant Daniel thought he intended somehow to smash his way in. But Hogue only turned the stone over, slid aside a small plastic panel that was attached to it, and pulled from its interior a shiny gold key. Then he slipped the false stone into the hip pocket of his jacket.

"Neat little things," he said. He slid the key into the lock without difficulty, and let them into the house. "Don't worry, it's quite all right," he added, when he saw how they were looking at him. "I'll just have to call about the lockbox. Happens all the time. Come on in."

They found themselves in a small foyer with plaster walls that were streaked like thick cake frosting, fir floors, and a built-in hatstand festooned with all manner of hats. Hogue hitched up the back of his trousers and stood looking around, blinking, mouth pinched, expression gone blank. The profusion of hats on the hatstand—three berets in the colors of sherbets, a tweedy homburg, a new-looking Stetson with a snakeskin band, several billed golf caps bearing the crest of Mr. Kite's club—seemed to bewilder him. He cleared his throat, and the young people waited for him to begin his spiel. But Hogue said nothing. Without gesturing for them to follow, he shuffled off into the living room.

It was like a page out of one of Mrs. Kite's magazines, furnished with a crewel love seat, two old-fashioned easy chairs that had been re-covered with pieces of a Persian kilim, a low Moroccan table with a hammered-brass top, an old blue Chinese Deco rug, and a small collection of art books and local Indian basketry, arranged with mock haphazardness on the built-in shelves. The desired effect was doubtless an eclectic yet contemporary spareness, but the room was very large, and to Daniel it just looked emptied.

"Are you all right, Mr. Hogue?" Christy said, elbowing Daniel.

Mr. Hogue stood on the Chinese rug, surveying the living room with his eyes wide and his mouth open, a hand pressed to his midsection as though he had been sandbagged.

"Eh? Oh, why, yes, it's just—they just—they changed things around a little bit," he said. "Since the last time I was here."

From his astonished expression it was hard to believe that Hogue had ever seen the place before. Daniel wondered if Hogue hadn't simply plucked it at random out of a listing book and driven them over here to satisfy some sense of obligation to Christy's parents. Clearly the owners had not been expecting anyone to come through this morning; there was an old knit afghan lying twisted on the love seat, a splayed magazine on one of the chairs, and a half-empty glass of tomato juice on the brass table.

"Mr. Hogue?" said Christy. "Are you sure this is okay?"

"Fine," said Hogue. He pointed to a pair of French doors at the far end of the living room. "I believe you'll find the dining room through there." Daniel followed Christy into the dining room, which was cool and shady and furnished with whitewashed birch chairs and a birchwood table with an immense glass top. In the center of the table sat a small black lacquer bowl in which a gardenia floated, its petals scorched at the edges by decay.

"Nice," Daniel said, although he always misgave at the odor of gardenias, which tempted with a promise of apples and vanilla beans but finished in a bitter blast of vitamins and burnt wire.

"Come on, Daniel. We can't afford this."

"Did I say we could?"

"Please don't be a bastard."

"Was I being a bastard?"

Christy sighed and looked back toward the living room. Hogue hadn't joined them yet; he seemed to have disappeared. He was probably back in the foyer, Daniel thought, looking around for the fact sheet on the house, so that he could pretend to be knowledgeable about it. Christy lowered her voice and spoke into Daniel's ear. Her breath played across the inner hairs of his ear and raised gooseflesh all down his forearms.

"Do you think he's not supposed to be doing this anymore?"

"What do you mean?" Daniel said, taking an involuntary step away from her. Her scarf had come loose at the back, allowing a thick lank strand of her unwashed dark hair to dangle alongside her face. It was not healthy to overwash the hair—that was why she was wearing the jazzy scarf—and Daniel imagined he could still smell smoke on it from the Astronomy Department barbecue they had attended the night before.

"I mean, with the lockbox, and all—do you think he's been disbarred? Or whatever they do to realtors?"

"They make them unreal," Daniel suggested. He reached up and took hold of her scarf, and teased it loose. All of her smoky hair spilled down around her head.

"Why did you do that?" she said.

"I don't know," he admitted. He handed her the scarf, and she bound up her hair once more. "I'll go check on Mr. Hogue."

He went through the French doors back into the living room. Hogue was standing at the far end, where it opened onto the foyer, with his back to Daniel. There were built-in shelves on this side of the room, also, peopled with a sparse collection of small *objets* and half a dozen framed photographs of infants and graduates and an Irish setter in an orange life preserver. As Daniel came in, Hogue was fingering something small and glittering, a piece of crystal or a glass animal. He picked it up, examined it, and then slipped it into the right hip pocket of his jacket.

"Coming," he said, after Daniel, rendered speechless, managed to clear his throat in alarm. Hogue turned, and for an instant, before his face resumed its habitual clench-jawed jet-pilot tautness, he looked grimly, mysteriously pleased with himself, like a man who had just exacted a small and glittering measure of revenge. Then he accompanied Daniel into the dining room, and Daniel tried to think of something plausible to ask him. What did normal husbands say to normal real-estate agents at this stage of the game? It occurred to him that Hogue had not yet mentioned the asking price of the house.

"So what do they want, anyway, Mr. Hogue?" he tried.

"God only knows," Hogue said. He reached down toward the black lacquer bowl and picked up the gardenia, holding it by the clipped, dripping stem underneath. He brought it to his nose, took a deep draft of it, and then let out a long artificial sigh of delight. With Daniel looking right at him, he slipped the flower into the pocket of his jacket, too. "Let's have a look at that kitchen, shall we?"

So Daniel followed him into the kitchen, where Christy was exclaiming with a purely formal enthusiasm over the alderwood cabinets, the ceramic stove burners, the wavering light off the lake.

"What a waste, eh?" Hogue said. A dark patch of dampness was spreading across the fabric of his pocket. "They put I don't know how many thousands of dollars into it." He reached over to a sliding rheostat on the wall and made the track lighting bloom and dwindle and bloom. He shook his head. "Now then, this way to the family room. TV room. It amounts to the same thing, doesn't it?"

He slid a louvered door aside and went into the next room. Christy gestured to Daniel to come and stand beside her. Daniel looked back at the dining room. A lone leaf spun on the surface of the water in the lacquer bowl.

"Daniel, are you coming?" said Christy.

"There's something weird about this house," said Daniel.

"I wonder what," Christy said, giving her eyes a theatrical roll toward the family room and Mr. Hogue. As he passed through the kitchen, Daniel looked around, trying to see if anything portable was missing—a paradoxical exercise, given that he had never laid eyes on the room before. Sugar bowl, saltshaker, pepper mill, tea tongs trailing a winding rusty ribbon of dried tea. On the kitchen counter, under the telephone, lay a neat pile of letters and envelopes, and Daniel thought Hogue might have grabbed some of these, but they had been rubber-banded together and they looked undisturbed. A business card was affixed with a paper clip to the uppermost letter, printed with the name and telephone number of a Sergeant Matt Reedy of the Domestic Violence Unit of the Seattle Police Department. Daniel peeled back the pleat of the letter it was clipped to—it was out of its envelope—and peeked at its salutation, typed on an old typewriter that dropped its O's.

"DEAR BITCH," he read. "ARE YOU AND HERMAN HAPPY NOW, YOU—"

"Daniel! What are you doing?"

"Nothing," Daniel said, letting the letter fall shut again. "They, uh, they seem to be having some problems, the people who live in this house."

"Nothing that's our business, Daniel," Christy said, with what seemed to him excessive primness, taking hold of his hand.

Daniel yanked his hand free. He could hear Mr. Hogue muttering to himself in the other room.

"Ouch!" said Christy, bringing her fingers to her lips to kiss the joints he'd wrenched. She eyed the pile of letters on the counter. "What did it say?"

"It said maybe they ought to try rubbing each other's feet a little more often."

Now Christy really looked hurt.

"If you didn't want to do it, Daniel, I wish—"

"What's going on in here?" said Mr. Hogue, returning from the family room.

"We're just coming now," Daniel said. "Sorry. It's just—man, this kitchen is incredible."

Hogue gave a sour nod, lips pressed together. There was an obvious bulge in his right hip pocket now, and what appeared to be a table-tennis paddle protruding from the left one.

"Incredible," he agreed.

In the family room, when they joined him there, Hogue stole a well-thumbed paperback copy of Donald Trump's autobiography which was lying out on the coffee table, and in the small, tobacco-stained den off the foyer he took a little brass paperweight in the shape of a re-clining pasha with curled slippers. When they went out to the garage, where, along with a long, slender automobile hidden under a canvas cover, there was a well-stocked workbench, he filched a box of nails, a Lufkin tape mea-sure, and something else that Daniel couldn't quite deter-mine the nature of. The thefts were blatant and apparently unself-conscious, and by the time they got upstairs to the second guest bedroom, Christy, too, was watching in a kind of jolly dread as Mr. Hogue worked the place over. He took a souvenir Space Needle, and a rubber coin purse, and a package of deodorizing shoe inserts. When he led the young couple at last into the master bedroom, his pockets were jangling.

He stopped short as he entered the room, so that Daniel and Christy nearly collided with him. He looked around at the big four-poster bed, the heavy Eastlake dresser and wardrobe, the walls covered in an unusual dark paper the red of old leather books. Once again Hogue marveled, in the same openmouthed, oddly crest-fallen manner, as if the bedroom's decor, like the living room's, came to him, somehow, as a blow. As in the liv-ing room, there was no indication that the sellers had been expecting anyone to come through. The bed was unmade, and there were some ruffled white blouses and several bras and pairs of women's underpants heaped on the floor by the door. Hogue crossed the dark red room to a door opposite, which appeared to give onto a screened-in sleeping porch. Windows on either side of the door let in some of the bright September light pouring through the outer windows of the porch.

"I'd sure like to lie down in that hammock out there,"
Hogue said, with surprising wistfulness. He gave the knob
an experimental twist. It was locked. He pressed his face
to the glass. "God, I'm tired."

He reached into his breast pocket for a cigarette and
found nothing there. He looked back and smiled thinly at
Daniel and Christy, as if they had played a cruel trick on
him, hiding the only solace of a weary and overworked
man. Then he patted down all his clattering pockets until
he came up with a tattered Pall Mall. He went over to a
marble-topped nightstand beside the bed and pulled open
its drawer. He scrabbled around inside until he found a
book of matches. His hands were shaking so badly now
that he dropped the cigarette. Then he dropped the
burning match. At last he succeeded in getting the thing
lit. He blew a plume of smoke toward the pillows of the
big, disorderly bed.

"You'll get the sun almost all day long in this room,"
he said, dreamily. "It's a shame to paper it over so dark."
Then he flicked ashes onto the polished fir floor.

"All right, Mr. Hogue," said Christy, with all the
sharpness of tone she was capable of mustering. "I guess
we've seen enough."

"All right," said Hogue, though he didn't move. He
just stood there, looking out at the canvas hammock that
was hung between two pillars of the sleeping porch.

"We'll meet you downstairs, how about?" Daniel said.
"How about you just give us a minute to talk things over
between ourselves. You know. Look around one more
time. You can't rush into something like this, right?"

Hogue swallowed, and some of the old flush of anger
seemed to return now to the tips of his ears and to the
skin at the back of his neck. Daniel could see that it was
Hogue who wanted to be left alone here, in this bedroom, contemplating all his untold mistakes and whatever
it was that was eating at him. He wanted them out of

there. Christy sidled up to Daniel and pressed herself against him, hip to his thigh, cheek against his shoulder. He put his arm around her, and pressed his fingers against the slight bulge of skin under the strap of her bra.

"You know how important the bedroom is," Christy said, in a strangled voice.

Hogue took a thoughtful drag on his cigarette, eyeing them. Then, as before, the fire seemed to go out of him, and he nodded.

"I'll meet you downstairs," he said. "You kids take all the time you want."

He went out of the room, but before he did so, he stopped by the pile of laundry, picked up a rather large pair of lobelia blue panties with a lace waistband, and stuffed them into his pocket with the rest of his loot. They heard his tread on the stairs, and then, a moment later, the sound of a cabinet door squealing open on its hinges.

"He's going for the silver," Daniel said.

"Daniel, what are we going to do?"

Daniel shrugged. He sat down on the unmade bed, beside the nightstand that Hogue had rifled for matches.

"Maybe I should call my parents," Christy said. "They know Bob. Maybe they know what to do when he gets this way."

"I think it's a little too late for us to snub him," said Daniel.

Christy looked at him, angry and puzzled by the persistence of his nastiness toward her.

"That's not fair," she said. "God! Just because my parents—"

"Check this out." Daniel had been rummaging around in the nightstand drawer, where he had found, in addition to a bag of Ricola cough drops, a silver police whistle, and a small plastic vial of a popular genital lubricant, a greeting card, in a pink envelope that was laconically addressed

"Monkey." He pulled out the card, on the cover of which Greta Garbo and John Gilbert were locked in a passionate black-and-white embrace. The greeting was handwritten: "I have tripped and fallen in love with you. Herman." After a moment Daniel looked up, feeling a little confused, and handed it to Christy. She took it with a disapproving frown.

"Herman," she read. "Herman Silk?"

"I guess it's a little extra service he provides."

"He must be selling his own house." She sat down on the bed beside him. "Do they do that?"

"Why not?" Daniel said. "Plenty of people sell their own houses."

"True."

He showed her the vial of lubricant.

"Maybe he should have said, 'I have *slipped* and fallen.' "

"Daniel, put that back. I mean it." She gestured downstairs. "Just because he's doing it doesn't mean you should." She snatched the little plastic bottle out of his hand, tossed it and the greeting card into the drawer, and then slammed the drawer shut. "Come on. Let's just get out of here."

They glared at each other, and then Daniel stood up. He felt a strong desire for his wife. He wanted to push her down onto the bed and pound her until his bones hurt and the smell of smoke from her hair filled the bedroom. But he would never do anything like that. And neither would she. Not in someone else's house, in someone else's bed. They were, both of them, hypochondriacs and low rollers, habitual occupants of the right lane on freeways, inveterate savers of receipts, subscribers to *Consumer Reports,* filterers of tap water, wearers of helmets and goggles and kneepads. And yet their prudence—prudence itself, it now seemed to Daniel, watching Christy's freckled breast fall and rise and fall—was an illusion, a thin padded blanket they drew around themselves to cushion the impact from the string of bad decisions each of them had made. For all their apparent caution, they had nonetheless married each other, willingly and without material compulsion, in the presence of the three hundred people. Christy had agreed to join herself in perpetuity to a man whose touch left her vagina as dry as a fist, and Daniel had consigned himself to a life spent as a hundred and sixty-two pounds of hair in her mouth and elbows in her rib cage and hot breath in her nostrils.

"I hate you," he said.

For a moment she looked very surprised by this admission. Then she stuck out her jaw and narrowed her eyes.

"Well, I hate you, too," she said.

Daniel fell on top of her. He was a little self-conscious at first about the animal sounds he heard them making and the way they were biting and tearing at each other's clothes. It was uncomfortably reminiscent of a key scene in *Spanking Brittany Blue*. Then some spasm sent Christy's hand flying, and she smacked Daniel in the eye. Inside his skull a bright red star flared and then winked out. After that, he forgot to pay attention to what they were doing. The bed underneath them smelled of its right occupants, of the night sweat and the aftershave and the skin lotion of Herman Silk and his Monkey. A loose board in the old fir floor rhythmically creaked. When the proper time came, Daniel reached into the drawer for Herman's little bottle of lubricant. He turned Christy over on her belly, and spread her legs with his knee, and greased her freely with the cold, clear stuff. His entry into her was, for the first time, effortless and quick.

"That was fun," Christy said, when it was over. She stretched her limbs across the wrecked bed as if to embrace it, and rolled, like a cat, back and forth, until it was smeared with the manifold compound of their lovemaking.

"Still hate me?" said Daniel.

She nodded, and that was when Daniel saw the mistake that they had made. Although sex was something they both regarded as perilous, marriage had, by contrast, seemed safe—a safe house in a world of danger; the ultimate haven of two solitary, fearful souls. When you were single, this was what everyone who was already married was always telling you. Daniel himself had said it to his unmarried friends. It was, however, a lie. Sex had everything to do with violence, that was true, and marriage was at once a container for the madness between men and women and a fragile hedge against it, as religion was to death, and the laws of physics to the immense quantity of utter emptiness of which the universe was made. But there was nothing at all safe about marriage. It was a doubtful enterprise, a voyage in an untested craft, across a hostile ocean, with a map that was a forgery and with no particular destination but the grave.

"I had lunch with your father the other day," he began.

"Shh!" Christy said.

He lay beside her, listening. From downstairs they could hear the sound of raised voices. A man and a woman were shouting at each other. The man was Mr. Hogue.

"I'm going to call the police, Bob," the woman said.

Daniel and Christy looked at each other. They stood up and scrambled to reassemble their clothes. Daniel slipped the vial of lubricant into his pocket. Then they went downstairs.

When they came into the kitchen, Mr. Hogue was lying on the floor, amid hundreds and hundreds of spilt threepenny nails, cupping his chin in his hands. Blood leaked out between his fingers and drizzled down his neck into the plaid of his madras jacket. The reclining brass pasha, the Ping-Pong paddle, Space Needle, and all the other things he had stolen lay scattered on the floor around him. A handsome woman with red spectacles, whom Daniel recognized as Mrs. Hogue, was kneeling beside him, tears on her face, wiping at the cut on his chin with a paper towel.

"Christy," she said. "Hello, Daniel."

She smiled ruefully and looked down at Mr. Hogue, moaning and whispering curses on the terra-cotta floor.

"Is he okay?" Daniel said, pointing to the realtor, who was, he saw now, no stranger to these troubled rooms.

"I certainly hope not. I hit him as hard as I could." Mrs. Hogue dabbed tenderly at the cut with the paper towel, then looked around at the kitchen she had renovated at such great expense. "So," she said, "what do you two think of the house?"

Daniel looked at Christy. She had lost her scarf sometime in the course of their struggle upstairs. Her face was a blur of smeared lipstick and streaked mascara and the radiant blood in her cheeks.

"It's perfect," he said.

Son of the Wolfman

WHEN THE man charged with being the so-called Reservoir Rapist was brought to justice, several of the women who had been his victims came forward and identified themselves in the newspapers. The suspect, eventually convicted and sentenced to fifteen years at Pelican Bay, was a popular coach and math instructor at a high school in the Valley. He had won a state award for excellence in teaching. Two dozen present and former students and players, as well as the principal of his school, offered to testify in behalf of his good character at his trial. It was the man's solid position in the community, and the mishandling of a key piece of evidence, that led some of his victims to feel obliged to surrender the traditional veil of anonymity which the LAPD and the newspapers had granted them, and tell their painful stories not merely to a jury but to the world at large. The second of the Reservoir Rapist's eight victims, however, was not among these women. She had been attacked on August 7, 1995, as she jogged at dusk around Lake Hollywood. This was the perpetrator's preferred time of day, and one of three locations he favored in committing his attacks, the other two being the Stone Canyon and Franklin Reservoirs; such regular habits led in the end to his capture, on August 29. A day before the arrest, the faint pink proof of a cross, fixed in the developing fluid of her urine, informed the Reservoir Rapist's second victim, Cara Glanzman, that she was pregnant.

Cara, a casting agent, was married to Richard Case, a television cameraman. They were both thirty-four years old. They had met and become lovers at Bucknell University and at the time of the attack had been married since 1985. In their twelve years together, neither had been unfaithful to the other, and in all that time Cara had never gotten pregnant, neither by accident nor when she was trying with all of her might. For the past five years this unbroken chain of menses had been a source of sorrow, dissension, tempest, and recrimination in Cara and Richard's marriage. On the day she was raped, in fact, Cara had called an attorney friend of her best friend, just to discuss, in a vague, strangely hopeful way, the means and procedures of getting a divorce in California. After the attack her sense of punishment for having been so disloyal to Richard was powerful, and it is likely that, even had she not found herself pregnant with Derrick James Cooper's child, she would never have counted herself among the women who finally spoke out.

The first thing Cara did after she had confirmed the pregnancy with her obstetrician was to make an appointment for an abortion. This was a decision made on the spur of the moment, as she sat on the crinkling slick paper of the examining table and felt her belly twist with revulsion for the blob of gray cells that was growing in her womb. Her doctor, whose efforts over the past five years had all been directed toward the opposite end, told her that he understood. He scheduled the operation for the following afternoon.

Over dinner that night, take-out Indian food, which they ate in bed because she was still unwilling to go out at twilight or after dark, Cara told Richard that she was pregnant. He took the news with the same sad calm he had displayed since about three days after the attack, when he stopped calling the detective assigned to the case every few hours, and dried his fitful tears for good. He gave Cara's hand a squeeze, then looked down at the plate balanced on the duvet in the declivity of his folded legs. He had quit his most recent job in midshoot, and for the three weeks that followed the attack had done nothing but wait on Cara hand and foot, answering her every need. But beyond sympathetic noises and gentle reminders to eat, dress, and keep her appointments, he seemed to have almost nothing to say about what had happened to Cara. Often his silence hurt and disturbed her, but she persuaded herself that he had been struck dumb by grief, an emotion which he had never been able adequately to express.

In fact Richard had been silenced by his own fear of what might happen if he ever dared to talk about what he was feeling. In his imagination, at odd moments of the day—changing stations on the radio, peeling back pages of the newspaper to get to the box scores—he tortured and killed the rapist, in glistening reds and purples. He snapped awake at three o'clock in the morning, in their ample and downy bed, with Cara pressed slumbering against him, horrified by the sham of her safety in his arms. The police, the lawyers, the newspaper reporters, the psychotherapists and social workers, all were buffoons, moral dwarves, liars, contemptible charlatans and slackers. And, worst of all, he discovered that his heart had been secretly fitted by a cruel hand with thin burning wires of disgust for his wife. How could he have begun to express any of this? And to whom?

That evening, as they ate their fugitive supper, Cara pressed him to say something. The looping phrase of proteins that they had tried so hard and for so long to produce themselves, spending years and running up medical bills in the tens of thousands of dollars, had finally been scrawled inside her, albeit by a vandal's hand; and now tomorrow, with ten minutes' work, it was going to be rubbed away. He must feel something.

Richard shrugged, and toyed with his fork, turning it over and over as if looking for the silver mark. There had been so many times in the last few years that he had found himself, as now, on the verge of confessing to Cara that he did not, in his heart of hearts, really want to have children, that he was haunted by an unshakable sense that the barrenness of their marriage might, in fact, be more than literal.

Before he could get up the courage to tell her, however, that he would watch her doctor hose the bastard out of Cara's womb tomorrow not only with satisfaction but with relief, she leapt up from the bed, ran into the bathroom, and vomited up all the matar paneer, dal saag, and chicken tikka masala she had just eaten. Richard, thinking that this would be the last time for this particular duty, got up to go and keep her hair from falling down around her face. She yelled at him to close the door and leave her alone. When she emerged from the bathroom she looked pale and desolate, but her manner was composed.

"I'm canceling the thing tomorrow," she told him.

At that point, having said nothing else for so long, there was nothing for him to say but, automatically, "I understand."

PREGNANCY SUITED Cara. Her bouts of nausea were intense and theatrical but passed within the first few weeks, leaving her feeling purged of much of the lingering stink and foul luster of the rape. She adopted a strict, protein-rich diet that excluded fats and sugars. She bought a juice machine and concocted amalgams of uncongenial fruits and vegetables, which gave off a smell like the underparts of a lawn mower at the end of a wet summer. She joined a gym in Studio City and struck up a friendship there with a woman who played a supporting character on a very bad sitcom and who was due a day before Cara. She controlled what entered her body, oiled and flexed and soaked it in emollients, monitored its emissions. It responded precisely as her books told her that it would. She put on weight at the recommended rate. Secondary symptoms, from the mapping of her swollen breasts in blue tracery to mild bouts of headaches and heartburn, appeared reassuringly on schedule.

For a time she marveled at her sense of well-being, the lightness of her moods, the nearly unwrinkled prospect that every day presented. In the wake of that afternoon at Lake Hollywood, which might have reduced her to nothing, she grew; every day there was more of her. And the baby, in spite of the evil instant of its origin—the smell of hot dust and Mexican sage in her nostrils, the winking star of pain behind her eyes as her head smacked the ground—she now felt to be composed entirely of her own materials and shaped by her hand. It was being built of her platelets and antibodies, strengthened by the calcium she took, irrigated by the eight squeeze bottles of water she daily consumed. She had quit her job; she was making her way through Trollope. By the end of her second trimester she could go for days on end without noticing that she was happy.

Over the same period of six months, Richard Case became lost. It was a measure, in his view, of the breadth of the gulf that separated Cara and him that she could be so cheerfully oblivious of his lostness. His conversation, never expansive, dwindled to the curtness of a spaghetti western hero. His friends, whose company Richard had always viewed as the ballast carried in the hold of his marriage, began to leave him out of their plans. Something, as they put it to each other, was eating Richard. To them it was obvious what it must be: the rapist, tall, handsome, muscled, a former All-American who in his youth had set a state record for the four hundred hurdles, had performed in one violent minute a feat that Richard in ten loving years had not once managed to pull off. It was worse than cuckoldry, because his rival was no rival at all. Derrick Cooper was beneath contempt, an animal, unworthy of any of the usual emotions of an injured husband. And so Richard was forced, as every day his wife's belly expanded, and her nipples darkened, and a mysterious purplish trail was blazed through the featureless country between her navel and pubis, into the awful position of envying evil, coveting its vigor. The half-ironic irony that leavened his and his friends' male amusements with an air of winking put-on abandoned him. For a month or two he continued to go with them to the racetrack, to smoke cigars and to play golf, but he took his losses too seriously, picked fights, sulked, turned nasty. One Saturday his best friend found him weeping in a men's room at Santa Anita. After that Richard just worked. He accepted jobs that in the past he would have declined, merely to keep himself from having to come home. He gave up Dominican cigars in favor of cut-rate cigarettes.

He never went with Cara to the obstetrician, or read any of the many books on pregnancy, birth, and infancy she brought home. His father had been dead for years, but after he told his mother what manner of grandchild she could expect, which he did with brutal concision, he never said another word to her about the child on the way. When his mother asked, he passed the phone to Cara, and left the room. And when in her sixth month Cara announced her intention of attempting a natural childbirth, with the assistance of a midwife, Richard said, as he always did at such moments, "It's your baby." A woman in the grip of a less powerful personal need for her baby might have objected, but Cara merely nodded, and made an appointment for the following Tuesday with a midwife named Dorothy Pendleton, who had privileges at Cedars-Sinai.

That Monday, Cara was in a car accident. She called Richard on the set, and he drove from the soundstage in Hollywood, where he was shooting an Israeli kung fu movie, to her doctor's office in West Hollywood. She was uninjured except for a split cheek, and the doctor felt confident, based on an examination and a sonogram, that the fetus would be fine. Cara's car, however, was a total loss—she had been broadsided by a decommissioned hearse, of all things, a 1963 Cadillac. Richard, therefore, would have to drive her to the midwife's office the next day.

She did not present the matter as a request; she merely said, "You'll have to drive me to see Dorothy." They were on the way home from the doctor's office. Cara had her cellular telephone and her Filofax out and was busy rearranging the things the accident had forced her to re-arrange. "The appointment's at nine."

Richard looked over at his wife. There was a large bandage taped to her face, and her left eye had swollen almost shut. He had a tube of antibiotic ointment in the pocket of his denim jacket, a sheaf of fresh bandages, and a printed sheet of care instructions he was to follow for the next three days. Ordinarily, he supposed, a man cared for his pregnant wife both out of a sense of love and duty and because it was a way to share between them the weight of a burden mutually imposed. The last of these did not apply in their situation. The first had gotten lost somewhere between a shady bend in the trail under the gum trees at the north end of Lake Hollywood and the cold tile of the men's room at Santa Anita. All that remained now was duty. He had been transformed from Cara's husband into her houseboy, tending to all her needs and requests without reference to emotion, a silent, inscrutable shadow.

"What do you even need a midwife for?" he snapped. "You have a doctor."

"I told you all this," Cara said mildly, on hold with a hypnotist who prepared women for the pain of birth. "Midwives stay with you. They stroke you and massage you and talk to you. They put everything they have into trying to make sure you have the baby naturally. No C-section. No episiotomy. No drugs."

"No drugs." His voice dropped an octave, and though she didn't see it she knew he was rolling his eyes. "I would have thought the drugs would be an incentive to you."

Cara smiled, then winced. "I like drugs that make you feel something, Richie. These ones they give you just make you feel nothing. I want to feel the baby come. I want to be able to push him out."

"What do you mean, 'him'? Did they tell you the sex? I thought they couldn't tell."

"They couldn't. I . . . I don't know why I said 'him.' Maybe I just . . . everyone says, I mean, you know, old ladies and whatever, they say I'm carrying high . . ."

Her voice trembled, and she drew in a sharp breath. They had come to the intersection, at the corner of Sunset and Poinsettia, where four hours earlier the bat-winged black hearse had plowed into Cara's car. Involuntarily she closed her eyes, tensing her shoulders. The muscles there were tender from her having braced herself against the impact of the crash. She cried out. Then she laughed. She was alive, and the crescent mass of her body, the cage of sturdy bones cushioned with fat, filled with the bag of bloody seawater, had done its job. The baby was alive, too.

"This is the corner, huh?"

"I had lunch at Authentic. I was coming up Poinsettia."

It had been Richard who discovered this classic West Hollywood shortcut, skirting the northbound traffic and stoplights of La Brea Avenue, within a few weeks of their

marriage and arrival in Los Angeles. They had lived then
in a tiny one-bedroom bungalow around the corner from
Pink's. The garage was rented out to a palmist who
claimed to have once warned Bob Crane to mend his
wild ways. The front porch had been overwhelmed years
before by a salmon pink bougainvillea, and a disheveled
palm tree murmured in the backyard, battering the roof
at night with inedible nuts. It had been fall, the only season in Southern California that made any lasting claim on
the emotions. The sunlight was intermittent and wistful
as retrospection, bringing the city into sharper focus while
at the same time softening its contours. In the afternoons
there was a smoky tinge of eastern, autumnal regret in the
air, which they only later learned was yearly blown down
from raging wildfires in the hills. Cara had a bottom-tier
job at a second-rate Hollywood talent agency; Richard
was unemployed. Every morning he dropped her off at
the office on Sunset and then spent the day driving around
the city with the bulging Thomas Guide that had been her
wedding gift to him. Though by then they had been lovers
for nearly two years, at times Richard did not feel that he
knew Cara at all well enough to have actually gone and
married her, and the happy panic of those early days found
an echo whenever he set out to find his way across that
bland, encyclopedic grid of boulevards. When he picked
Cara up at the end of the day they would go to Lucy's or
Tommy Tang's and he would trace out for her the route
he had taken that day, losing himself among oil wells,
palazzos, Hmong strip malls, and a million little bunga-
lows like theirs, submerged in bougainvillea. They would
drink Tecate from the can and arrive home just as the
palmist's string of electric jalapeños was coming on in her
window, over the neon hand, its fingers outspread in wel-
come or admonition. They slept with the windows open,
under a light blanket, tangled together. His dreams would
take him once more to El Nido, Bel Air, Verdugo City.

In the morning he sat propped on a pillow, drinking coffee from a chipped Bauer mug, watching Cara move around the bedroom in the lower half of a suit. They had lived in that house for five years, innocent of Cara's basal temperature or the qualities of her vaginal mucus. Then they had moved to the Valley, buying a house with room for three children that overlooked the steel-bright reservoir. The Thomas Guide was in the trunk of Richard's car, under a blanket, missing all of the three pages that he needed most often.

"I can't believe you didn't see it," he said. "It was a fucking hearse."

For the first time she caught or allowed herself to notice the jagged, broken note in his voice, the undercurrent of anger that had always been there but from which her layers of self-absorption, of cell production, of sheer happy bulk, had so far insulated her.

"It wasn't my fault," she said.

"Still," he said, shaking his head. He was crying.

"Richard," she said. "Are you . . . what's the matter?"

The light turned to green. The car in front of them sat for an eighth of a second without moving. Richard slammed the horn with the heel of his hand.

"Nothing," he said, his tone once again helpful and light. "Of course I'll drive you anywhere you need to go."

MIDWIVES' EXPERIENCE of fathers is incidental but proficient, like a farmer's knowledge of bird migration or the behavior of clouds. Dorothy Pendleton had caught over two thousand babies in her career, and of these perhaps a thousand of the fathers had joined the mothers for at least one visit to her office, with a few hundred more showing up to do their mysterious duty at the birth. In the latter setting, in particular, men often revealed their characters, swiftly and without art. Dorothy had seen angry husbands before, trapped, taciturn, sarcastic, hot-tempered, frozen over, jittery, impassive, unemployed, workaholic, carrying the weight of all the generations of angry fathers before them, spoiled by the unfathomable action of bad luck on their ignorance of their own hearts. When she called Cara Glanzman and Richard Case in from the waiting room, Dorothy was alert at once to the dark crackling effluvium around Richard's head. He was sitting by himself on a love seat, slouched, curled into himself, slapping at the pages of a copy of *Yoga Journal*. Without stirring he watched Cara get up and shake Dorothy's hand. When Dorothy turned to him, the lower half of his face produced a brief, thoughtless smile. His eyes, shadowed and hostile, sidled quickly away from her own.

"You aren't joining us?" Dorothy said in her gravelly voice. She was a small, broad woman, dressed in jeans and a man's pin-striped oxford shirt whose tails were festooned with old laundry tags and spattered with blue paint. She looked dense, immovable, constructed of heavy materials and with a low center of gravity. Her big plastic eyeglasses, indeterminately pink and of a curvy elaborate style that had not been fashionable since the early 1980s, dangled from her neck on a length of knotty brown twine. Years of straddling the threshold of blessing and catastrophe had rendered her sensitive to all the fine shadings of family emotion, but unfit to handle them with anything other than tactless accuracy. She turned to Cara. "Is there a problem?"

"I don't know," said Cara. "Richie?"

"You don't know?" said Richard. He looked genuinely shocked. Still he didn't stir from his seat. "Jesus. Yes, Dorothy, there is a little problem."

Dorothy nodded, glancing from one to the other of them, awaiting some further explanation that was not forthcoming.

"Cara," she said finally, "were you expecting Richard to join you for your appointment?"

"Not—well, no. I was supposed to drive myself." She shrugged. "Maybe I was hoping . . . But I know it isn't fair."

"Richard," said Dorothy, as gently as she could manage, "I'm sure you want to help Cara have this baby."

Richard nodded, and kept on nodding. He took a deep breath, threw down the magazine, and stood up.

"I'm sure I must," he said.

They went into the examination room and Dorothy closed the door. She and another midwife shared three small rooms on the third floor of an old brick building on a vague block of Melrose Avenue, to the west of the Paramount lot. The other midwife had New Age leanings, which Dorothy without sharing found congenial enough. The room was decorated with photographs of naked pregnant women and with artwork depicting labor and birth drawn from countries and cultures, many of them in the Third World, where the long traditions of midwifery had never been broken. Because Dorothy's mother and grandmother had both been midwives, in a small town outside of Texarkana, her own sense of tradition was unconscious and distinctly unmillenarian. She knew a good deal about herbs and the emotions of mothers, but she did not believe, especially, in crystals, meditation, creative visualization, or the inherent wisdom of preindustrial societies. Twenty years of life on the West Coast had not rid her attitude toward pregnancy and labor of a callous East Texas air of husbandry and hard work. She pointed Richard to a battered fifth-hand armchair covered in gold Herculon, under a poster of the goddess Cybele with the milky whorl of the cosmos in her belly. She helped Cara up onto the examination table.

"I probably should have said something before," Cara said. "This baby. It isn't Richie's."

Richard's hands had settled on his knees. He stared at the stretched and distorted yellow daisies printed on the fabric of Cara's leggings, his shoulders hunched, a shadow on his jaw.

"I see," said Dorothy. She regretted her earlier brusqueness with him, though there was nothing to be done about it now and she certainly could not guarantee that she would never be brusque with him again. Her sympathy for husbands was necessarily circumscribed by the simple need to conserve her energies for the principals in the business at hand. "That's hard."

"It's extra hard," Cara said. "Because, see . . . I was raped. By the, uh, by the Reservoir Rapist, you remember him." She lowered her voice. "Derrick James Cooper."

"Oh, dear God," Dorothy said. It was not the first time these circumstances had presented themselves in her office, but they were rare enough. It took a particular kind of woman, one at either of the absolute extremes of the spectrum of hope and despair, to carry a baby through from that kind of beginning. She had no idea what kind of a husband it took. "I'm sorry for both of you. Cara." She opened her arms and stepped toward the mother, and Cara's head fell against her shoulder. "Richard." Dorothy turned, not expecting Richard to accept a hug from her but obliged by her heart and sense of the proprieties to offer him one.

He looked up at her, chewing on his lower lip, and the fury that she saw in his eyes made her take a step closer to Cara, to the baby in her belly, which he so obviously hated with a passion he could not, as a decent man, permit himself to acknowledge.

"I'm all right," he said.

"I don't see how you could be," Dorothy said. "That baby in there is the child of a monster who raped your wife. How can you possibly be all right with that? I wouldn't be."

She felt Cara stiffen. The hum of the air-conditioning filled the room.

"I still think I'm going to skip the hug," Richard said.

The examination proceeded. Cara displayed the pale hemisphere of her belly to Dorothy. She lay back and spread her legs, and Dorothy, a glove snapped over her hand, reached up into her and investigated the condition of her cervix. Dorothy took Cara's blood pressure and checked her pulse and then helped her onto the scale.

"You are perfect," Dorothy announced as Cara dressed herself. "You just keep on doing all the things you tell me you've been doing. Your baby is going to be perfect, too."

"What do you think it is?" Richard said, speaking for the first time since the examination had begun.

"Is? You mean the sex?"

"They couldn't tell on the ultrasound. I mean, I know there's no way to really know for sure, but I figured you're a midwife, maybe you have some kind of mystical secret way of knowing."

"As a matter of fact I am never wrong about that," Dorothy said. "Or so very rarely that it's the same as always being right."

"And?"

Dorothy put her right hand on Cara's belly. She was carrying high, which tradition said meant the baby was a boy, but this had nothing to do with Dorothy's feeling that the child was unquestionably male. It was just a feeling. There was nothing mystical to Dorothy about it.

"That's a little boy. A son."

Richard shook his head, face pinched, and let out a soft, hopeless gust of air through his teeth. He pulled Cara to her feet, and handed her her purse.

"Son of the monster," he said. "Wolfman Junior."

"I have been wrong once or twice," Dorothy said softly, reaching for his hand.

He eluded her grasp once more.

"I'm sort of hoping for a girl," he said.

"Girls are great," said Dorothy.

• • •

CARA WAS due on the fifth of May. When the baby had not come by the twelfth, she went down to Melrose to see Dorothy, who palpated her abdomen, massaged her perineum with jojoba oil, and told her to double the dose of a vile tincture of black and blue cohosh which Cara had been taking for the past week.

"How long will you let me go?" Cara said.

"It's not going to be an issue," Dorothy said.

"But if it is. How long?"

"I can't let you go much past two weeks. But don't worry about it. You're seventy-five percent effaced. Everything is nice and soft in there. You aren't going to go any two weeks."

On the fifteenth of May and again on the seventeenth, Cara and a friend drove into Laurel Canyon to dine at a restaurant whose house salad was locally reputed to contain a mystery leaf that sent women into labor. On the eighteenth, Dorothy met Cara at the office of her OB in West Hollywood. A nonstress test was performed. The condition of her amniotic sac and its contents was evaluated. The doctor was tight-lipped throughout, and his manner toward Dorothy Cara found sardonic and cold. She guessed that they had had words before Cara's arrival or were awaiting her departure before doing so. As he left to see his next patient, the doctor advised Cara to schedule an induction for the next day.

"We don't want that baby to get much bigger."

He went out.

"I can get you two more days," said Dorothy, sounding dry and unconcerned but looking grave. "But I'm going out on a limb."

Cara nodded. She pulled on the loose-waisted black trousers from CP Shades and the matching black blouse that she had been wearing for the past two weeks, even though two of the buttons were hanging loose. She stuffed her feet into her ragged black espadrilles. She tugged the headband from her head, shook out her hair, then fitted the headband back into place. She sighed, and nodded again. She looked at her watch. Then she burst into tears.

"I don't want to be induced," she said. "If they induce me I'm going to need drugs."

"Not necessarily."

"And then I'll probably end up with a C-section."

"There's no reason to think so."

"This started out as something I had no control over, Dorothy. I don't want it to end like that."

"Everything starts out that way, dear," said Dorothy. "Ends that way, too."

"Not this."

Dorothy put her arm around Cara and they sat there, side by side on the examining table. Dorothy relied on her corporeal solidity and steady nerves to comfort patients, and was not inclined to soothing words. She said nothing for several minutes.

"Go home," she said at last. "Call your husband. Tell him you need his prostaglandins."

"Richie?" Cara said. "But he . . . he can't. He won't."

"Tell him this is his big chance," Dorothy said. "I imagine it's been a long time."

"Ten months," said Cara. "At least. I mean unless he's been with somebody else."

"Call him," Dorothy said. "He'll come."

Richard had moved out of the house when Cara was in her thirty-fifth week. As from the beginning of their troubles, there had been no decisive moment of rupture, no rhetorical firefight, no decision taken on Richard's part at all. He had merely spent longer and longer periods away from home, rising well before dawn to take his morning run around the reservoir where the first line of the epitaph of their marriage had been written, and arriving home at night long after Cara had gone to sleep. In week thirty-four he had received an offer to film a commercial in Seattle. The shoot was scheduled for eight days. Richard had never come home. On Cara's due date, he had telephoned to say that he was back in L.A., staying at his older brother Matthew's up in Camarillo. He and Matthew had not gotten along as children, and in adulthood had once gone seven and a half years without speaking. That Richie had turned to him now for help filled Cara with belated pity for her husband. He was sleeping in a semiconverted garage behind Matthew's house, which he shared with Matthew's disaffected teenage son Jeremy.

"He doesn't get home till pretty late, Aunt Cara," Jeremy told her when she called that afternoon from the doctor's office. "Like one or two."

"Can I call that late?"

"Fuck yeah. Hey, did you have your baby?"

"I'm trying," Cara said. "Please ask him to call me."

"Sure thing."

"No matter how late it is."

She went to Las Carnitas for dinner. Strolling mariachis entered and serenaded her in her magic shroud of solitude and girth. She stared down at her plate and ate a tenth of the food upon it. She went home and spent a few hours cutting out articles from *American Baby,* and ordering baby merchandise from telephone catalogs in the amount of five hundred and twelve dollars. At ten o'clock she set her alarm clock for one-thirty and went to bed. At one o'clock she was wakened from a light uneasy sleep by a dream in which a shadowy, hirsute creature, bipedal and stooped, whom even within the dream itself she knew to be intended as a figure of or stand-in for Derrick James Cooper, mounted a plump *guitarrón,* smashing it against the ground. Cara shot up, garlic on her breath, heart racing, listening to the fading echoes in her body of the twanging of some great inner string.

The telephone rang.

"What's the matter, Cara?" Richard said, for the five thousandth time. His voice was soft and creased with fatigue. "Are you all right?"

"Richie," she said, though this was not what she had intended to say to him. "I miss you."

"I miss you, too."

"No, I . . . Richie, I don't want to do this without you."

"Are you having the baby? Are you in labor now?"

"I don't know. I might be. I just felt something. Richie, can't you come over?"

"I'll be there in an hour," he said. "Hold on."

Over the next hour Cara waited for a reverberation or renewal of the twinge that had awakened her. She felt strange; her back ached, and her stomach was agitated and sour. She chewed a Gaviscon and lay propped up on the bed, listening for the sound of Richard's car. He arrived exactly an hour after he had hung up the telephone, dressed in ripped blue jeans and a bulging, ill-shaped, liver-colored sweater she had knit for him in the early days of their marriage.

"Anything?" he said.

She shook her head, and started to cry again. He went over to her and, as he had so many times in the last year, held her, a little stiffly, as though afraid of contact with her belly, patting her back, murmuring that everything would be fine.

"No it won't, Richie. They're going to have to cut me open. I know they will. It started off violent. I guess it has to end violent."

"Have you talked to Dorothy? Isn't there some, I don't know, some kind of crazy midwife thing they can do? Some root you can chew or something?"

Cara took hold of his shoulders, and pushed him away from her so that she could look him in the eye.

"Prostaglandins," she said. "And you've got them."

"I do? Where?"

She looked down at his crotch, trying to give the gesture a slow and humorous Mae West import.

"That can't be safe," Richard said.

"Dorothy prescribed it."

"I don't know, Cara."

"It's my only hope."

"But you and I—"

"Come on, Richie. Don't even think of it as sex, all right? Just think of that as an applicator, all right? A prostaglandin delivery system."

He sighed. He closed his eyes, and wiped his open palms across his face as though to work some life and circulation into it. The skin around his eyes was crepey and pale as a worn dollar bill.

"That's a turn-on," he said.

He took off his clothes. He had lost twenty-five pounds over the past several months, and he saw the shock of this register on Cara's face. He stood a moment, at the side of the bed, uncertain how to proceed. For so long she had been so protective of her body, concealing it in loose clothing, locking him out of the bathroom during her showers and trips to the toilet, wincing and shying from any but the gentlest demonstrations of his hands. When she was still relatively slender and familiar he had not known how to touch her; now that she loomed before him, lambent and enormous, he felt unequal to the job.

She was wearing a pair of his sweatpants and a T-shirt, size extra large, that featured the face of Gali Karpas, the Israeli kung fu star, and the words TERMINATION ZONE. She slid the pants down to her ankles and lifted the shirt over her head. Her brassiere was engineered like a suspension bridge, armor plated, grandmotherly. It embarrassed her. Under the not quite familiar gaze of her husband, everything about her body embarrassed her. Her breasts, mottled and veined, tumbled out and lay shining atop the great lunar arc of her belly, dimpled by a tiny elbow or knee. Her pubic bush had sent forth rhizoids, and coarse black curls darkened her thighs and her abdomen nearly to the navel.

Richard sat back, looking at her belly. There was a complete miniature set of bones in there, a heart, a pleated brain charged with unimaginable thoughts. In a few hours or a day the passage he was about to enter would be stretched and used and inhabited by the blind, mute, and unknown witness to this act. The thought aroused him.

"Wow," Cara said, looking at his groin again. "Check that out."

"This is weird."

"Bad weird?" She looked up at Richard, reading in his face the unavoidable conclusion that the presence of the other man's child in her body had altered it so completely as to make her unrecognizable to him. A stranger, carrying a stranger in her womb, had asked him into her bed.

"Lie back," he said. "I'm going to do this to you."

"There's some oil in the drawer."

"We won't need it."

She lowered herself down onto her elbows and lay, legs parted, looking at him. He reached out, cautiously, watching his hands as they assayed the taut, luminous skin of her belly.

"Quickly," she said, after a minute. "Don't take too long."

"Does it hurt?"

"Just—please—"

Thinking that she required lubrication after all, Richard reached into the drawer of the nightstand. For a moment he felt around blindly for the bottle of oil. In the instant before he turned to watch what his hand was doing, his middle finger jammed against the tip of the X-Acto knife that Cara had been using to cut out articles on nipple confusion and thrush. He cried out.

"Did you come?"

"Uh, yeah, I did," he said. "But mostly I cut my hand."

It was a deep, long cut that pulsed with blood. After an hour with ice and pressure they couldn't get it to stop, and Cara said that they had better go to the emergency room. She wrapped the wound in half a box of gauze, and helped him dress. She threw on her clothes and followed him out to the driveway.

"We'll take the Honda," she said. "I'm driving."

They went out to the street. The sky was obscured by a low-lying fog, glowing pale orange as if lit from within, carrying an odor of salt and slick pavement. There was no one in the street and no sound except for the murmur of the Hollywood Freeway. Cara came around and opened the door for Richard, and drove him to the nearest hospital, one not especially renowned for the quality of its care.

"So was that the best sex of your life or what?" she asked him, laughing, as they waited at a red light.

"I'll tell you something," he said. "It wasn't the worst."

THE SECURITY guard at the doors to the emergency room had been working this shift for nearly three years and in that time had seen enough of the injuries and pain of the city of Los Angeles to render him immobile, smiling, very nearly inert. At 2:47 on the morning of May 20 a white Honda Accord pulled up, driven by a vastly pregnant woman. The guard, who would go off duty in an hour, kept smiling. He had seen pregnant women drive themselves to have their babies before. It was not advisable behavior, certainly, but this was a place where the inadvisable behaviors of the world came rushing to bear their foreseeable fruit. Then a man, clearly her husband, got out of the passenger side and walked, head down, past the guard. The sliding glass doors sighed open to admit him. The pregnant woman drove off toward the parking lot.

The guard frowned.

"Everything all right?" he asked Cara when she reappeared, her gait a slow contemplative roll, right arm held akimbo, right hand pressing her hip as though it pained her.

"I just had a really big contraction," she said. She made a show of wiping the sweat from her brow. "Whew." Her voice sounded happy, but to the guard she looked afraid.

"Well, you in the right place, then."

"Not really," she said. "I'm supposed to be at Cedars. Pay phone?"

He directed her to the left of the triage desk. She lumbered inside and called Dorothy.

"I think I'm having the baby," she said. "No, I'm not. I don't know."

"Keep talking," said Dorothy.

"I've only had three contractions."

"Uh-huh."

"Contractions hurt."

"They do."

"But, like, a lot."

"I know it. Keep talking."

"I'm calling from the emergency room." She named the hospital. "Richard cut his hand up. He . . . he came over . . . we . . ." A rippling sheet of hot foil unfurled in her abdomen. Cara lurched to one side. She caught herself and half-squatted on the floor beside the telephone cubicle, with the receiver in her hand, staring at the floor. She was so stunned by her womb's sudden arrogation of every sensory pathway in her body to its purposes that, as before, she forgot to combat or work her way through the contraction with the breathing and relaxation techniques she had been taught. Instead she allowed the pain to permeate and inhabit her, praying with childish fervor for it to pass. The linoleum under her feet was ocher with pink and gray flecks. It gave off a smell of ashes and pine. Cara was aware of Dorothy's voice coming through the telephone, suggesting that she try to relax the hinge of her jaw, her shoulder blades, her hips. Then the contraction abandoned her, as swiftly as it had arrived. Cara pulled herself to her feet. Her fingers ached around the receiver. There was a spreading fan of pain in her lower back. Otherwise she felt absolutely fine.

"You're having your baby," Dorothy said.

"Are you sure? How can you tell?"

"I could hear it in your voice, dear."

"But I wasn't talking." Though now as she said this she could hear an echo of her voice a moment earlier, saying, *Okay . . . okay . . . okay.*

"I'll be there in twenty minutes," Dorothy said.

When Cara found Richard, he was being seen by a physician's assistant, a large, portly black man whose tag read COLEY but who introduced himself as Nordell. Nordell's hair was elaborately braided and beaded. His hands were manicured and painted with French tips. He was pretending to find Richard attractive, or pretending to pretend. His hand was steady, and his sutures marched across Richard's swollen fingertip as orderly as a line of ants. Richard looked pale and worried. He was pretending to be amused by Nordell.

"Don't worry, girlfriend, I already gave him plenty of shit for you," Nordell told Cara when she walked into the examination room. "Cutting his hand when you're about to have a baby. I said, boyfriend, this is not your opera."

"He has a lot of nerve," said Cara.

"My goodness, look at you. You are big. How do you even fit behind the wheel of your car?"

Richard laughed.

"You be quiet." Nordell pricked another hole in Richard's finger, then tugged the thread through on its hook. "When are you due?"

"Two weeks ago."

"Uh-huh." He scowled at Richard. "Like she don't

already have enough to worry about without you sticking your finger on a damn X-Acto knife."

Richard laughed again. He looked like he was about to be sick.

"You all got a name picked out?"

"Not yet."

"Know what you're having?"

"We don't," said Cara. "The baby's legs were always in the way. But Richard would like a girl."

Richard looked at her. He had noticed when she came into the room that her face had altered, that the freckled pallor and fatigue of recent weeks had given way to a flush and a giddy luster in her eye that might have been happiness or apprehension.

"Come on," said Nordell. "Don't you want to have a son to grow up just like you?"

"That would be nice," Richard said.

Cara closed her eyes. Her hands crawled across her belly. She sank down to the floor, rocking on her heels. Nordell set down his suturing clamp and peeled off his gloves. He lowered himself to the floor beside Cara and put a hand on her shoulder.

"Come on, honey, I know you been taking those breathing lessons. So breathe. Come on."

"Oh, Richie."

Richard sat on the table, watching Cara go into labor. He had not attended any but the first of the labor and delivery classes and had not the faintest idea of what was expected of him or what it now behooved him to do. This was true not just of the process of parturition but of all the duties and grand minutiae of fatherhood itself. The rape, the conception, the growing of the placenta, the nurturing and sheltering of the child in darkness, in its hammock of woven blood vessels, fed on secret broth—all of these had gone on with no involvement on his part. Until now he had taken the simple, unalterable fact of this rather brutally to heart. In this way he had managed to prevent the usual doubts and questions of the prospective father from arising in his mind. For a time, it was true, he had maintained a weak hope that the baby would be a girl. Vaguely he had envisioned a pair of skinny legs in pink high-topped sneakers, crooked upside down over a horizontal bar, a tumbling hem conveniently obscuring the face. When Dorothy had so confidently pronounced the baby a boy, however, Richard had actually felt a kind of black relief. At that moment, the child had effectively ceased to exist for him: it was merely the son of Cara's rapist, its blood snarled by the same abrading bramble of chromosomes. In all the last ten months he had never once imagined balancing an entire human being on his forearm, never pondered the depths and puzzles of his relationship to his own father, never suffered the nightly clutch of fear for the future that haunts a man while his pregnant wife lies beside him with her heavy breath rattling in her throat. Now that the hour of birth was at hand he had no idea what to do with himself.

"Get down here," said Nordell. "Hold this poor child's hand."

Richard slid off the table and knelt beside Cara. He took her warm fingers in his own.

"Stay with me, Richie," Cara said.

"All right," said Richard. "Okay."

While Nordell hastily wrapped Richard's finger in gauze and tape, a wheelchair was brought for Cara. She was rolled off to admissions, her purse balanced on her knees. When Richard caught up to her a volunteer was just wheeling her into the elevator.

"Where are we going?" Richard said.

"To labor and delivery," said the volunteer, an older man with hearing aids, his shirt pocket bulging with the outline of a pack of cigarettes. "Fourth floor. Didn't you take the tour?"

Richard shook his head.

"This isn't our hospital," Cara said. "We took the tour at Cedars."

"I wish I had," Richard said, surprising himself.

When the labor triage nurse examined Cara, she found her to be a hundred percent effaced and nearly eight centimeters dilated.

"Whoa," she said. "Let's go have you this baby."

"Here?" Cara said, knowing she sounded childish. "But I . . ."

"But nothing," said the nurse. "You can have the next one at Cedars."

Cara was hurried into an algae-green gown and rolled down to what she and the nurse both referred to as an LDR. This was a good-sized room that had been decorated to resemble a junior suite in an airport hotel, pale gray and lavender, oak-laminate furniture, posters on the walls tranquilly advertising past seasons of the Santa Fe Chamber Music Festival. There was a hospital smell of air-conditioning, however, and so much diagnostic equipment crowded around the bed, so many wires and booms and monitors, that the room felt cramped, and the effect of pseudoluxury was spoiled. With all the gear and cables looming over Cara, the room looked to Richard like nothing so much as a soundstage.

"We forgot to bring a camera," he said. "I should shoot this, shouldn't I?"

"There's a vending machine on two," said the labor nurse, raising Cara's legs up toward her chest, spreading them apart. The outer lips were swollen and darkened to a tobacco-stain brown, gashed pink in the middle, bright as bubble gum. "It has things like combs and toothpaste. I think it might have the kind of camera you throw away."

"Do I have time?"

"Probably. But you never know."

"Cara, do you want pictures of this? Should I go? I'll be right back. Cara?"

Cara didn't answer. She had slipped off into the world of her contractions, eyes shut, head rolled back, brow luminous with pain and concentration like the brow of Christ in a Crucifixion scene.

The nurse had lost interest in Richard and the camera question. She had hold of one of Cara's hands in one of hers, and was stroking Cara's hair with the other. Their faces were close together, and the nurse was whispering something. Cara nodded, and bit her lip, and barked out an angry laugh. Richard stood there. He felt he ought to be helping Cara, but the nurse seemed to have everything under control. There was nothing for him to do and no room beside the bed.

"I'll be right back," he said.

He got lost on his way down to the second floor, and then when he reached two he got lost again trying to find the vending machine. It stood humming in a corridor outside the cafeteria, beside the men's room. Within its tall panel of glass doors, a carousel rotated when you pressed a button. It was well stocked with toiletry and sanitary items, along with a few games and novelties for bored children. There was one camera left. Richard fed a twenty-dollar bill into the machine and received no change.

When he got back to the room he stood with his fingers on the door handle. It was cold and dry and gave him a static shock when he grasped it. Through the door he heard Cara say, "Fuck," with a calmness that frightened him. He let go of the handle.

There was a squeaking of rubber soles, rapid and intent. Dorothy Pendleton was hurrying along the corridor toward him. She had pulled a set of rose surgical scrubs over her street clothes. They fit her badly across the chest and one laundry-marked shirttail dangled free of the waistband. As Dorothy hurried toward him she was pinning her hair up behind her head, scattering bobby pins as she came.

"You did it," she said. "Good for you."

Richard was surprised to find that he was glad to see Dorothy. She looked intent but not flustered, rosy-cheeked, wide-awake. She gave off a pleasant smell of sugary coffee. Over one shoulder she carried a big leather sack covered in a worn patchwork of scraps of old kilims. He noticed, wedged in among the tubes of jojoba oil and the medical instruments, a rolled copy of *Racing Form*.

"Yeah, well, I'm just glad, you know, that my sperm finally came in handy for something," he said.

She nodded, then leaned into the door. "Good sperm," she said. She could see that he needed something from her, a word of wisdom from the midwife, a pair of hands to yank him breech first and hypoxic back into the dazzle and clamor of the world. But she had already wasted enough of her attention on him, and she reached for the handle of the door.

Then she noticed the twenty-dollar cardboard camera dangling from his hand. For some reason it touched her that he had found himself a camera to hide behind.

She stopped. She looked at him. She put a finger to his chest. "My father was a sheriff in Bowie County, Texas," she said.

He took a step backward, gazing down at the finger. Then he looked up again.

"Meaning?"

"Meaning get your ass into that room, deputy." She pushed open the door.

The first thing they heard was the rapid beating of the baby's heart through the fetal monitor. It filled the room with its simple news, echoing like a hammer on tin.

"You're just in time," said the labor nurse. "It's crowning."

"Dorothy. Richie." Cara's head lolled toward them, her

cheeks streaked with tears and damp locks of hair, her eyes red, her face swollen and bruised looking. It was the face she had worn after the attack at Lake Hollywood, dazed with pain, seeking out his eyes. "Where did you go?" she asked him. She sounded angry. "Where did you go?"

Sheepishly he held up the camera.

"Jesus! Don't go away again!"

"I'm sorry," he said. A dark circle of hair had appeared between her legs, surrounded by the fiery pink ring of her straining labia. "I'm sorry!"

"Get him scrubbed," Dorothy said to the nurse. "He's catching the baby."

"What?" said Richard. He felt he ought to reassure Cara. "Not really."

"Really," said Dorothy. "Get scrubbed."

The nurse traded places with Dorothy at the foot of the bed, and took Richard by the elbow. She tugged the shrink-wrapped camera from his grasp.

"Why don't you give that to me?" she said. "You go get scrubbed."

"I washed my hands before," Richard said, panicking a little.

"That's good," said Dorothy. "Now you can do it again."

Richard washed his hands in brown soap that stung the nostrils, then turned back to the room. Dorothy had her hand on the bed's controls, raising its back, helping Cara into a more upright position. Cara whispered something.

"What's that, honey?" said Dorothy.

"I said Richard I'm sorry too."

"What are you sorry about?" Dorothy said. "Good God."

"Everything," Cara said. And then, "Oh."

She growled and hummed, snapping her head from side to side. She hissed short whistling jets of air through her teeth. Dorothy glanced at the monitor. "Big one," she said. "Here we go."

She waved Richard over to her side. Richard hesitated.

Cara gripped the side rails of the bed. Her neck arched backward. A humming arose deep inside her chest and grew higher in pitch as it made its way upward until it burst as a short cry, ragged and harsh, from her lips.

"Whoop!" said Dorothy, drawing back her arms. "A stargazer! Hi, there!" She turned again to Richard, her hands cupped around something smeary and purple that was protruding from Cara's body. "Come on, move it. See this."

Richard approached the bed, and saw that Dorothy balanced the baby's head between her broad palms. It had a thick black shock of hair. Its eyes were wide open, large and dark, pupils invisible, staring directly, Richard felt, at him. There was no bleariness, or swelling of the lower eyelids. No one, Richard felt, had ever quite looked at him this way, without emotion, without judgment. The consciousness of a great and irrevocable event came over him; ten months' worth of dread and longing filled him in a single unbearable rush. Disastrous things had happened to him in his life; at other times, stretching far back into the interminable afternoons of his boyhood, he had experienced a sense of buoyant calm that did not seem entirely without foundation in the nature of things. Nothing awaited him in the days to come but the same uneven progression of disaster and contentment. And all those moments, past and future, seemed to him to be concentrated in that small, dark, pupilless gaze.

Dorothy worked her fingers in alongside the baby's shoulders. Her movements were brusque, sure, and indelicate. They reminded Richard of a cook's, or a potter's. She took a deep breath, glanced at Cara, and then gave the baby a twist, turning it ninety degrees.

"Now," she said. "Give me your hands."

"But you don't really catch them, do you?" he said. "That's just a figure of speech."

"Don't you wish," said Dorothy. "Now get in there."

She dragged him into her place, and stepped back. She took hold of his wrists and laid his hands on the baby's head. It was sticky and warm against his fingers.

"Just wait for the next contraction, Dad. Here it comes."

He waited, looking down at the baby's head, and then Cara grunted, and some final chain or stem binding the baby to her womb seemed to snap. With a soft slurping sound the entire child came squirting out into Richard's hands. Almost without thinking, he caught it. The nurse and Dorothy cheered. Cara started to cry. The baby's skin was the color of skimmed milk, smeared, glistening, flecked with bits of dark red. Its shoulders and back were covered in a faint down, matted and slick. It worked its tiny jaw, snorting and snuffling hungrily at the sharp first mouthfuls of air.

"What is it?" Cara said. "Is it a boy?"

"Wow," said Richard, holding the baby up to show Cara. "Check this out."

Dorothy nodded. "You have a son, Cara," she said. She took the baby from Richard, and laid him on the collapsed tent of Cara's belly. Cara opened her eyes. "A big old hairy son."

Richard went around to stand beside his wife. He leaned in until his cheek was pressed against hers. They studied the wolfman's boy, and he regarded them.

"Do you think he's funny-looking?" Richard said doubtfully. Then the nurse snapped a picture of the three of them, and they looked at her, blinking, blinded by the flash.

"Beautiful," said the nurse.

Green's Book

SHE WAS the type of girl that Green always noticed right away: too thin, dressed wrong, foulmouthed, already drunk and laughing too loud—a shimmying funnel of dust, lightning, and uprooted houses working its way across the room. She had coarse dyed-black hair worn chopped off at the jawline, a wide mouth painted the color of a grape Tootsie Pop, brilliant teeth, pointy black boots, black stockings, and a crinkly black dress that showed off exactly too much of her shoulders and breasts. It was a few seconds, standing in Emily Klein's living room, shaking hands all around, before Green realized that he knew the girl. And then one moment more of erotic doubt, mingled with a pleasant sense of trouble, before he recognized her. She spotted him. Green hooked an arm around his young daughter's waist, hoisted her into the air, and turned back toward the door.

"I left something in the trunk," he told Emily Klein. He fled down the front steps with his squirming burden, looking for all the world like a man who was stealing a child. He stepped back out into the afternoon. The light of a Washington summer, of his earliest childhood, spilled over the dilapidated lawns and trees of the Kleins' neighborhood, rippling and golden and rank as a pool of gasoline. Green hurried toward his car.

"Put me down!" Jocelyn cried. "You're mooshing my new dress."

"Sorry," said Green, as if he had bumped a passerby. He was not listening to his daughter's protests.

"Daddy!" It was a cry of fury—choked, deeply offended—such as Jocelyn rarely expressed to Green. The heel of her shoe glanced sharply off his cheekbone. That was when he realized that she had been kicking him the whole way out to the street. No doubt he had made a spectacle of them both.

They reached Green's car, a new black German sedan with a turbocharged engine. Green stopped, his cheek stinging. He turned the little girl over and set her on her feet. Her cheeks were bright red, her breathing frantic. Green realized that in his haste to flee the woman in the Kleins' living room he had been constricting the very wind out of his daughter's lungs.

"I'll fix your dress," he said, glancing over his shoulder at the house. "I'm sorry."

The dress was a gray-and-white seersucker dirndl, appliquéd on the bib with a basket of blue asters, worn over a stiff white blouse trimmed at the collar with crocheted lace. The shoes, also new, were patent T-straps, liquid and black as the pupil of an eye. Jocelyn's legs, their pudgy thighs the only trace that now remained of a rather corpulent babyhood, Green had stuffed carefully into a pair of white tights. When Green exercised his rights of visitation—one weekend a month, three weeks during the summer—he dressed her with surprising care and according to outmoded notions of proper feminine attire that horrified his former wife but that, for reasons he chose not to examine, Green found he could not suppress.

Green knelt in front of Jocelyn and tugged down on the hem of her skirt, smoothing it with one hand. He hiked the waistband of the tights, lifting his daughter a full half inch off the ground, and held her suspended until her skinny little bottom—she was just out of diapers—sank back snugly into place. He straightened her lacy collar, setting it to lie flat on her heaving chest. Jocelyn observed these attentions with an air of approval and of being very conscious of her decision to forgive her father for his bad behavior.

"I can feel my heart," she told him. She pressed a dimpled hand against the basket of blue asters. The presence of her heart in her chest had come to her attention only within the last week. Its activities, when they became palpable, were still an accidental enchantment that startled and delighted her, like the metallic blur of a hummingbird at the window or the sound of her mother's voice emerging from Green's answering machine.

"What's it doing?"

"It's beading." She had mangled his explanation of the circulatory system and must, he thought, see the production of her blood as an amusing inward pastime of her body in moments of exertion, an endless stringing of bright red beads. "Where are we going?"

"Daddy has to get something out of the trunk."

"What?"

"Something."

"Is it a surprise?"

"I don't know. It might be."

"A surprise for me? Is it a toy?"

"No," he said. "It isn't a toy."

"What is it, then?"

"Jocelyn, please. It isn't anything."

In the trunk of his car, when he opened it, along with his overnight bag, Jocelyn's pink plastic suitcase, and a zippered case of compact discs, was an implausible crate of grapefruit he had bought five weeks ago, on a briefer than fleeting impulse, at a roadside stand near his home in Fort Lauderdale, then forgotten until two days earlier as he loaded up for the drive north. Green ran a hand through his hair; there was enough sweat on his forehead to slick back and hold the thinning strands in place. He tried to decide just how idiotic he would look struggling into the Kleins' house with a crate full of shriveled Indian River grapefruit. Now that they were safely out on the street again, he considered the possible consequences of their simply splitting. Caryn, his ex-wife, who lived in Philadelphia, was not expecting Jocelyn for another two days. Green had accepted an invitation to stay with the Kleins, but now that seemed impossible. He had always wanted to go out to Chincoteague and take a look at those half-feral ponies from the Marguerite Henry books; maybe Jocelyn would like that. At any rate, he was certain his absence from Seth Klein's graduation party could not possibly make a great deal of difference to Seth, who hadn't seen Green since he was a very little boy and even then had not evinced any great interest in Green. Green burned his forehead for an instant on the black roof of his car. Go, he told himself.

"Marty?"

They were supposed to be the descendants of horses that survived the sinking of a Spanish galleon in the age of plunder, those ponies, but Green had read recently that natural historians now doubted this. It was much more likely that the ponies had been deliberately driven onto their island by local farmers looking for convenient pastureland. Green wondered if by the end of his life, or perhaps sooner, every single beautiful lie he had been told during the course of his childhood, great or small, would have been exposed.

"Marty? It's Ruby. Klein."

Green turned. Ruby came scraping and clattering down

the drive in her witch boots, trailing cigarette smoke, holding a can of Pabst, looking amazed. She had a long, handsome, heavy-chinned face, flawless skin tinged faintly blue like skimmed milk, with the plump purple-jelly-bean mouth. Evidently her natural endowments were insufficient—or perhaps superfluous—for her purposes. Not only were her lips heavily painted but her eyelashes were rimed like a chimney sweep's bristles with thick black flakes of mascara, and she had pierced the ridge of her left eyebrow, both nostrils, and every available centimeter of both earlobes. Several ounces of sterling were involved, and there was an unmistakable promise, not just in this but in something halting and surreptitious in her walk, of hidden posts, clasps, and metal rings concealed elsewhere on her body. Her machete-cut hair scraped against his cheek as she lurched wholeheartedly into his arms. Green held her for as long as he could bear, then let go. His heart seemed to shrink in his chest, to collapse itself into a tight, tiny black fist of shame. Her brilliant loose smile was a reproach, her beauty a reminder of all that was ugly inside him.

"Look at you," he said. The last time he had seen her, she was seven, dressed for an ice-skating class, wearing a pair of mittens strung through the sleeves of a pink coat trimmed with white fake fur. "Ruby. My."

"I'm kind of drunk; you probably noticed."

Green had schooled himself never to tell lies. It was a constant battle with his natural impulses.

"I did," he said.

"I'm so pissed. My father is coming." She pronounced the word *father* by deepening her voice to a Mister Ed baritone and nickering it, rolling her eyes. "I haven't seen the bastard in five years. Last time I saw him, I scratched his bastard face. There was skin under my fingernails."

"My goodness," said Green. He had never met Emily Klein's ex-husband, though tucked away in some inner

closet drawer he found a small shoe box in which scorn
for Dr. Harvey Klein, who had left his pregnant wife and
daughter and fled to Texas with his receptionist, lay
wrapped in yellowing tissue paper. Still, the expression of
naked parricidal impulses within the hearing of his own
loving daughter made him uneasy. He cleared his throat
and pushed Jocelyn forward, a bit like Van Helsing brandishing a cross, both as a reproach to Ruby and as a form
of protection against her.

"Hi, cutie," Ruby said. She bent forward, hands on her
knees, in an effort to put herself at eye level with Jocelyn.
Green's daughter turned her face away and buried it in
the billow of his trouser leg. He was wearing a pair of
loose linen Florida pants, the color of a boiled shrimp.
"What's your name?"

"This is Jocelyn," said Green. "My little girl. We're on
our way back to her mother's in Philly. In fact—this is
embarrassing—well, I just realized that she's expecting us
today and not—"

"Your mom said you might show up," Ruby said, her
eyes still searching out Jocelyn's in the pink folds of
Green's pants. A strand of hair fell across her face. She
peeled it back and tucked it behind her right ear. It sprang
loose. "She called." She pointed at Jocelyn with a finger-
nail painted a dark purple the exact shade of a hammer-
blow bruise. "She said you were a little angel."

This information made no apparent impression on
Jocelyn. She had worked a large patch of Green's pant leg
into her mouth and was chewing on it with alacrity.

"Jocelyn," Green said, breaking one of his personal rules
of fatherly conduct, which was never to employ his
child's name, alone, to reprimand her. Green was writing
a book of rules of fatherly conduct. "A child's name is a
gift," he had written in his manuscript, which was under
contract to a New York publisher, "an object of power;
in many cases, with the passing of years and the accretion

of character traits and personality quirks, a richly descrip-
tive adjective. It must never be, however, an expression of
reproach." The irony of Green's writing a textbook on
fatherhood while at the same time spending a total of less
than two months a year with his own daughter was not
lost on him. Few if any ironies ever were. Ironicism, by
the way, was another typical resource of fathers proscribed
by the rules in Green's book.

"She told me you were in Europe someplace," Green
said to Ruby. It was only, in fact, because his mother had
led him to believe that Ruby would not be present that
Green had accepted the suggestion from his mother, who
lived now in Denver, that as long as he and little Jocelyn
were going to be passing through Washington, D.C., they
might as well drop by the Kleins' party and see Emily
Klein, whose ovarian cancer appeared to be on the verge
of killing her.

"Yeah, with my band," Ruby said, rolling her eyes.
"Ex-band. Fuckin' losers. I came home early. The tour
fuckin' blew, oh, my God. Shit Jesus, it's hot out here.
What are you guys doing? You ran out of there like
someone was chasing you."

It was a mark of Green's bewilderment that he allowed
this torrent of foul language to flow over his child without
comment, without even the minimally disapproving eyebrow arch that he reserved in situations where the swearer
was, for example, an extremely large and menacing man.

"Oh," he said. "Yes. I don't know. Let's go in. We
were just . . ."

"Damn, I was so glad when you walked in there," she
said. "That whole scene is so fuckin' tedious; all Seth's
friends are such morons—"

"Tedious," Green said. He returned the car keys to his
pocket. He would never make it out to see the wild
ponies of Assateague Island, and this knowledge, for some
reason, stirred in him a wave not so much of sadness as of

self-loathing, as if he had already promised to take Jocelyn there and was now going to be forced to renege. "I'm afraid I'm pretty tedious myself these days."

"Tedious is, like, not an absolute," Ruby said, licking her lips. "There are degrees."

Green recognized the humor in her remark and produced what he hoped would pass for a plausible smile. Everything he saw was bordered with a sparkle of nausea, and the blood boiled in his ears like the ocean. He picked up Jocelyn and settled her onto his forearm. "I'll do my best to be entertaining."

Ruby took his arm and pulled him toward the house.

"That's what I always liked about you," she said.

ONE NIGHT when he was thirteen years old, Green had put Ruby Klein into her bed and waited for her to fall asleep. On Friday and Saturday nights, when Emily Klein and Green's mother—girlhood chums from Richmond whose divorces had beached them within a mile of each other in Rockville, Maryland—went out to drink wine and meet men, Ruby Klein was often left in Green's care. Ruby was four, shy, docile, afraid of darkness, and Green's feeling for her had always been one of impatient indifference tempered by occasional moments of embarrassed gratitude. He was a little-esteemed boy, and she looked up to him. He was often lonely, and she was always there. Then Green had begun to be driven mad by the idea of sex. He found books published by the Grove Press that described perversions and lewd acts that in the mind of an adult would easily have been judged inhuman, fanciful, or at least ill-advised. He masturbated on buses, in public rest rooms, lying across his grandmother's bed. A desire overcame him to have sex with almost every woman he knew, from his mother and Emily Klein, to the French teacher Ms. Ball, to a retarded girl named Rojean whom he often saw after swim-team practice happily hosing down the pool deck in her tight red Speedo. The books he had discovered at the back of his mother's closet gave him the impression that such polymorphous and indiscriminate behavior was not only possible but appropriate and common. On this one night, then, he had felt himself aroused by the glinting down on the neck of little Ruby Klein, by the tracery of pale blue veins at her armpits, by the sound of her water in the toilet. When he determined that she had fallen asleep, he drew the covers back and lifted the hem of the overlong T-shirt she wore and contemplated her pale belly and her tiny boy's nipples. He bent forward to kiss her at the junction of her skinny thighs.

"Marty, what are you doing?" she had asked him, in a soft, strangely adult voice.

He pretended to her that he had been afraid she was developing a rash; he said it was something they had eaten. He dressed her and covered her and kissed her on the forehead as a hundred times before.

"Now be quiet," he said. "And go to sleep."

The madness had seemed to abate somewhat after this. He was shocked by his own audacity and unable to relinquish a certainty of having done, for the first time in his life, something genuinely bad. Shortly afterward his mother had moved them out to Denver, and although no one treated him any differently than before, he often wondered if he were not responsible for this imposition of a thousand miles between him and Ruby. Eventually he had made love in the conventional fashion to a girl his own age and had been introduced to the joys and limitations of conventional sex in the company of women he had professed to love. He studied psychology in college and graduate school, an education that provided him with any number of interesting, credible theories that might have explained the Saturday night in Ruby Klein's bedroom years before.

He did not, however, seek such an explanation. He did not think of that night at all. He got married and fathered a girl and went into practice as a family therapist in the flat wastes of Broward County. He got divorced and took new lovers, and then one day awoke to discover that he had turned thirty-one.

THE FRONT lawn, hemmed in by a concrete driveway and a cracked slate patio that wrapped around two thirds of the house, was the setting for a hard-fought contest between dandelions and death. A pair of broad stumps, like the lids of two buried jars, marked the place where great trees must once have stood, cooling the house with their leafy shadows. Emily Klein's rented house—she had been forced to sell the big neocolonial in Winding Way Woods when Harvey Klein refused to comply with his alimony and child-support obligations—was a modest box of Roman brick, in faded Froot Loop colors, tangled in a bramble of burnt-out Christmas lights, with a big, black iron cursive letter *L* bolted to the side of the chimney. It had an asymmetrical shape, a ribbon window in the living room, and a jutting flat roof and, like many modernist houses that have long been inhabited by humans, a defeated aspect, a look of having been stranded, of despairing of the world for which it had been intended but which never came to pass.

Just beside the front steps, some long-ago hobbyist had set a goldfish pond. It was a small, irregular circle of greenish cement, encrusted at its edges with globules of brownish cement that had been molded and striated to suggest natural rock formations. As during their first journey up to the front door, Jocelyn was arrested once more by the sight of this forlorn puddle, with its skin of algae, dandelion fluff, and iridescent oil, and its lone occupant, a listless twist of gold floating like a discarded candy wrapper near the surface. She squatted beside it, wobbling, hands on her knees, and pointed toward the somnolent fish, the toe of one shining shoe dangerously near to the water. His daughter had a remarkable capacity for fascination with anything filthy, broken, or pathetic, from derelicts to dog dung, which in the book he was writing Green would have accounted as evidence of sensitivity and imagination but which in practice irritated and disturbed him.

"Daddy, what's that?"

"It's a bowl of tapioca pudding."

"No, it's a goldfish."

"Oh," said Green, through his teeth, wrestling her from the water's edge, "so it is."

"How long have you had her?" said Ruby, as Green scooped up his daughter again and this time toted her struggling form into the house.

"Three weeks," said Green, attempting to mask his utter exasperation with a show of utter exasperation. Then he regretted his response. Ruby's tone had been conspiratorial, implying sympathy with the trial of shepherding a toddler and with the fatigue it must be causing him, but the premise of her question was not merely that, since he was a divorced father with limited access to his daughter and hence limited experience with her, there must be a finite limit to his tolerance of her misbehaviors, but also that, on a more fundamental level, he must view Jocelyn as inherently inconvenient, annoying, even undesirable, as if she were a flu he had picked up and could not shake, or a cast on his leg. Once again Green found himself confronted with making the painful admission that he did not love his daughter in any way that was meaningful or passionate or useful to her. Their three weeks together had crawled by in an endless, desperate quest on his part to fill her hours with healthy amusements of the sort he recommended in his book and in a constant, successful effort on hers to exhaust the

potential for amusement of each, with thrilling intensity
and utter finality, within fifteen minutes. She was a well
behaved enough child, remarkably so given the circumstances of her life, but every time she went into hysterics
or pushed things too far or merely refused to surrender
the wonder of consciousness at the end of the day, Green
had found himself miserably, devoutly wishing for the
visitation to end. The long drive up from Florida had
been a nightmarish marathon of squirming, gas-station
lavatories, and the sound-track albums from animated
movies whose values, and lyrics, he deplored. Now he
was having regrets. He ought to have driven them out to
the ocean, to see the horses. He ought to have offered to
keep her for the entire summer. He ought to have spent
the rest of his life married to Caryn and pretending that he
loved her even though, as he now must acknowledge, all
the love of which he was capable had somehow been sacrificed in that one dark kiss eighteen years before.

Inside the house, the climate was hot, malarial, absolutely still. All the doors and windows were open, and
flies chased one another from room to room. Rap music,
or what sounded to Green like rap music, was playing
loud enough in the backyard to make the glass in the
living-room picture frames hum like tissue on a comb.
The adoption of rap as the theme music of teenage white
boys was one of the clearest symptoms, along with pierced
eyebrow ridges, of the substitute world that had eventually shown up to claim the future in which the Kleins'
stark and crumbling house now languished.

Seth Klein's graduation party was largely an affair of
such white boys. Although it was hard for Green to tell
them apart, and a certain amount of perceptual cloning
may have exaggerated their numbers in his gaze, there
were perhaps twenty-five of them. They threatened the
ceilings with their brush-cut heads and angled their bodies

out over the teenage girls, of whom there seemed to be substantially fewer in attendance. There were also a number of relatives, friends of the family, and inexplicable near-strangers like Green himself, with paper plates that they balanced on their laps or used to fan themselves against the heat. The only one Green knew, though time and illness had altered her in ways that made his stomach tighten, was Emily. He had no idea which boy might be Seth.

"Well," said Emily. She canted her head to one side and looked askance at Green, exactly as she might have done twenty years earlier, when he tried to persuade her that there had once been another letter in the alphabet, called thorn, or that the television reporter Roger Mudd was a direct descendant of the Dr. Mudd who went to prison for setting John Wilkes Booth's broken leg. She had always treated him like a bullshit artist, Green remembered, long before he'd ever had something to lie to her about, and the more sincere he became in his efforts to convince her of whatever unlikely truth he was trying to expound, the greater her doubt of him would grow. Now her thick hair, always, like Ruby's, a mass of unplaited dark rope, was gone. In its place grew a sweet pale tuft of dark blond baby down. She had been plump and drinking and frowsy the last time Green saw her, at a fortieth-birthday party for his mother in Las Vegas ten years earlier, but the cancer had honed her and brightened her eyes. She did not look well, but being sick brought out something in her, a peppery, droll quality that went back to Green's earliest memories of the first woman he had ever desired. "So what was that all about?" She looked Green up and down, then tried to peer around his back. "What did you forget?"

"He didn't forget anything," said Ruby. "He was just afraid of me."

"And I was afraid of her, too," said Jocelyn, loyally.

"That shows real sense," Emily said. "Your reputation precedes you, Rube."

"Ha. How are you?" said Green.

She shrugged. "Not great. Not dead." She smiled, and her crooked teeth, with their coffee and tobacco stains, seemed to afford a glimpse of her yellowing skull, tinged with the residues of soil and water. He smiled back, feeding himself neat little dietetic packets of raw, unrefined panic. The cancer in Emily Klein—surely that was not his fault, too? But something inside him—a schizophrenic or a clergyman would have called it a voice—told him that it was. That it was all his fault—rap music, labial piercing, his divorce, everything that had come to pass since that long-ago night in Ruby Klein's bedroom. What had become of little Ruby Klein? He felt like the poor time-traveling dolt in the Bradbury story who returned from stepping on a butterfly in the Triassic to find his own epoch altered abruptly, inevitably, with signs misspelled and everyone under the foot of a murderous and ignorant tyrant. How could one ever begin to repair the damage that he had so obviously done?

"I'm sorry," he said at last.

Emily shrugged. She thought he was merely condoling her for the cancer. She pointed to her daughter. "So, what do you make of that face full of metal, Doctor? You ought to see her tattoos. On the other hand, considering their location, maybe you ought to not."

"He'll see them," said Ruby. "Everybody will." She looked at her wristwatch. "I'm just, you know, waiting for Dad to turn up before I start the show."

"I wish you would," said Emily, looking a little dreamy.

"Don't think I won't."

"Would he just die?"

"With any luck."

"Especially the monkey," Emily said thoughtfully.

Ruby punched her on the arm. "Goddamn it, Mom, you know it's a fuckin' Sasquatch."

"A Sasquatch is not that skinny." Emily turned to Green. "What is it with this tattoo shit, Marty? Can you explain this phenomenon?"

"Well," Green said. He could feel the weak grin guttering on his lips. He knew what Freud had said about tattooing, of course, and he had his own private theory that people who tattooed themselves, particularly the young men and women one saw doing it today, were practicing a kind of desperate act of self-assertion through legerdemain, holding a candle to a phrase written in invisible ink, raising letters and lines where before there had been only the blankest sheet of paper. *Don't throw me away,* they were saying. *I bear a hidden message.* "It's difficult to say."

"I hope you don't have one."

"Not yet," said Green. "Ha-ha." He struggled to relax, to regain his therapeutic cool, to pick up the scattered index cards on which he had jotted down all his notes about who he was. Green was an excellent therapist, kindly but distant, supportive but ineluctable, deferential yet sure of himself, solitary but self-sufficient. None of these qualities had stood him in any good stead during the three years of his marriage to Caryn or given him the faintest clue of how to connect to his daughter, that wild, random compound of Caryn and him that they had, in their fantastic ignorance, set to wander loose in the world.

"Daddy," Jocelyn said. She pointed to the buffet table, spread from end to end with a motley assortment of barbecue favorites, vegetarian fare, and polychrome latex-based snacks. She seemed to be indicating a pile of Toll House cookies. "What are those?"

She twisted herself in his arms, trying to get free. Again Green gripped her tightly. He could not rid himself of the erroneous sensation that this was the house in which, sometime around his twelfth birthday, something crucial inside of him had broken, never to be repaired. He was afraid to put Jocelyn down here, to let her wander its rooms alone.

"What are what, honey?" he said.

"Those. Those round brown things."

"What things?"

"Those things that look like chocolate-chip cookies."

"Those are chocolate-chip cookies."

"Can I have one?"

"Yes, you may."

"Can I get down?"

Green looked at her. What difference did it make whether he said yes to her or no? In forty-eight hours, she would slip across the border, into another jurisdiction, where his laws and statutes did not apply.

"Yes," he said, "you may."

He put her down, and she ran over to the table and reached for the cookie, rising up onto the balls of her feet.

"What a sweetheart," said Ruby.

"Thank you," said Green. "Now, tell me, which one of these boys is Seth?"

Emily turned to scan the room. "Which one of these boys is Seth? You tell me. I'm serious. I mean," she said, "look at these kids. I swear, I couldn't pick him out of a lineup, which isn't too far-fetched, I'm afraid. Just look at them. Look at this one." She slapped a young man on the back of his stubbly head as he passed. He grinned at her. "I tell Seth he looks like a penis, with his bald head and his pants all sagging down around his ankles like a big scrotum. It's a room full of penises. Then again, I suppose that's always true, isn't it? Even when they're wearing suits and ties."

The screen door banged. Ruby jumped.

"Every time I walk into this house," said the man who came in through the door, "someone is saying the word *penis*. I don't know why that is."

Harvey Klein was a small, solid, almost top-heavy man, jut-jawed and broad-shouldered. He wore a knit short-sleeve polo shirt of soft summer-weight wool, gray with black flecks, and tight black jeans, creased down the front like a pair of suit pants. His brushed-aluminum hair was cut short, except at the very back, where he wore it pulled into a neat little pigtail. His sunglasses hung on a cord around his neck. A few thick silver hairs curled up through the open collar of his shirt. He stood in the doorway, waiting for his eyes to adjust to the gloom.

"You've never been in this house before," said Emily.

"But I'm certain I'm right nonetheless."

"Harvey."

"Em."

They embraced. Green could see him taking stock of her, palpating her bones with his long, sentient fingers. He looked at least fifteen years younger than his ex-wife, though Green suspected that they were exactly the same age.

"This is your daughter," Emily said, pulling away. "In case you don't recognize her."

"She's hard to miss," said Dr. Klein.

"Penis," said Ruby. "Penis, penis, penis."

He spread his arms wide, waiting for her to step into them. She set her hands on her hips and gave him a look, through lowered lids, face half-averted, lips pursed, mulling him over. She kept him waiting a long time, long enough for Green to wonder if she hated her father enough to leave him hanging there like a fool with his hands in the air. The expression on Dr. Klein's face didn't waver. He stood there, smiling like a man who had just come home from the track, up a couple of grand, to take everyone out for steaks and dancing. And, at the last possible moment, Ruby threw herself into his arms. Her feet kicked into the air, and she swung from his neck, tethered to him at one end, dangling loose at the other. She mur-

mured something in her father's ear. He closed his eyes
and inhaled deeply the smell of her hair. Green understood, though he could not have said quite how, that
there had never been any other possible outcome.

"Yo, Duncan," said one of the big boys elbowing one
another in the living room. "Go tell Feeb his dad's here."

Dr. Klein unhooked Ruby's hands from the back of his
neck and restored her spindly bootheels to the terrazzo
floor of the living room. He was looking around her now,
past her, studying the room, taking in its motley population and random furnishings—some of which must have
chimed dimly in his memory—with the remote but
friendly air of a busy doctor, a study that eventually led
him to Green. He looked puzzled. Then he turned back
to Ruby and took hold of her chin with the fingers of one
hand. He switched her face from side to side. "Christ,
what is all this shit, Ruby Ellen? You look like a goddamn
charm bracelet." He let go of her chin, and her face
seemed to hang there a moment, in midair, as if suspended on the lingering tension of his regard. Dr. Klein
returned his pleasant, clinical gaze to Green. "You look
like a hurricane fence." He winked at Green and held out
his hand. "Harvey Klein."

"Martin Green. I, uh, I used to baby-sit Ruby."

"Martin Green. Your mother was Carol, sure, sure. I
remember her. Baby-sit. Hard to believe that"—he nodded
toward Ruby, winking again—"was ever a baby. Isn't it?"

"I—"

"Never have children, Mr. Green. They'll break your
heart."

Ruby simulated the sound of vomiting.

"Ruby," said Emily, "isn't there something you wanted
to show your father?"

Ruby blushed. "Maybe later," she said. "Shut up,
Mom."

"Now," said Dr. Klein, "where is my son?"

"Where is my daughter?"said Green.

Jocelyn was no longer standing by the buffet table. Green craned his head to get a better look. An elderly uncle of Emily's and one of the ersatz hoodlums were engaged in a transgenerational analysis of the *Planet of the Apes* series of films, while at the same time, armed with a couple of plastic forks, they made their way through the remnants of a macaroni casserole. The only other occupants of the buffet line were great black flies. Green called out to the two men, over the heads of several intervening partygoers. "Have you seen my little girl?" The men shook their heads and went back to their conversation. "Excuse me," Green said to Dr. Klein. "I seem to have lost my child."

Making his way over to the buffet table, Green crouched down to see if Jocelyn was hiding underneath it. She had never hidden from him before, but as his book would have been only too happy to confirm, rapid tactical innovation was a hallmark of her age, and the acute sense of embarrassment he felt, getting down on hands and knees to look for her, seemed to confirm that he had fallen neatly into one of her traps. All that he found under the buffet table, however, was a back issue of *Allure* splattered with mayonnaise, a loose skateboard truck with neon orange wheels, and a small rubber pig.

Green checked the kitchen. He checked the laundry room. He traveled down a dim back hallway of the house, checking in the bathrooms, the bedrooms, the closets, ending up in a recreation room, where, under a skylight, on top of a bumper pool table covered in tangerine felt, two young people were asymptotically approaching copulation. Nobody he asked had seen her; he didn't interrupt the lovers.

"Jocelyn," he called out, again and again, his voice

densely layered with irritation, embarrassment, anxiety, and an attempt to sound good-humored and accustomed to her mischief. "Jocelyn!"

As he searched the house, Green's calm inner therapist's voice seemed to swell within him, repeating its stock reassurances and sensible explanations—his daughter was playing a trick on him, had gotten into a sewing basket or toolbox, was punishing him for leaving her, for taking her, for sending her back—with increasing imperturbability and lack of sense, like the intoner of useful foreign phrases nattering on about bus depots and the price of a postage stamp on a language tape playing in the dashboard of a car that is spinning out of control. All the while, in a dank, spiderwebbed corner of his thoughts, the story of his daughter's disappearance from the world was being rehearsed, in flat and unexceptional newspaper prose: a graduation party in a down-at-heel suburban neighborhood, a divorced father returning his daughter to her mother, one terrible moment of inattention—

"Uh, Marty?"

It was a hoarse, raspy young voice, calling from the front of the house. Green ran back along the hallway from the rec room and nearly ran into a small, bony, frail-looking young man with large black eyeglasses, dressed in a Charlotte Hornets basketball jersey blazoned with the number one, carrying Jocelyn in his arms. She was crying, muddy, soaked to the skin, alive.

"She fell into the pond," said the young man, handing her over to him. "I think she's all right. I'm Seth."

"Thanks, Seth," said Green. "I'm sure she's going to be fine."

Green carried his daughter into the bathroom and stood her on an oval of worn pink chenille. Her socks, dress, and blouse looked as though they had been splashed with thin coffee. Her cheeks were splattered with mud.

She was incoherent and apneic with outrage and relief. Green spoke to her softly.

"Did you fall into the pond?" He pulled the ruined dirndl up over her head. "Were you trying to see the fish?" He unbuttoned her blouse, rolled the tights down her legs, slipped off her shoes. "Did you hurt anything?" The murky water had soaked through to her panties. Green pulled them off. "Are you okay? Were you trying to see the fish, silly girl? Okay. I know. All right. You're all right. Come, we'll get you into a nice, warm bath." He reached across her with his right arm, cradling her in his left, and opened the tap in the bathtub. "Okay. I know. All right."

The sound of the water seemed to calm or distract her. She left off sobbing and pressed a hand to her chest, feeling for the agitated throb under the bone. Green had undressed her without thinking, without hesitation, and now, after his encounter with Ruby Klein, the sight of her pouting, chubby vagina, glinting with down, filled him with an unaccustomed tenderness. It occurred to him that, in all but the most glancing and utilitarian of ways, he never looked at her genitals, or touched them, or allowed himself to think about them at all, and it seemed to him, as he lifted her into the air and set her down into the green, clear water of the tub, that this prohibition of consciousness, born on that night in Ruby's bedroom eighteen years before, had somehow grown to include all of Jocelyn Green, his daughter. Because he was afraid of what he might do to her, he had removed himself from her life, for her own protection, as it were.

"Daddy," said Jocelyn. She was calm again. "I want you to take a bath with me."

"No, honey," said Green, as he always did, refusing even to consider the suggestion. "A bath is something you do by yourself."

"Mommy takes a bath with me."

"I know she does." His steadfast refusal to join mother and daughter for their nightly romp in the tub was one of several small but collectively fatal disappointments Green had caused Caryn during their marriage. "And you two have a lot of fun." Green looked around for something that might pass as a bath toy and so distract Jocelyn. He picked up a flat soap holder, caked with green scum, studded on both sides with rubbery spikes. He rinsed the scum away in the bathwater and handed the thing to Jocelyn. "Look," he said, his tone sickly and bright, "a hedgehog."

She knocked it away. It struck the tiled wall beside Green and ricocheted into his face.

"No!" Blood flowed into her face, and she went limp with rage. He caught her before she slipped under the water, drenching his forearms and the front of his shirt. "I don't want a headhog! I want you to take a bath with me!"

"Honey. Sweetie. I'm sorry. I know you think it could be fun for us to do that, too. And I love to do things with you . . ." Jocelyn did not appear to be listening. She had curled herself into a ball, kicking at him, splashing him, screaming so loudly that it was all Green could do to keep from covering her mouth with his hand. There was an entire chapter in Green's book devoted to dealing with the anger of children. None of the techniques he recommended involved gagging or straitjacketing the child. They were all about listening to and accepting a child's emotional outbursts, in a supportive way, without giving in to them. The use of such techniques, however, was predicated on the parent's staunch certainty of having the child's best interests at heart. You were not to forbid things to your children simply and for no other reason than because you were afraid of doing them yourself. You were not to oblige your children to pay for the errors and calamities of your own upbringing. And you were never, not if there was a milligram of love in your heart for your children, to deny them the incalculable comfort of your own body.

"Oh, all right," said Green, gripping the slippery, squirming girl by the upper arms. "All right!"

The transformation was breathtaking. She stopped crying at once, and the blood drained away from her cheeks. She laughed.

Green took off his pants and folded them neatly, laying them on the closed lid of the toilet, with his underpants folded on top. He hung his shirt from the hook on the back of the door. Quickly he stepped into the tub with one foot, hesitating, his unfettered penis flapping like a tattered rag knotted to his body. Jocelyn looked at it with great interest, the way she had looked at the goldfish in the pond and the studs and pendants in Ruby Klein's face. She pointed.

"What do you have?" she said.

"I have a penis," he said. "How about that?"

"It looks wobbly."

"It is," he said. "Very wobbly."

He settled himself in beside her, around her, enclosing her small form in the slick black fur and protuberances of his thin, bony shanks. There was a knock at the door. Green jumped. He put a hand to his chest.

"Marty?" It was Ruby. "Everything all right in there?"

"Everything's fine," said Green. He took hold of his daughter's hand and pressed it against his chest, over the breastbone.

"Feel that?" he said.

Mrs. Box

THE FARNHAM Building stood on a hillside in the northwest corner of Portland, overlooking the Nob Hill district and the Willamette River, from 1938 until late last year, when an elderly electric blanket belonging to one of the building's many elderly residents started a fire that killed six people and left the Farnham a whistling black skeleton in the center of a ring of rubble and ash. Fifteen stories tall, painted throughout the course of its existence a somber and unwavering shade of wintergreen, bearing more than a passing resemblance to a hospital tower, the Farnham never aspired to a landmark brand of beauty—it was just imposing enough to pass for stately, just Moderne enough to qualify as hip—but it had been home to a number of decrepit, rich widows and fashionable restaurateurs and interior designers, its lines and fenestration had a certain Bauhaus gravity, and its unusual color and prominent site lent it, in the esteem of Portlanders, some of the authority of a brilliant cathedral or a domed capitol. It was visible from all over town and from as far away as Vancouver, Washington, where one summer afternoon it was spotted by Eddie Zwang, a bankrupt optometrist in a Volvo station wagon who was at that moment crossing from Washington to Oregon on the I-5, headed for someplace like Mexico or Queen Maud Land, the hatch of his car filled with twenty thousand dollars' worth of stolen optical equipment. His cheeks, as he drove, were already wet with tears, and a heavy muscle of sorrow pounded in his chest, and when he saw the cool, green Farnham rising from its lush hillside, he made a sudden, sentimental, and, under the circumstances, unwise decision to stop and say hello to Mrs. Horace Box, his ex-wife's grandmother, who lived on its ninth floor, in Apartment G.

Eddie left the clamor of the freeway and plunged into the calm, alphabetical streets of Northwest, then headed west on Burnside, toward Willamette Heights. Although he had spent most of his adult life amid the vast, amorphous, pale cities of the West Coast, cities built in rain forests and bone deserts and on the shoulders of terrible mountains, he had been raised in the corroded redbrick river towns of the old Midwest—nine years in Pittsburgh, eight in Cleveland, college at Cincinnati—and he had always found great comfort in the modest hills, narrow streets, and rusty brown riverscape of Portland. He thought of it as a city in which painted advertisements for five-cent cigars faded from the sides of empty brick warehouses. He drove past the ballpark where he and Dolores had taken Oriole Box to watch her beloved Beavers lose baseball games, and past Muller's, her favorite restaurant, and then, heart beating as in anticipation of a wild tryst, he turned into the street that led up the hill to the Farnham.

After Eddie nosed the Volvo into one of the visitors' parking spaces, he got out and watched the street for any sign of the black LTD that had been following him, on and off, for the past two days. Its driver—Eddie had gotten a good look at him this morning on the ferry dock back at Southworth, on the Olympic Peninsula, where Eddie had made an unsuccessful attempt, in a deserted high school parking lot outside Sequim, to sell off some of the fancy Bausch & Lomb hardware he was carrying to a skittish medical-equipment fence with the improbable name of Seymour Lenz—was a florid man in a Sikh turban and a gray seersucker jacket, with sleepy eyes and a sharp black beard that jutted out from his face at a furious angle. The Sikh had been following him in the hope, Eddie imagined, of repossessing Eddie's Volvo, although there were certainly a number of alternative explanations, upon which Eddie, who had suffered all his life from a debilitating tendency to hope for the best, didn't care to dwell.

At this moment, however, there was nothing in the steep Portland street but the turbulence of light and air rising from the hot blacktop, and a pinch-faced young woman, dressed in a grimy parka and a red-and-black Trail Blazers ski cap, pushing uphill a broken baby stroller that she had filled with empty bottles and cola cans. Eddie was running away from so many disasters and errors of judgment, had left behind him so many injured parties, angry creditors, and broken hearts, that for an instant it occurred to him—a parka and a ski hat! in this heat!—to suspect the young woman of being somebody's agent or repo man or spy. But of course she was only a crazy girl pushing and singing a lullaby to a stroller full of garbage; and Eddie felt sorry for her, and ashamed of himself for suspecting her. He had become paranoid—a thought that made him feel sorry, now, for himself. Then he bolted his steering wheel with a red Club lock and armed the Volvo's alarm.

He entered the Farnham through the basement and rode up alone in the elevator, carrying in his left hand the neat leather briefcase, a birthday present from Dolores's parents, that contained all the grim documents and bitter receipts of his financial and marital dismantlement, the importunities of the creditors of his failed practice, the sheet that divorced him from Dolores, as well as an expensive satellite-uplink telephone pager that had not uttered a beep for several months, a well-thumbed copy of the April issue of *Cheri,* and the remains of a three-day-old Deluxe hamburger from Dick's, wrapped in a letter from the bankruptcy law firm of Yost, Daffler & Traut. He would have liked just to throw away the briefcase, but he had loved his former in-laws and he felt obliged to carry their last present to him everywhere he went, as if to make up for having managed to lose the other, more precious gift they had given him. Eddie sighed. It was hot in the moaning old elevator, and there was the smell of benzoin, rotten flowers, old women. His hair was slick with perspiration and his white oxford shirt clung to the small of his back. He was sorry he would not be looking his best for Oriole (she was particular about such things), but he had left his pastel neckties and fine madras blazers and white duck trousers behind him in Seattle, along with his wife and his livelihood and his optometrist's faith in the ultimate correctability—*Now, which is clearer:* this? *or* this?—of everything. He hoped that the old woman would recognize him. It had been more than a year.

"Yes?" said Oriole, when she opened her door, peering at him through the narrow gap that the chain permitted. He could make out her thick eyeglasses and the little white cloud of her hair.

"It's me, Gam," said Eddie. "It's Eddie."

She stared at him, mouth open, eyes looking huge and crooked behind her half-inch lenses. She had on her blue summer housecoat and slippers. Her makeup, normally thickly applied, and her hair, normally arranged into a nice, round old-lady 'do, were uneven and haphazard. Neither Oriole nor he was looking too sharp, then, on this hot summer day. She surveyed him carefully, from his high forehead to his worn-heeled shoes, finally settling, it seemed, on the trim calfskin briefcase in his hand as the key to the mystery of his identity.

"I'm sorry, young man," she said, her voice pleasant but cool and slightly wheezy, as though it were being produced by a ripped concertina. "I mustn't talk to salesmen. My husband doesn't approve of it one bit."

"Gam, it's *Eddie*." Eddie set down the briefcase. He swallowed. "*Dolores's* Eddie."

"Oh, my." Oriole looked worried. She knew that she ought to recognize him. She stroked the soft white down on her chin and gave it another try. "Did you call me?" she said.

"No, I'm sorry, Gam, I didn't. I'm just passing through Portland and I thought I'd stop by."

"Yes," she said, nodding her heavy head, her eyebrows knit, her watery blue eyes studying his face. "Well, isn't this a nice surprise!" She closed the door to undo the chain, then opened it wide to him. "Won't you come in?" He could see she still had no idea who he was. "And to think that I was just thinking of you, too! How do you like that?"

"Hi, Gam," said Eddie, putting his arms around the old woman and kissing her cheek. Raised by her German parents on a farm outside Davenport at the beginning of the century, Oriole was a big, broad-backed woman, ample and plain and quadrangular as the state of Iowa itself. Hugging her, Eddie felt comforted, as by the charitable gaze of a cow. He picked up the briefcase and followed her into the apartment, a suite of four rooms with two baths, a tiny kitchen, and a view from two sides of roofs and bridges, the dull, shining band of the river, and, on this hot, clear summer afternoon, the distant white ghost of Mt. Hood. Oriole passed most of her time in the small, bright room just off the entryway, sitting in a green chintz chair, with her feet propped up on a green chintz hassock,

reading large-print editions of the novels of Barbara Cart-
land, whom she somewhat resembled, solving word-
search puzzles, and spying on the next-door neighbors
through a pair of Zeiss binoculars nearly as old as she
was—Eddie thought she must be ninety—brought back
from the Great War by Dolores's grandfather, Horace.
The Farnham was built on the plan of a Greek cross, and
Oriole, whose apartment was in the eastern arm, had only
to gaze along an angle reaching some twenty feet to the
northwest to see into the windows of 9-F. There was
never much to see—the occupants were a Persian cat and
a couple of maiden sisters named Stark who kept their
blinds drawn most of the time and whose chief occupa-
tions seemed to be drinking tea and reading religious
magazines—but Oriole never stopped hoping, and once
she had been fortunate enough to witness a brief foray by
the housebound cat out onto the narrow window ledge,
and the sisterly panic that ensued. It was a momentous
event that Oriole rarely neglected to renarrate to visitors.

"Why don't you put your darling little suitcase in the
guest room?" she said to Eddie now, patting at the wispy
cloud of her hair, tugging at the collar of her housecoat.
"I'm just going to get dressed." She chuckled. "You must
think I'm awfully lazy! I guess I just lost track of the time
this morning. What time is it?"

Eddie blushed for her sake and pretended to look at his
watch. "It's still early," he said. "But, Gam, I'm afraid I'm
not staying. I only—"

"I'll bring you some clean towels," said Oriole, steering
herself into her bedroom. "I know we'll have *such* a nice
time."

Eddie shrugged, set down his burden, and sank onto a
cheap vinyl-and-chrome kitchen chair, beside a scarred
old walnut table whose matching chairs and sideboard
had long since disappeared. Besides the well-worn armchair and hassock, the only other furniture in this room,

which served as Oriole's parlor, study, and dining room, was an overlarge piece of Empire cabinetry that held her romance novels, Dresden shepherds and shepherdesses, and a heartbreakingly beautiful photograph of a homely sixteen-year-old debutante Dolores, with a snaggled smile, being devoured by a vast pink chiffon ball gown. There was a formal living room, in which a few other relics of Oriole's life—a scrollworked Victorian chesterfield, a gilt mirror, some chairs with feet carved into lions' heads—had been set on display, but she rarely used it, preferring to entertain guests from the lumbar comfort of her green chintz armchair. All the rest of her furniture— and, according to the dentally sound but no less heartbreaking woman who'd emerged from the clutches of that vast pink dress, there had been rooms and rooms of it—had been sold, along with the big house on Alameda Street which Eddie had never seen, or dispersed among Oriole's eventual heirs, or, as Oriole always claimed, stolen, by the gang of crooked servants, nurses, and kleptomaniacal beings by whom the old lady imagined herself to be plagued. "There!" said Oriole, emerging from her bedroom in a loose sleeveless dress, belted at the waist and patterned with pink daisies, purple irises, red carnations, and gold fleurs-de-lis against a background of green lattice. Eddie wondered if such dresses were, for old ladies, the fashion equivalent of large-print books and shouted conversations. "That's much better. It's awfully warm today."

"It is hot," said Eddie. It was stuffy, as well, and there was a faint sweet tang from the kitchen trash. Despite the heat of the afternoon, none of the windows were open, and the apartment felt even more close and airless than the elevator. "You look very nice."

"Thank you." She made her way over to her green chair and lowered herself slowly and with an air of deep satisfaction into it. She and Eddie looked at each other, smiling across the gap of years and nonblood relationship and a fundamental lack of acquaintance. It occurred to Eddie, for the first time, that he and Mrs. Box were nothing to each other. Eddie mopped his forehead. Oriole tapped her knobby fingers on the arm of her chair and studied him, eyes screwed, head cocked to one side.

"Do I know you from Davenport?" she said at last.

"No, Gam," said Eddie. "I've never been to Davenport. You know me from here in Portland. From your granddaughter. Dolores?"

"Of course," said Oriole. She nodded. "I like her."

"So do I," said Eddie.

"Did you know my husband?"

"No, I didn't, Gam. But I know what a nice man he was." In point of fact, old Horace Box, an executive with the Great Northern Railroad who died when Dolores was a little girl, had always been described to Eddie as a formidable person—a strikebuster, a perfectionist. His photograph looked out from the wall above Oriole's head—square jaw, rimless spectacles, brilliantined hair, an expression of unsurprised disappointment.

"Oh, he was a wonderful man," said Oriole. "I miss him to this day."

"I know you do."

"You know," she said, lowering her voice as though about to impart a confidence. She fingered a gold chain that hung amid the satiny pleats of her throat—an ornate, inch-thick, and not particularly attractive piece of jewelry, a sort of gnarled golden tree branch across which crawled beetle-size diamonds surrounded by swarms of emerald-chip aphids. "This beautiful necklace he gave me never leaves my body."

"Wow," said Eddie. Oriole had revealed the secret of her necklace to him many times in the past, in exactly these terms, following the script of the tour she conducted for visitors through a fragmentary scale model of her vanished life. But this time, as he watched her run her swollen fingers along the twisted branch that Horace Box had presented her with on the occasion of their fiftieth anniversary, Eddie was moved, and somehow disturbed, by the enduring habit of her grief. For twenty-two years the necklace had not left her withered throat except on two calamitous and oft-narrated occasions, when the clasp had given way—once on the beach at Gearhart, and once as she bent to draw a bath.

"I sleep with it on, you know," she said. "Though at times it lies quite heavy on my windpipe."

"Seventy-two years," said Eddie, enviously, too softly for Oriole to hear. He and Dolores had been married thirty-one months before parting. There had been an extramarital kiss, entrepreneurial disaster, a miscarried baby, sexual malaise, and then very soon they had been forced to confront the failure of an expedition for which they had set out remarkably ill-equipped, like a couple of trans-Arctic travelers who through lack of preparation find themselves stranded and are forced to eat their dogs. Eddie had known for a long time—since his wedding day—that it was not a strong marriage, but now, for the first time, it occurred to him that this was because he and Dolores were not strong people; they had not been able to bear the weight of married love upon their windpipes.

The principal reason for his divorce, Eddie believed, was that throughout their marriage he had foolishly devoted most of his time to the development of an ill-starred device called the Stylevision. This was to be a combination of video camera, liquid-crystal screen, keyboard, hard-wired image-manipulating software, and a six-thousand-entry fashion-eyewear database that would enable the optical consumer to "try on" six thousand different pairs of eyeglasses without moving a muscle. "A face processor," Dolores had half derisively called it. He had sunk tens of thousands of dollars, not primarily his own, into the device, only to see his plans founder on the unfortunate tendency of the Stylevision's screen to display, in addition to the face and prospective spectacles of the horrified client, the shadows of his nasal cavity and eye sockets, the naked grin of his teeth, all the delicate architecture of his skull. The device emitted neither radiation nor sonographic waves; the X-ray trick was simply an intermittent and unpredictable side effect— Geoff Eisner, Eddie's wirehead partner, had called it "an artifact"—of the program which enabled it to manipulate images of the human face, so that every fifteenth or sixteenth trial, the machine produced not a fashionably bespectacled client in a range of attractive and affordable frames but a grinning death's-head. Eddie's investors withdrew their support and sued him for a return on their investment, while Dolores also viewed the failure of the Stylevision, after so many months of marital neglect, as a kind of broken agreement, and a perplexed Geoff Eisner— that bastard—who had done most of the soldering and software development and who had been the all-too-willing recipient of that extramarital kiss, vanished back into the cannabinaceous wastes of Oregon. In the end Eddie lost his patents and his wife through the inexorable efforts of attorneys, and found himself the prey and plaything of collection agencies and subpoena artists.

"I believe it's quite valuable," Oriole was saying. "Though I've never had it—oh, thingamajiggy." Sadly she shook her head. "I don't know what's becoming of my memory! What do you call it when they take a look at your jewelry and—you know—"

"An appraisal," said Eddie.

She snapped her fingers. "That's it. I've never had it appraised. But I believe it's quite valuable."

"I believe," said Eddie, as a thrilling and unwelcome idea entered his brain, "that you're probably right."

It was a kind of fantasy, at first—another foolhardy

Eddie Zwang scheme. Stiff-necked old Mr. Box had been burdened by a romantic soul and over the years had given his wife all manner of baubles and gems, and although none of them alone was worth as much as the necklace, one ought, Eddie imagined, to be able to pawn her things for enough to install himself in Mexico in the miserable style to which he planned to grow accustomed. If they dined at Muller's, say, where it was always Oriole's habit to drink two cocktails, a thief would be able to lift her earrings and bracelets and watches while she slept, without fear of waking her. The kindness Oriole had always shown him, the affection that had drawn him from the freeway this afternoon into this misbegotten visit to the Farnham, the outrage and meanness of his contemplated crime—all of these he dismissed as the qualms of a man who had the luxury of having faith in himself. Nothing he did surprised him anymore. He would leave her the ugly gold necklace that lay so heavy on her windpipe. He told himself it was the only thing she really had.

"That certainly isn't a very big suitcase," said Oriole, pointing to the calfskin satchel at his feet.

"Well, I can't stay very long," said Eddie. The muscles of his face clenched into a hard knot, and as he smiled at Oriole his heart was filled with low enthusiasm. "But I think I will stay the night."

THEY TOOK a taxicab to Muller's. The fare was $2.75, which Oriole insisted on paying, tipping the driver with the change from three one-dollar bills. Eddie was embarrassed. (He and Dolores had once tried to determine at what point her grandmother's mind had ceased to notice increases in the cost of living, presidential-election results, the disappearance of unkind racial and ethnic generalizations from polite conversation. They'd figured the date of her last glance down at the instrument panel of life to be sometime in the early 1970s; that was when her husband had died, struck down in the middle of Tenth Avenue by a truck full of crawfish on ice, bound for Jake's Famous.) The taxi driver made no effort to conceal his disgust at the proffered gratuity, and Oriole no effort to remark it. Eddie searched his pockets for change but found only a ten-dollar bill and the 1943 zinc penny that he carried for luck. He held on to his last ten dollars and his luckless lucky charm and slunk into the darkness of Muller's cocktail lounge, which Oriole for some reason favored over the dining room. It was a morose and shadowy lounge—red Naugahyde, soft Muzak, favored by a certain type of quiet, middle-aged alcoholic—but Oriole seemed oblivious of its unsavory air and had a table she liked in the corner, under a chiefly orange but somewhat brown painting of a lighthouse. They ordered from the large, cholesterol-rich menu. They each drank a pair of vodka tonics, and the old woman told him, for what Eddie reckoned to be the fifteenth or sixteenth time and with steadily increasing divagation, about her mother's summer kitchen in the backyard of the house in Davenport, about her trip West as a newlywed in 1920 on her husband's railroad and her disappointment at not seeing any wild Red Indians along the way, and about her sisters—Robin and Linnet—both of them now passed on. They ate their tan-and-beige meals of gravy and crust. While Oriole's attention was focused on her dessert, Eddie contrived to order a third drink for each of them. Then Oriole paid the bill, stiffing the waitress, and they made their hazy way back to the Farnham.

Although Eddie and Oriole went to bed at eight-thirty, the drinks he had poured into her appeared to have the unexpected effect of making her wakeful, and Eddie lay for what seemed like hours waiting for her to stop humming and commenting to herself in the next room and finally fall asleep. He was miserable. The fried food and all those ounces of cheap well vodka had begun to give rise to monsoon winds and tsunamis in his gut. There was still a narrow band of blue on the horizon, and he felt tormented by this last faint banner of daylight wavering at the limits of his vision. Although he had cranked open the windows, it was a warm evening, and the small guest bedroom was stifling. The weak breeze off the river did little to cool the room and carried with it a rich and bitter odor of hops from the Blitz brewery downtown. This was an unwelcome and nostalgic smell that seemed to intensify the weight of the summer night upon him. Every once in a while he thought he caught the cheering of the crowd and the flat patter of the announcer, wafted from the distant ballpark like the summertime smell of beer. He lay fully dressed upon the still-made bed, already regretting the crime that he was about to commit, forcing himself to concentrate on his own fitness for such a reprehensible act and on the bacon-and-flowers smell of a woman he had known for an evening in Juárez, many years ago.

At last silence descended over the apartment, tentative and provisional at first, then all-encompassing. Eddie got up from the bed and tiptoed down the hall to Oriole's bedroom. Her drapes were drawn, and it was impossible to see. The old woman's alcohol-slowed breathing was so shallow that Eddie couldn't even hear it, and the unexpected blackness and quiet of the room almost turned him back. He took a long, deep breath and tried to visualize the layout of the room. Many times in the past he had watched Dolores help the old woman dress, and it seemed to him that Oriole kept her jewelry box in the upper-left-hand drawer of her Empire dresser, which ought to be immediately behind him and about three feet to his left. Reaching back with the fingers of one hand outstretched, he felt his way along the wall to her dresser, which he did not so much discover as collide with, producing a loud report that fortunately did not seem to awaken Oriole. He pulled open the top left drawer, and immediately his hand brushed against a smooth, firm surface that his fingers told him must be the green morocco lid of the jewelry box.

His heart leaping, he tucked the box under his arm, slid the drawer softly back in, and crept out of the room. He stepped into the relatively dazzling light of the hallway, and stood for a moment, breathing, his forehead against the cool plaster wall. There was no doubt in his mind that he had just broken something that could never be repaired. His old life lay on the other side of a jagged tear in the earth. He would never see Dolores again, although all at once he knew that seeing her again was the only thing he wanted to do. He remembered the photograph of her, on the Empire shelf in the sitting room, and went to look at it, indulging a brief and hopeless fantasy of returning the box to its drawer, getting in his car, driving back to Seattle, waking Dolores, pleading with her to take him back.

As he came into the darkened living room, he saw something that nearly caused him to drop the box of jewelry. Oriole was sitting in the green chair, her old Zeiss binoculars trained on some place away to the north.

"Gam?" said Eddie, after he recovered from the shock of finding her awake and in her chair, dressed in only a short, sleeveless white nightgown—more naked than he had seen her, or any old lady, for that matter, ever before. "Can't you sleep?"

She seemed not to hear him. She sat still and ghostly in the reflected light of the city below, in her transparent nightgown; her cheeks, her bare arms and shoulders and thighs were streaked with veins and fissures, mysterious and mottled as the face of the moon. He found it an oddly beautiful sight. She was staring out at a point across the river, on the heights of the opposite bank of the Willamette, scanning slowly back and forth across a line high above the horizon. She was looking, he guessed, for the house on Alameda Street.

"I wonder if these goggles need a cleaning," said Oriole. Her voice was little more than a whisper. "Do you know anyone who might be able to do the job?"

"Are you looking for your old house?" Discreetly he set down the jewelry box on the dining table and went over to stand beside her.

She nodded. "But I don't seem to be able to make it out."

"I think it's too dark, Gam. It's awfully far away, too. I'm not even sure you'd be able to pick it out in the daytime."

"Oh, *there* it is," she said. "It has a pair of stone lions on the lawn."

"I know it does," said Eddie. "You can see it from here?"

Again she nodded her stolid head, without lowering the binoculars.

"Oh, yes," she said. "You can see it perfectly well. The azaleas have been lovely this year. Have a look."

She handed him the heavy old pair of 10x binoculars, through which, Dr. Zwang felt reasonably certain, it would be impossible to distinguish the old brown house, tucked into the shade of its fir trees, five miles away. He closed his eyes, and fit the field glasses to the sockets of his skull.

"Lovely," he said, keeping his eyes firmly shut. "I see the lions, too," he added.

"They're colored, the people who live there now," said Oriole. "But very nice."

He turned his head and trained the glasses on the luminous cup of the ballpark, at those far-off happy men dressed in suits of brilliant white.

"I'll be right back," he said. He handed her the binoculars, picked up the box of jewels, and walked brazenly into her bedroom, where, as though she had asked him to, he replaced the box in the drawer. Perhaps it was no extravagance, after all, to have faith in oneself, or perhaps he was not quite down to his last dime in that regard. He closed the drawer with a feeling of renewed hopefulness. As he did so, however, he heard Oriole moaning, out in the living room—a long, slow, devastated sound, as of someone faced with the ruin of a dream. Eddie thought she might have fallen. He hurried back out to the living room to find the old woman standing, pointing at him with one outstretched arm that trembled from fingertip to shoulder, and he saw the real reason she had looked so oddly naked to him a moment earlier.

"You!" she cried. "You've stolen my beautiful necklace!" She clawed with one hand at the emptiness at her throat.

"What?" Eddie took a step backward. Was he that drunk? Had he stolen the necklace without knowing it? "No," he said. "Gam, I didn't! It—it must have fallen off."

"It isn't here! You've stolen it!"

Eddie held out his hands, palms upward, and took a step toward the old woman, but she drew back, and covered her face with her shaking arm.

"No, no, no, no! Don't you come near me!"

As quickly as that, placid old Oriole Box became hysterical, and started to shriek. Eddie had heard such shrieking issuing only from the worst and most desperate corners of the world—from the back room of a police station in downtown Los Angeles at four o'clock in the morning, on the shoulder of a highway in the wake of a bloody accident that had killed a young husband, from some distant corridor of the Swedish Hospital emergency room as he sat beside Dolores through the evening of her miscarriage.

"Gam," said Eddie helplessly. "Please. Calm down." He switched on a lamp, and the sudden efflorescence of light seemed to take the old woman by surprise. Abruptly she fell silent. Again Eddie started toward her, but as he did so he tripped on something and fell forward. The old woman reached out as if to catch him, and although Eddie knew she had only meant to ward him off, he lay happy in her arms, and for an instant she bore the weight of him. Then she shook herself free, and he sank to his knees before her, and something glittering caught his eye. It was Oriole's necklace, lying in a crooked coil on the carpet underneath the green hassock.

"There it is," he sang out, with a cheerfulness he didn't feel. "I found it."

Eddie crawled over to the hassock on his hands and knees. He reached under it and fished out the necklace, then handed it up to Oriole. He had made a narrow escape, for the second time that evening. What if Oriole had awakened the neighbors with her screaming? What if she had summoned the police? How it would have confirmed all of Dolores's worst opinions of him to learn that he had been arrested for robbing her grandmother! He looked around for the thing that had tripped him up, and saw that the fine calfskin briefcase, heavy with the authentications and certificates of his defeat, was lying flat on the floor behind him.

"Oh," said Oriole. "Oh, thank heavens." Her hands and fingers were still trembling badly, and he had to help her fasten the necklace around her soft old throat once more.

"You just sit down for a minute in this chair," he said.

"My necklace," said Oriole, running her fingers along the heavy gold branch, her voice coming breathless and faint. "It never leaves my body, you know."

"I know," said Eddie. Perhaps he had not escaped quite as cleanly as all that. It was proving very difficult for him to look Oriole in the eye. He bowed his head. Pretty soon, if he kept on this way, there would be no one left in the world with whom he would be able to make eye contact.

"What time is it?" said Oriole.

"Almost nine-thirty." He wondered if it wouldn't be better for him just to get back into his loaded-down Volvo and be on his way. If he drove straight through he could be in Rosario by this time tomorrow.

The telephone rang. Oriole lifted the receiver to her ear.

"Yes? Oh, *hello*." She patted at her hair, and drew upon all her ninety-odd years' practice at the dissimulation of happiness and the repression of despair. "Yes, I know it is. And to think that I was just thinking of you!"

Eddie went to the window and looked north across the city, to the river and the lights and the distant black ribbon of his old life.

"You did?" Oriole was saying. "Well, and I'm sure you got a good price for it. It's such a darling house."

Dolores; their house in Juanita had been on the market for months. She hadn't wanted to sell it, but Eddie needed the cash, and on her gym teacher's salary she'd had no way of buying him out. A part of him was anxious to find out how much Dolores had gotten for the house, but just now that part seemed a small one, with a weak and ineffectual voice in the council of his heart.

Just as he understood that he really did belong in the morass of debt and hopelessness in which he had become mired, he looked down, into the Farnham's parking lot, and saw that the familiar black LTD, gleaming orange in the halogen light of the parking lot, had pulled up alongside his Volvo station wagon. Eddie reached for the Zeiss binoculars and watched, with a bleak fascination, as the man in the turban climbed out of the passenger side of the long black car, accompanied by the woman in the red-and-black ski hat. The Sikh went around to force the lock on the Volvo's door, and if the alarm went off, Eddie couldn't hear it. In another moment the man with the angry beard had disengaged the Club lock (Eddie had heard you could freeze them brittle with a squirt of Freon, then shatter them with a gentle tap), hot-wired the engine, and driven off in Eddie's car, taking with him all of Eddie's stolen equipment—his slit lamp, Phoroptor, tonometer, ophthalmoscope—and his clothing and legal documents, his Al Hibbler records, his photographs of Dolores.

Eddie didn't move. He felt as though he himself had been blasted with a paralyzing dose of some cold, cold gas.

"Now tell me," said Oriole, to the abandoned woman on the other end of the line. "How's that darling husband of yours?"

Spikes

ONE AFTERNOON toward the middle of April, Kohn's lawyer, her patience exhausted, called and said she was giving him one last chance. He was to come into Chagrin Harbor that afternoon and sign the petition in which he and his wife informed the state of Washington that their marriage was irretrievably broken. If he once again failed to show, his lawyer regretted she would have to toss his file into a bottom drawer, send him a bill, and forget about him. His wife, and *her* lawyer, would then be free to reap uncontested the rewards of his recalcitrance. So Kohn pulled on his big rubber boots and slogged up the path to the slough of gravel where he and his neighbors on Valhalla Beach parked their mud-encrusted Jeeps and pickups. There was a chill in the air, and Kohn's large, unshaven head with its spectacles and stunned features was zipped deep into the hood of a parka the vague color of boiled organ meat. He peered out at the world through a tiny porthole trimmed with synthetic fur and heard only the sound of his own respiration.

His marriage had been short-lived, a brief tale of blind

hopefulness, calamity, and then the dismantling ministra-
tions of psychotherapists and lawyers. Jill was ten years
older than Kohn, a Chubb Island native, a Lacan scholar
who taught at Reed College. She yearned to have a child.
Kohn was an Easterner, socially awkward, obsessive. He
was an instrument maker who built custom electric guitars, mostly for the Japanese market, and he preferred to
keep his own yearnings pressed between the clear panes of
a marijuana habit where he could safely observe them. He
spoke with a slight stammer. His only good friend was
one he had made in his freshman year of high school. Jill
had mistaken his carpenterial silences, and a shyness that
was purely physiological, for the marks of a sensitive soul.
She was thirty-five and perhaps not interested in looking
too closely or too far.

She had gotten pregnant right after the wedding. They
left Portland and moved back up to the Puget Sound, to
her parents' old brown-shingled house on Probity Beach.
The baby, a son, arrived in March, and for the length of a
baseball season the three of them were contented, in a
blurred way that at certain moments resolved itself into
sharp foci of happiness no wider than a dime, no more
substantial than a smell of salt in the hollow of the baby's
neck as Kohn carried him up the beach to his grand-
parents' whitewashed porch. In October, the baby spiked
a fever of 106°. He lost consciousness on the ferryboat, in
his mother's arms, on the way into Swedish Hospital. He
was buried, along with his parents' marriage, in a corner
of Chubb Island Cemetery, with some of his ancestors
and cousins. They got therapy, but it was a waste of
money and time because Kohn didn't like to talk in front
of the therapist. He grieved at odd moments, privately,
minutely, invisibly almost even to himself. He did not, it
was certainly true, grieve enough. He withdrew. Jill left
him. She left the island and moved to a Siddha Yoga
ashram, a former hotel in the Catskill Mountains once

patronized by Kohn's great-grandparents. She would never completely recover, Kohn knew, from what had happened, but complete recovery was probably not necessary. At least she had managed to put some solid geographical distance between herself and their disaster. It was as if she had been blown clear, while Kohn continued to camp, snowbound, on the steaming wreckage. He had moved out of her parents' house, rented the tiny cabin on Valhalla Beach, set up his workbench, and resumed the slow production of his signature model, the Kohn Six, a flying wedge of flamed maple with locking tremolo and tuners and deluxe hum-bucking pickups with coil taps. He waited for the next intervention of fate, hoping this time to miss it when it came.

When Kohn reached the muddy parking area, out of breath from the climb, he saw Bengt Thorkelson standing in the rain beside his mother's Honda Civic, with a length of PVC pipe, swinging for the fences.

Bengt was eleven years old and lived with his widowed mother in the Wayland house, three doors down the beach from Kohn. He was short for his age, and pudgy, with wiry dark hair and big eyeglasses. He ran with a slight wobble in his hips. On the beach at dusk, when he thought no one was looking, he practiced seagull impersonation, with some success. His best friend, Malcolm Dorsey, was currently the only black child on Chubb Island. That was all Kohn knew about him, except that walking on the beach one stoned morning the winter before, Kohn had come upon Bengt sitting on a driftwood log, in the rain, with his orange Lab mongrel Nerf, holding a polka-dot Minnie Mouse umbrella over both their heads, and sobbing. Kohn had hurried past him, head down, zipped tight into his parka. The boy's father, Kohn knew vaguely, had drowned or somehow been killed at sea. His mother was a buxom, energetic, foul-mouthed, kind of sexy woman who had once brought

Kohn a strange casserole involving tofu, buckwheat noodles, and currants. Kohn avoided her, too. He kept his distance from all his neighbors, whose lives extended across Chubb Island from Valhalla Beach to Rhododendron Beach, from Chagrin Harbor to Point Probity, from the tops of the transmitter towers along Radio Beach down to the deep Cretaceous bones of the island. Kohn's life fit into the back of an Econoline van.

"Hi, Bengt," Kohn said, moving slowly toward his van, the mud sucking in and spitting out the soles of his boots as he went. He was never comfortable saying the boy's name, which must be the curse of his entire existence. Generally he veered between leaving off the *t* and trying to slip in as much of the *g* as he felt Swedish custom would allow.

"Hi, Mr. Kohn," Bengt said glumly. He crouched and picked up a penny from the ground by his feet. He was dressed in a bright red-and-white hooded sweatshirt that said RANGERS in blue script across the chest, stiff new dungarees, rolled, and a pair of ancient, pointy men's cleats, tied with dress laces, much too large for his feet and apparently a hand-me-down from some remote ball-playing ancestor. A brand-new fielder's glove lay on the ground at his feet. His fingers on the length of plastic pipe were pink with cold. He rocked back on his heels, raised the pipe like a hatchet behind his head, and tossed the penny into the air. Then he swung, as Kohn had seen him swing before, putting everything he had into a huge, wild hack that spun him around so far he almost fell over. The penny hit the mud with a splatter of rude commentary on his form.

"Shit. I mean, shoot." He picked the penny up, tossed it, and took another swing. He missed again. "Shoot." He tossed the penny and swung wild again. "Shoot!" He glanced toward Kohn, then away, his cheeks reddening. "I can hit it," he assured Kohn. He pointed, and Kohn saw that the ground before him was sprinkled lightly with pennies.

"You have a game today?" said Kohn. He had spoken to no one but his lawyer in days, and the bassoon twang of his voice struck his ears oddly. He unzipped his hood a little.

"No, I have practice. Today's the first day."

"In the rain?"

"It's not raining." Kohn guessed that he was right; it had *rained* all winter, every day but January 11 and February 24, from early December to mid-March, a magical-realist deluge that made fence posts sprout green leaves and restored Chubb Lake, lost thirty years earlier to a failed Army Corps of Engineers drainage project. This spring weather was something different, hardly weather at all—a thin, drifting blanket of sparkling grayness that would not prevent islanders from mowing their lawns, washing their cars, or working on their home-run swings. Again Bengt tossed the elusive cent into the air. This time he connected, and the coin chimed an E-flat against the tube. It hooked foul, toward the Civic, ricocheted, and landed in the mud ten feet from Bengt's shoes, leaving a white scar in the blue flank of the car. "Yes!" he cried grimly. He reached into his pocket, fished around, and brought out another penny. "I suck."

"Pennies are small."

"Baseballs are small, too," Bengt observed. He probed at the mud with the end of his pipe. "I'd like to shoot a crossbow one time," he went on irrelevantly. He operated an invisible crank, took aim along the stock of his PVC pipe, and then let a bolt fly with a *thwok!* of his tongue. He looked down at his feet. "These shoes were my uncle Lars's. I know they're stupid-looking."

"No," said Kohn. "Not really." Kohn looked at his wristwatch. A few seconds later he looked at it again. Lately he was always checking his watch, but the next moment he never seemed to remember what it had told him.

"Huh," said Bengt finally. "Well, okay. I'm late now. I guess I must be pretty late. I guess I might as well not go. I hate baseball." He glanced up at Kohn, then away, looking to see if he had shocked Kohn. Kohn tried to look shocked. "I'm much more interested in archery."

"Is your mom driving you?"

"She's with my gran in the hospital. She fell off a step stool in the kitchen, my gran I mean, and broke her hip. My uncle Lars is staying with me supposally but I don't know where he is. I called Tommy Latrobe and his dad is supposed to come over to pick me up. But I guess they forgot."

Bengt tossed a penny and connected again, pulling it to the left but keeping it more or less fair this time. Then he dug down into his pocket again.

"You sure have a lot of pennies in there," Kohn said.

Bengt brought out a handful of fifty-cent penny rolls, in crisp, tight, red-and-white wrappers. He held them out for Kohn to inspect, then slipped all but one back into his pocket. From this one he peeled down a quarter-inch of wrapper, and loosened another handful of coins.

"They were my dad's," he said. "My mom said he used to have a lot of time on his hands. On the boats." The Chubb Island Thorkelsons ran an outfit that went up to Alaska, rounded up ice floes, and drove them to Japan, where they were sold, suitably shaved and crushed, in elegant bars. Wondrous the things a Japanese person would buy. "There's a whole box of penny rolls under my mom's bed." He tossed a penny, swung, and drove it toward the ivy- or vinyl-covered wall of his imagination.

"Don't hit them into the mud!" Kohn was appalled. "Your father's pennies!"

"I don't need them."

Bengt pressed another penny between his thumb and forefinger and tossed it into the air. He brandished the length of pipe and reached back to take his hack. Kohn reached out and grabbed hold of his wrist and cupped the spinning penny like a moth. The boy looked at him, astonished. He wrenched his hand away and gave it a shake. His arm bore briefly the pale impression of Kohn's fingers.

"Oh, my God, I'm sorry," said Kohn, surprised by himself. They were only pennies. They rolled under the refrigerators of the world, wedged themselves into the joints of desk drawers, disappeared into the bowels of auto seats, slipped behind breakfronts, bureaus, and toilets. No one bothered to fish them out. They fell from the hands of careless pedestrians and lay for hours on the sidewalk without anyone stopping to pick them up. Kohn himself had tossed ringing handfuls into the garbage. "Did I hurt you? God, I'm sorry. Let me give you a ride to practice. I'm on my way into town."

Bengt studied Kohn, his forehead wrinkling. He checked Kohn's adequate build. He appraised Kohn's knotted, strong-looking hands. "Do you like baseball?" he said.

Kohn considered the question. He had first come to the game at the age of eight, in Washington, D.C., and had fallen in love with Frank Howard, but at the end of the season Howard and the Senators had departed for Texas. That November, his parents had ended their own marriage. The candy manufacturer for whom Mr. Kohn worked as an accountant transferred him to Pittsburgh. After a nasty legal battle the young Kohn went with him. The following spring his father took him many times down to the big ugly ballpark at the Confluence. The Pirates had a handsome Puerto Rican outfielder who hit in the clutch and cut down runners at the plate with strikes from deep right. He collected his three thousandth career hit on the last day of the season, and died the following winter in a plane crash. After that Kohn gave up on the organized versions of the sport.

He shook his head. "To be honest I kind of hate it, too."

"I know," said Bengt, banging the ground with the end of his pipe. "God!"

"But I play a little softball sometimes." Kohn had played on an intramural team in college. He had been the second-worst player on a team that finished in ninth place out of twelve.

Bengt looked a little surprised. "What position?"

"Outfield." Kohn had a sudden craving for the broad skewed vista from far right, the distant buzz of chatter from the bench, the outfielder's blank bovine consciousness of grass and sky. If you backed up far enough out there on a hot summer day you could sometimes see the curvature of the earth. "Mostly left."

"Do you have a glove?" Bengt was getting a little excited now.

"Somewhere in my van, I think."

"Cool," said Bengt. He dropped the piece of pipe, picked up his own mitt, and started toward Kohn's van, cleats spraying clodlets of mud as he went. Kohn trudged after him. When he climbed in behind the wheel he saw to his dismay that the boy was smiling.

"I have to go see my lawyer," Kohn said. "Did I mention that?"

Ordinarily Kohn drove the island roads with unstudied recklessness. His work demanded that hours of intense care be paid to very small things and when he got behind the wheel of a car he always came a little unwound. But he drove his twitchy, voluble young passenger toward town carefully and slowly. He worked at it. He was doing a good deed and a part of him was afraid of doing good deeds. They often seemed to result, he had noticed, in tragedy and newspaper articles. A kindly, heartbroken neighbor drives a troubled young fatherless boy to his baseball practice. Their van flips over and bursts into flames.

"My uncle Lars is like eighty years old," Bengt was saying, warily watching his shoes. "He played for the St. Louis Browns. He was the pitcher who killed somebody, you know? With a baseball, I mean, in a game. Johnny something, I don't remember. It was in a book. Strange but true baseball stories."

"Lars *Larssen*?" said Kohn. Kohn had read this same book, or one like it, as a child. "That's your uncle Lars? Wow. Johnny Timberlake, wasn't it?"

"Timberlake."

"What happened to him after that?"

"He died!"

"I mean, your uncle. Did he have to go to jail, or anything?"

Bengt shook his head. "He had to retire, I guess was all," he said. "It was a wild pitch. It was just bad luck."

At the intersection of Cemetery Road and Chubb Island Highway they pulled up to the traffic signal, one of only two on the island. The light turned from green to yellow, and Kohn slowed the car to a stop. He looked over at Lars Larssen's old spikes, with their reptile skin, their rats' snouts, their laces like quivering feelers. Kohn would not have wanted to put his own feet inside them.

"I have to wear six pairs of socks," said Bengt.

"Can't you just buy new ones?"

Bengt didn't immediately reply. He looked at the cursed shoes that were swallowing his feet, at the curling, scarred black toes of bad luck itself.

"I wish," he said. There was more to it, his tone suggested, than lack of money. It seemed to have been impressed on him that these shoes were his inheritance.

In spite of Kohn's fears, they arrived safely at practice.

Kohn cut the engine, and they sat. They stared through the windshield at the men and boys gathered on the grass. The team practiced on the dirt-infield diamond behind Chagrin Harbor Elementary School, on the edge of a cow pasture frequented, autumn midnights, by the local island coven of shroomheads. The fathers were standing around in their baseball caps, in a knot, smoking and talking. They looked over at Kohn's van, trying to identify it. Many of them would have known each other all their lives. On this field they would have tormented the chubby, bespectacled goat of their generation. Their sons sat clumped along the bench like pigeons on the arm of a statue. One boy stood off to one side, taking practice swings with a red aluminum bat, and two others were practicing some private martial art that involved kicking each other repeatedly in the behind. At last a tall, heavyset man separated himself from the group of fathers and approached the boys, clapping his hands. The men spread out behind him, arms folded across their chests, suddenly all business. The boys scrambled to their feet and went to string themselves out along the third base line.

"You'd better get going," Kohn said, looking at his watch.

"I can't," said Bengt.

"Go on. You'll be fine."

"Aren't you coming?"

"Some other time," Kohn said. "I'm serious, I really do have to see my lawyer."

Bengt didn't say anything. He affected to study the engineering of his fielder's mitt, picking at its knots and laces. Kohn checked his watch again. He was already ten minutes late for his appointment.

"Who's your lawyer?" Bengt said at last. "Mr. Crofoot? Mr. Toole? Ms. Banghart?"

"Ms. Banghart."

Bengt nodded. "Are you making out your will?"

"Yes," said Kohn. "And I'm leaving everything to you. Now, go on."

Bengt looked down at his lap. His glasses started to slide off, but he caught them and pushed them back up his nose. His eyelids fluttered and he took a deep breath. Kohn was afraid he might start to cry. Then he opened the door. Before he got out of the car, he reached into the muff of his sweatshirt and took out a neat, tight roll of pennies. He handed it Kohn.

"I can get someone to bring me home," he said. "Thank you for the ride."

Kohn hesitated, but he felt that because of Bengt's father, because of the fruitless nights the late Mr. Thorkelson had spent rolling stacks of coins as he drove the broken ice across the sea, he could not refuse payment. He took the pennies, then watched as Bengt, slow, hunched forward as if he were dragging some huge, cumbersome object, trudged over to join the other boys. Kohn put the pennies in his pocket and got out of the car.

The boys stood in a broken line along the base path between third and home, in bits and pieces of outgrown and hand-me-down uniforms, ripped jeans, dusty caps bearing the insignia of a dozen different major league teams, but all of them wearing complicated polychrome athletic shoes tricked out with lights, air pumps, windows, fins, ailerons, spoilers. They were skinny, mean-looking boys, scratch hitters and spikers of second basemen, dirt players, brushback artists. One of them was almost as tall as a man, with a faint pencil sketch of a mustache on his upper lip. They all stared at Bengt as he sidled up to the line. He was shorter than any of them, ten pounds heavier, and as he looked up at the coach he blushed, and gave an apologetic little laugh, which, amid that gang of tiny hard cases, came off inevitably as shrill and unbecoming. Standing with the other boys Bengt reminded Kohn of the leather button used in his family for many years to replace the shoe in Monopoly, ranged at Go alongside the race car, the top hat, and the scrappy little dog, plump and homely and still trailing a snippet of brown thread. When he saw Kohn he colored again, and looked down at his feet. This time his glasses fell off. They landed in the mud. A few of the boys laughed. Bengt picked them up and wiped the lenses on his sweatshirt.

"I guess now we know what happened to Joe Jackson's shoes," said a father, and all the men and boys laughed.

"Hello," said the coach, walking over to Kohn, looking a little suspicious. "Glad you could make it. You must be . . ."

He held out his hand, waiting for Kohn to supply the explanation, the narrative that would plausibly connect him to Bengt Thorkelson.

"I'm just a neighbor," Kohn said.

"Hey, that's okay," the coach said. He was a large man, rubicund in the face, hard and fat in the Boog Powell style. A pure pull hitter. He forced his genial features onto a grid of seriousness, and looked at Bengt, who was looking down at his uncle's shoes. "We understand."

Kohn was handed third base, a heavy mysterious parcel, and stepped out onto a ball field for the first time in ten years. It was not much of a field; mangy, pebbly, two-thirds-sized, with the hulk of a commercial henhouse collapsing in the field on the other side of the fence in deep right. But the dirt was a rich brown, the color of fir-tree bark, and where there was grass it was thick and spongy and freshly cut. Bengt led him to the square pipe buried in the dirt at the hot corner, and they tamped the pegged base down into it. The boy kicked at the base, circled it, then climbed up onto it and kicked at it again, affecting the taut air of a base runner stranded at third, waiting for somebody to hit one, anything, a blooper, a cheap little broken-bat single.

"I've never been on third before," he said presently.

"It's nice," Kohn said.

"It's not bad," said Bengt. He looked at his watch, black plastic with a liquid-crystal face. "Don't you have to go?"

"Don't worry about it."

"But you can't stay, can you?"

"I'd better not."

"They don't really do anything," Bengt said. "Mostly they just stand around talking."

"That doesn't sound too tough," Kohn said. "I could probably manage that."

For the first ten minutes the coach had the boys stretch, alternate crunches with push-ups, and focus their mental energies, since the key to good baseball, in spite of what they might have seen or observed, was mental effort. All of the fathers appeared relieved to be exempted from this portion of the proceedings. They stood around behind home plate, smoking, leaning against the backstop. Then when practice began—ball tossing, bunting and base-running exercises, followed by an intrasquad game—the men, as Bengt had suggested, mostly stayed put. From time to time they exhorted their sons, or teased them, not always kindly. The boys made a study of ignoring the men and the things they said. And yet Kohn felt that the presence of their fathers on the other side of the chain-link backstop was as indispensable to them as bats, dirt, spikes, grass, the reliable pain of a baseball smacking against the heels of their mitts. If a boy's father somehow missed a play, a nice catch, a bunt laid down stiff and in-flexible as rebar, the boy acted quite put out.

Kohn found himself standing with the fathers, neither included in their conversation nor made to feel particu-larly unwelcome. Some of the men seemed to recognize him; they exchanged pleasantries and agreed that it had, finally, stopped raining. At one point there was a low chuckle at the far end of the group of fathers, some of the men looked at him, and Kohn heard the name of Bengt's mother mentioned. He wondered if he should say something to explain, to correct their misapprehension. The coach hit a soft line drive toward Bengt, who stumbled, knocked the ball to the ground, and chanced to fall on top of it. He stood up, looking stunned, then remembered to pick up the ball and shag it back in to the coach. His throwing style managed nonchalance without troubling much about accuracy.

"Nice stop!" Kohn called.

Half an hour into the practice, a station wagon pulled up. The door sprang open, and a boy ran onto the field. Kohn gathered that this was Tommy Latrobe, who had been taken ill during school hours with an illness now unaccountably cured. The other boys hectored him like crows until he told them to shut up.

Tommy Latrobe's father walked up and stood beside Kohn. He was fair, freckled, dressed in the full, pin-striped regalia of the Chubb Tavern Mudcats, carrying a glove and a pair of bats. He looked Kohn up and down. "Cold?" he said.

Kohn unzipped his parka as far as he could; the zipper always jammed at the last two inches.

"Uh-oh," Latrobe said, pointing. "That one's through."

Kohn looked out at the field, where Bengt Thorkelson, at short, down on one knee, with boys running wild on the base paths, waited for the slowest ground ball in the history of baseball to roll into his mitt, his small face bright with wonder and dread.

"So which one is yours?" said Latrobe.

AFTER PRACTICE was over, Kohn drove them both back to Valhalla Beach. The boy was silent. He seemed to be reviewing all of the errors he had made, the rallies he had scotched. Kohn searched for the appropriate platitudes and encomiums. Before he knew it they were home. He steered the van back into the swamped half-acre of mud and gravel.

"Well," he began.

"That's my gran's car," Bengt said, pointing to a sober gray Dart parked beside the Civic. He jumped out of the van and ran down the rickety wooden steps that led to his house, without remembering to say good-bye. Kohn walked down the hill to his own house, and called his lawyer to apologize. The secretary said she wasn't in, and would not be able to take his calls anymore.

A few days later when Kohn went into Seattle to buy lumber and saw blades and screens for his bong, he spotted a pair of flashy baseball shoes in the window of an athletic shoe store on Forty-fifth. They were absurdly beautiful things, a cross between architecture and graffiti, wrapped in blue tissue. They cost a hundred and fifty-two dollars and forty-two cents. Kohn laid down two fifties, two twenties, a ten and three ones, then reached into the pocket of his coat.

"I believe I have the two cents," he said.

The Harris Fetko Story

THE HOTEL in Tacoma was a Luxington Parc. There was one in Spokane, one in Great Falls, and another in downtown Saskatoon. It was half motor lodge, half state-of-the-art correctional institution, antacid pink with gun-slit windows. There was a stink of chlorine from the waterfall in the atrium where the chimes of the elevators echoed all night with a sound like a dental instrument hitting a cold tile floor. A message from Norm Fetko, Harris's father, was waiting at the desk on Friday night when the team got in. It said that on the previous Friday Fetko's wife had given birth to a son and that the next afternoon, at three o'clock, they were going to remove his little foreskin, of all things, in a Jewish religious ceremony to be held, of all places, at Fetko's car dealership up in Northgate. Whether by design or hotel policy, the message was terse, and Harris's invitation to his half brother's bris was only implied.

When Harris got upstairs to his room, he sat with his hand on the telephone. The passage of four years since his last contact with Fetko had done little to incline him to forgiveness. He tended, as did most commentators on the

Harris Fetko story, to blame his father for his own poor character and the bad things that had happened to him. He decided it would be not only best for everyone but also highly satisfying not to acknowledge in any way his father's attempt at renewing contact, an attempt whose motives, with an uncharitableness born of long experience, Harris suspected at once.

He picked up the receiver and dialed Bob Badham. There was no answer. Harris set the receiver down on the floor of his room—it was in his contract that he got a room to himself—lay down alongside it, and squeezed out the one thousand abdominal crunches he had been squeezing out every night since he was eleven years old. When he had finished, he got up, went into the bathroom, and looked at himself in the mirror with approval and dispassion. He was used from long habit to thinking of his body as having a certain monetary value or as capable of being translated, mysteriously, into money, and if it were somehow possible, he would have paid a handsome sum to purchase himself. He turned away from the mirror and sat down on the lid of the toilet to trim the nails of his right hand. When his nails were clipped and filed square, he went back out to pick up the telephone. It was still ringing. He hung up and dialed Bob's work number.

"Screw you, Bob," Harris said cheerfully to Bob Badham's voice-mail box. "I mean, hello." He then left a detailed account of his current whereabouts and telephone number, the clean result of his most recent urine test, and the next destination on the team's schedule, which was Boise, a Holiday Inn, on July 5. Harris possessed the sort of wild, formless gift that attracted the gaze of harsh men and disciplinarians, and the whole of his twenty-six years had been lived under the regimens of hard-asses. Bob Badham was merely the latest of these.

There was a knock at the door. Harris went to answer it in his pin-stripe bikini briefs, hoping, not quite unconsciously, that he would find an attractive female member of the Western Washington Association of Mortgage Brokers (here for their annual convention) come to see if it was really true that the briefly semi-notorious Harris Fetko was in the hotel.

"Why aren't you in bed?" said Lou Sammartino.

The coach of the Regina Kings club of the North American Professional Indoor Football League was not, as it happened, a hard-ass. He indulged his players far more than most of them deserved—housing them with his family when things went badly for them; remembering their birthdays; nudging them to save receipts, phone their wives, pay their child support. He was an intelligent man of long experience who, like many coaches Harris had played for, believed, at this point in his career rather desperately, in the myth of the football genius, a myth in which Harris himself, having been raised by a football genius, had learned by the age of seventeen to put no stock whatever. Lou Sammartino believed that the problem of winning at football was surely one susceptible to the systematic application of an inspired and unbiased mind. His lifetime record as a coach, including a stint in the short-lived Mexican Football League of 1982, was 102–563. He pushed past Harris and barked at his quarterback to close the door. He was hunched and rotund, with a jowly, pocked face and immense black-rimmed spectacles. The smell of his cologne was exactly like that of the tiny red cardboard pine trees that dangle from the rearview mirrors of taxicabs.

"What's the matter?" said Harris. He looked out into the hallway, in both directions, then closed the door against the stiff artificial breeze that came howling down the deserted corridor.

"We need to talk." Lou sat down on the bed and studied Harris. His watery brown eyes behind the lenses of his glasses were beautiful in a way that suited his losing record. "You called your PO?"

"I left a message."

"Aren't you supposed to see him in person when you're home?"

"I'm *not* home," said Harris. "Technically. My *home* is Seattle. We're in *Tacoma*."

"Technically," said Lou. "A word much beloved of fuckups."

"Something to drink?" Harris went to the minibar. There was nothing in it except for a rattling ice tray and a ghostly smell of caulk. The minibars were always empty in Luxington Parcs and in most of the other hotels the Regina Kings patronized. Often they were not even plugged in. "I'm supposed to have six bottles of mineral water," Harris said. He tried not to sound petulant, but it was difficult, because he was feeling petulant.

"Aw," said Lou.

"I'm sick of this!" Harris slammed the refrigerator door shut. "Every fucking time I walk into my room and open the minibar door, there's supposed to be six fucking bottles of mineral water in there." The slammed door rebounded and bashed into the wall beside the minibar. Its handle gouged a deep hole in the wallboard. Crumbs of plaster spattered the floor. Harris ran his fingers along the edges of the hole he had made in the wall. A feeling of remorse took wing in his chest, but with an old, sure instinct, he caught it and neatly twisted its neck. He turned to Lou, trying to look certain of himself and his position. The truth was that Harris didn't even like mineral water; he thought it tasted like saliva. But it was in his contract. "So, okay, talk. It's past my bedtime."

"Harris, in a minute or two there's someone coming up here with a proposition for you." Just as he said this, there was another knock at the door. Harris jumped. "He wants to offer you a job."

"I already have a job."

Lou turned up the corners of his mouth but somehow failed to produce a viable smile.

"Lou," said Harris, and his heart started to pound. "Please tell me the league isn't folding."

There had been rumors to this effect since before the season even began; attendance at games in all but a few sports-starved cities was declining by a thousand or more every weekend, the owner of the Portland team had been murdered by Las Vegas wiseguys, and the Vancouver bank on whose line of credit the NAPIFL depended for its operating costs was under investigation by the government of Canada.

Lou stroked the bedspread, smoothing it, watching the back of his hand.

"I just want to play out the schedule," he said sadly. "I could be happy with that."

"Harris?" said a man on the other side of the door. "You there?"

Harris put on his jeans and went to the door.

"Oly," he said. He took a step back into the room. The man at the door was enormous, six feet eight inches tall, just shy of three hundred pounds. Like Norm Fetko a member of the 1955 national champions and—unlike Fetko—a successful businessman, purveyor of a popular topical analgesic, Oly Olafsen had always been the biggest man Harris knew, a chunk of the northern ice cap, a piece of masonry, fifteen tons of stone, oak, and gristle supporting eight cubic inches of grinning blond head. He wore silver aviator eyeglasses and a custom-tailored suit, metallic gray, so large and oddly proportioned that it was nearly unrecognizable as an article of human clothing and appeared rather to have been designed to straiten an obstreperous circus elephant or to keep the dust off some big, delicate piece of medical imaging technology.

"How's my boy?" said Oly.

It had been Oly Olafsen's money, more or less, that

Harris had used, more or less without Oly's knowing about it, to purchase the pound of cocaine the police had found under the rear bench of Harris's 300ZX when they pulled him over that night on Ravenna Avenue. He gave Harris's hand a squeeze that compressed the very bones.

"So," he went on, "the coach has got himself another son after all these years. That's a thought, isn't it? Wonder what he's got cooked up for this one."

This remark angered Harris, whom the sporting world for two hectic and disappointing collegiate seasons had known as Frankenback. Among the failings of his character exposed during that time was a total inability to stand up to teasing about any aspect of his life, his father's experimentation least of all. With a great effort and out of an old habit of deference to his father's cronies, he got himself to smile, then realized that Oly wasn't teasing him at all. On the contrary, there had been in Oly's soft voice a disloyal wrinkle of concern for the fate, at his great idol's hands, of the latest little Fetko to enter the world.

"Yeah, he asked me out to the showroom tomorrow," Harris said. "To the thing where they, what's that, circumcise the kid."

"Are you people Jewish?" said Lou, surprised. "I didn't know."

"We're not. Fetko isn't. I guess his new wife must be."

"I'll be there. Ah!" Gingerly—his knees were an ancient ruin of cartilage and wire—Oly lowered himself into the desk chair, which creaked in apparent horror at the slow approach of his massive behind. "As a matter of fact, I'm paying for the darn thing." Oly smiled, then took off his glasses and pinched the bridge of his nose. When he put the glasses back on, he wasn't smiling anymore. "The coach has got himself into a little bit of a tight spot out there in Northgate," he said, pressing his palms together as if they represented the terrific forces that were putting the squeeze on Fetko. "I know things haven't been, well, the greatest between you two since . . . everything that happened, but the coach—Harris, he's really putting his life back together. He's not—"

"Get to the point," said Harris.

An odd expression came over Oly's generally peaceful and immobile face. His eyebrows reached out to each other over the bridge of his nose, and his tiny, pale lips compressed into a pout. He was unhappy, possibly even actively sad. Harris had never imagined that Oly might ever be feeling anything but hunger and gravitation.

"Harris, I'm not going to lie to you, the old man could really use a little help," said Oly. "That's what I want to talk to you about. I don't know if Lou has mentioned it, but the coach and I—"

"I told him," said Lou. "Harris isn't interested."

"Isn't he?" Oly looked at Lou, his face once again a region of blankness, his eyes polite and twinkling. He had pleasant, vacant little eyes that, along with his bulk and a recipe purchased in 1963 from a long-dead Chinese herbalist in the International District for $250, had enabled him to do what was necessary to make Power Rub the number-three topical analgesic in the western United States. "Somebody might think he would be very interested in finding another job, seeing as how this outfit of yours is about to go belly-up." He turned his flashbulb eyes toward Harris now. "Seeing as how what they call gainful employment is a condition of his parole."

"If that happens, and I don't personally feel that it will, Harris can find another job. He doesn't need any help from you."

"What is he going to do? He doesn't know how to do anything but be a quarterback! It's in his genes, it's in his blood particles. It's wired into his darn brain. No, I figure he has to be very interested in hearing about an opportunity like this. A chance to actually *redefine the position,* at twice his present salary, in front of a guaranteed national cable audience of *forty-four million homes.*"

Harris was accustomed to having his disposition discussed and his fate decided, in his presence, by other people; it was part of that same mysterious alchemy that could transmute his body into cash and of the somewhat less obscure process that had sent him to Ellensburg for nineteen months. But at the mention of cable television, he could not restrain himself.

"What is it?" he said. "What opportunity?"

Oly reached into the breast pocket of his jacket and withdrew a manila envelope, folded in half. He took a color brochure from the envelope and handed it to Harris. Harris sat down on the bed to read. It was a prospectus designed to attract investors to a league that would feature a sport that the brochure called Powerball, "the first new major American sport in a hundred years," to be played in every major city in the United States, apparently by men in garish uniforms that were part samurai armor and part *costume de ballet,* one of whom was depicted, on the airbrushed cover of the brochure, swinging across the playing arena from a striped rappelling cable. The description was vague, but, as far as Harris could tell, Powerball appeared to be an amalgam of rugby, professional wrestling, and old pirate movies. It was not football or anything close to football. Once Harris realized this, he skimmed through such phrases as "speed, drama, and intense physical action . . . the best elements of today's most popular sports . . . our proposed partnership with the Wrestling Channel . . . all the elements are in place . . . revolutionary, popular, and, above all, profitable . . ." until he turned to the last page and found a photograph of his father beside a caption that identified him as "coaching great Norm Fetko, inventor of Powerball, part owner and coach of the Seattle franchise."

"Fetko invented this crap?" said Harris, tossing the brochure onto the floor.

"It came to him in a dream," said Oly, looking solemn. He raised his hands to his eyes and spread his thick fingers, watching the air between them as it shimmered with another one of Norm Fetko's lunatic visions. "A guy . . . with a football under his arm . . . swinging from a rope." Oly shook his head as if awestruck by the glimpse Harris's father had vouchsafed him into the mystic origins of the future of American sport. "This will be big, Harris. We already have a line on investors in nine cities. Our lawyers are working out the last few kinks in the TV contract. This could be a very, very big thing."

"Big," said Harris. "Yeah, I get it now." For he saw, with admiration and to his horror, that at this late stage of his career Fetko had managed to come up with yet another way to ruin the lives and fortunes of hapless elevens of men. None of Fetko's other failures—his golf resort out in the Banana Belt of Washington, his "revolutionary" orange football, his brief (pioneering, in retrospect) foray into politics as a candidate with no political convictions, his attempt to breed and raise the greatest quarterback the world would ever see—had operated in isolation. They had all roped in, ridden on the backs of, and ultimately broken a large number of other people. And around all of Fetko's dealings and misdealings, Oly Olafsen had hovered, loving sidekick, pouring his money down Fetko's throat like liquor. "That's why he called. He wants me to play for him again."

"Imagine the media, Harris, my gosh," said Oly. "Norm and Harris Fetko reunited, that would sell a few tickets."

Lou winced and sat down on the bed next to Harris. He put his hand on Harris's shoulder. "Harris, you don't want to do this."

"No kidding," said Harris. "Oly," he said to Oly. "I

hate my father. I don't want to have anything to do with him. Or you. You guys all fucked me over once."

"Hey, now, kid." Another crack of grief opened in the glacial expanse of his face. "Look, you hate me, that's one thing, but I know you don't—"

"I hate him!"

Inside Harris Fetko the frontier between petulance and rage was generally left unguarded, and he crossed it now without slowing down. He stood up and went for Oly, wondering if somewhere in the tiny interval between the big man's jaw and shoulders he might find a larynx to get his thumbs around. Oly started to rise, but his shattered knees slowed him, and before he could regain his feet, Harris had kicked the tiny chair out from under him. A sharp pain went whistling up Harris's shin, and then his foot began to throb like a trumpet. The right foreleg of the wooden chair splintered from the frame, the chair tipped, and Oly Olafsen hit the flecked aquamarine carpet. His impact was at once loud and muffled, like the collision of a baseball bat and a suitcase filled with water.

"I'm sorry," Harris said.

Oly looked up at him. His meaty fingers wrapped around the broken chair leg and clenched it. His breath blew through his nostrils as loud as a horse's. Then he let go of the chair leg and shrugged. When Harris offered a hand, Oly took it.

"I just want to tell you something, Harris," he said, smoothing down his sleeves. He winched up his trousers by the belt, then attended to the tectonic slippage of the shoulder pads in his jacket. "Everything the coach has, okay, is tied up in this thing. Not money. The coach doesn't have any money. So far the money is mostly coming from me." With a groan he stooped to retrieve the fallen brochure, then slipped it back into its envelope. "What the coach has tied up in this thing, it can't be paid back or defaulted on or covered by a bridge loan." He tapped the rolled manila envelope against the center of his chest. "I'll see you tomorrow."

"No, you will not," said Harris as Oly went out. He tried to sound as though he were not in terrible pain. "I'm not going."

Lou lifted Harris's foot and bent the big toe experimentally. Harris groaned. A tear rolled down his cheek.

"You broke it," said Lou. "Aw, Harris."

"I'm sorry, Coach," said Harris, falling backward on the bed. "Fucking Fetko, man. It's all his fault."

"Everything else, maybe it was Fetko's fault," said Lou, though he sounded doubtful. He picked up the telephone and asked room service to bring up a bucket of ice. "This was your fault."

When the ice came, he filled a towel with it and held it against Harris's toe for an hour until the swelling had gone down. Then he taped the big toe to its neighbor, patted Harris on the head, and went back to his room to revise the playbook for tomorrow. Before he went out, he turned.

"Harris," he said, "you've never confided in me. And you've never particularly followed any of the copious advice I've been so generous as to offer you over the last few months."

"Coach—"

"But regardless of that, I'm foolishly going to make one last little try." He took off his glasses and wiped them on a rumpled shirttail. "I think you ought to go to that thing tomorrow." He put his glasses back on again and blinked his eyes. "It's your brother that'll be lying there with his little legs spread."

"Fuck the little bastard," said Harris, with the easy and good-natured callousness that, like so much about the game of football, had always come so naturally to him. "I hope they slice the fucking thing clean off."

Lou went out, shaking his big, sorrowful head. Ten minutes later there was another knock at the door. This time it was not a lady mortgage broker but a reporter for the *Morning News Tribune* come to poke around in the embers of the Harris Fetko conflagration. Harris lay on the bed with his foot in an ice pack and told, once again, the sorry tale of how his father had ruined his life and made him into all the sad things he was today. When the reporter asked him what had happened to his foot and the chair, Harris said that he had tripped while running to answer the phone.

THEY BEAT Tacoma 10–9, on a field goal in the last eight seconds of the game. Harris scrambled for the touchdown, kicked the extra point with his off foot, and then, when in the last minute of the game it became clear that none of the aging farm implements and large pieces of antique cabinetry who made up his backfield and receiving corps were going to manage to get the ball into the end zone, he himself, again with his left foot, nailed the last three points needed to keep them happy for one more day back in Regina.

When the team came off the field, they found the Kings' owner, Irwin Selwyn, waiting in the locker room, holding an unlit cigar in one hand and a pale blue envelope in the other, looking at his two-tone loafers. The men from the front office stood around him, working their Adam's apples up and down over the knots of their neckties. Selwyn had on blue jeans and a big yellow sweater with the word KINGS knit across it in blue. He stuck the cigar between his teeth, opened the blue envelope, and unfolded the letter from the league office, which with terse, unintentional elegance regretfully informed the teams and players of the NAPIFL that the standings at the end of that day's schedule of games would be duly entered into the record books as final. Lou Sammartino, having coached his team to first place in its division and the best record in the league, wandered off into the showers and sat down. Irwin Selwyn shook everyone's hand and had his secretary give each player a set of fancy wrenches (he owned a hardware chain) and a check for what the player would have been owed had Lou Sammartino been granted his only remaining desire. Shortly thereafter, twenty-five broken giants trudged out to the parking lot with their socket wrenches and caught the bus to the rest of their lives.

Harris went back to his room at the Luxington Parc, turned on the television, and watched a half-hour commercial for a handheld vacuum device that sheared the bellies of beds and sofas of their eternal wool of dust. He washed his underpants in the sink. He drank two cans of diet root beer and ate seven Slim Jims. Then he switched off the television, pulled a pillow over his head, and cried. The serene, arctic blankness with which he was rumored, and in fact did struggle, to invest all his conscious processes of thought was only a hollow illusion. He was racked by that particular dread of the future that plagues superseded deities and washed-up backs. He saw himself carrying an evening six-pack up to his rented room, wearing slacks and a name tag at some job, standing with the rest of the failures of the world at the back of a very long line, waiting to claim something that in the end would turn out to be an empty tin bowl with his own grinning skull reflected in its bottom. He went into the bathroom and threw up.

WHEN HE reemerged from the bathroom, the queasiness was gone but the dread of his future remained. He picked up the phone and called around town until he found himself a car. His tight end, a Tacoma native, agreed, for a price they finally fixed at seventeen dollars—seventeen having been the number on the tight end's 1979 Washington State Prep Championship jersey—to bring his brother's car around to the hotel in half an hour. Harris showered, changed into a tan poplin suit, seersucker shirt, and madras tie, and checked out of his room. When he walked out of the Luxington Parc, he found a 1979 Chevrolet Impala, eggplant with a white vinyl top, waiting for him under the porte cochere.

"Don't turn the wipers on," said Deloyd White. "It blows the fuse on the radio. Be honest, it blows a lot of fuses. Most of them."

"What if it rains?"

Deloyd looked out at the afternoon, damp and not quite warm, the blue sky wan and smeary. He scratched at the thin, briery tangle of beard on his chin.

"If it rains you just got to drive really fast," he said.

As Harris drove north on I-5, he watched nervously as the cloak of blue sky grew threadbare and began to show, in places, its eternal gray interfacing of clouds. But the rain held off, and Harris was able to make it all the way out to Northgate without breaking the speed laws. The Chevy made a grand total of seven cars parked on the lot of Norm Fetko's New and Used Buick-Isuzu, an establishment that had changed hands and product lines a dozen times since Pierce Arrow days. It sat, a showroom of peeling white stucco, vaguely art deco, next to a low cinder-block garage on one of the saddest miles of Aurora Avenue, between a gun shop and a place that sold grow lights. Fetko had bought the place from a dealer in Pacers and Gremlins, banking on his local celebrity to win him customers at the very instant in history when Americans ceased to care who it was that sold them their cars. Harris pulled in between two Le Sabres with big white digits soaped onto their windshields, straightened his tie, and started for the open door of the dealership.

A tall, fair-haired salesman, one of the constantly shifting roster of former third-stringers and practice dummies Fetko could always call upon to man the oars of his argosies as they coursed ever nearer to the maelstrom, was propped against the doorway, smoking a cigarette, as Harris walked up. He was stuffed imperfectly into his cheap suit, and his face looked puffy. He lounged with a coiled air of impatience, tipping and rocking on the balls of his feet. His hair was like gold floss.

"Hey, Junior," he said. He gestured with a thumb. "They're all in the back room."

"Did they do it already?"

"I don't think so. I think they were waiting for you."

"But I said I *wasn't* going to come," said Harris, irritated to find that his change of heart had come as a surprise only to him.

He walked across the showroom, past three metal desks, three filing cabinets, and three wastebaskets, all enameled in a cheery shade of surgical glove; three beige telephones with rotary dials; a dismantled mimeograph; and an oak hat rack that was missing all of its hooks but one, from which there hung an empty plastic grocery sack. There was no stock on the floor, a bare beige linoleum expanse layered with a composite detritus of old cigarette ash and the lost limbs of insects. The desk chairs were tucked neatly under the desks, and the desktops themselves were bare of everything but dust. Aside from a bookshelf filled with the binders and thick manuals of the automobile trade and a few posters of last season's new models tacked up amid black-and-white photographs of the owner, in his glory days, fading back to pass, there was little to suggest that Norm Fetko's New and Used was not a defunct concern and had not been so for a very long time.

"I knew you'd come," said Fetko's wife, hurrying across the back room to greet him. She was not at all what he had imagined—an ample, youngish bottle blonde with an unlikely suntan and the soft, wide-eyed look, implying a certain preparedness to accept necessary pain, that Fetko had favored in all the women he had gotten involved with after Harris's mother. She was small, with thin arms and a skinny neck, her hair like black excelsior. Her eyes were deep set. She was certainly no younger than forty. Her name was Marilyn Levine.

"I almost didn't," he insisted. "I'm, uh, not too wild about . . . these things."

"Have you been to a bris before?"

Harris shook his head.

"I'm not even going to be in the room," Marilyn said. "That's what a lightweight I am." She was wearing a loose burgundy velvet dress and ballet shoes. This was another surprise. Over time, most of the women in Fetko's life allowed themselves to become, as it were, themed, favoring grass-green muumuus patterned with stiff-arming running backs, goalposts, and footballs turning end over end. Marilyn touched a hand to Harris's arm. "Did you know the coach stopped drinking?"

"When did he do that?"

"Almost a year ago," she said. "Not quite."

"That's good news," said Harris.

"He isn't the same man, Harris," she told him. "You'll see that."

"Okay," said Harris doubtfully.

"Come say hi."

She led him past the buffet, three card tables pushed together and spread with food enough for ten times as many guests as there were in attendance. Aside from one or two of Fetko's employees and a dozen or so members of Marilyn's family, among them an authentic-looking Jew, with the little hat and the abolitionist beard, whom Marilyn introduced as her brother, the room was empty. A few women were huddled at the back of the room around a cerulean football that Harris supposed must be the blanketed new Fetko.

In the old days, at a function like this, there would have been a great ring of standing stones around Fetko, dolmens

and menhirs in pistachio pants, with nicknames like Big
Mack and One-Eye. Some of the members of the '55
national champions, Harris knew, had died or moved to
faraway places; the rest had long since been burned, used
up, worn out, or, in one case, sent to prison by one or
another of Fetko's schemes. Now there remained only Oly
Olafsen, Red Johnnie Green, and Hugh Eggert with his
big cigar. Red Johnnie had on a black suit with a funereal
tie, Oly was wearing another of his sharkskin tarpaulins,
and Hugh had solved the troublesome problem of dressing
for the dark ritual of an alien people by coming in his very
best golf clothes. When they saw Harris, they pounded
him on the back and shook his hand. They squeezed his
biceps, assessed his grip, massaged his shoulders, jammed
their stubbly chins into the crook of his neck, and, in the
case of Hugh Eggert, gave his left buttock a farmerly slap.
Harris had been in awe of them most of his life. Now he
regarded them with envy and dismay. They had grown old
without ever maturing: quarrelsome, salacious boys zipped
into enormous rubber man-suits. Harris, on the other
hand, had bid farewell to his childhood aeons ago, without
ever having managed to grow up.

"Harris," said Fetko. "How about that." The tip of his
tongue poked out from the corner of his mouth, and he
hitched up the waist of his pants, as if he were about to
attempt something difficult. He was shorter than Harris
remembered—fatter, grayer, older, sadder, more tired,
more bald, with more broken blood vessels in his cheeks.
He was, Harris quickly calculated, sixty-one, having already been most of the way through his thirties, a head
coach in Denver with a master's in sports physiology,
before he selected Harris's mother from a long list of
available candidates and began his grand experiment in
breeding. As usual he was dressed today in black high-
tops, baggy black ripstop pants, and a black polo shirt.
The muscles of his arms stretched the ribbed armbands of

his shirtsleeves. With his black clothes, his close-cropped hair, and his eyes that were saved from utter coldness by a faint blue glint of lunacy, he looked like a man who had been trained in his youth to drop out of airplanes in the dead of night and strangle enemy dictators in their sleep.

"Son," he said.

"Hey there, Coach," said Harris.

The moment during which they might have shaken hands, or even—in an alternate-historical universe where the Chinese discovered America and a ten-year-old Adolf Hitler was trampled to death by a passing milk wagon—embraced, passed, as it always did. Fetko nodded.

"I heard you played good today," he said.

Harris lowered his head to hide the fact that he was blushing.

"I was all right," he said. "Congratulations on the kid. What's his name?"

"Sid Luckman," said Fetko, and the men around him, except for Harris, laughed. Their laughter was nervous and insincere, as if Fetko had said something dirty. "Being as how he's a Jewish boy." Fetko nodded with tolerant, Einsteinian pity toward his old buddies. "These bastards here think it's a joke."

No, no, they reassured him. Sid Luckman was an excellent choice. Still, you had to admit—

"Luckman's the middle name," said Harris.

"That's right."

"I like it."

Fetko nodded again. He didn't care if Harris liked it or not. Harris was simply—had always been—there to know when Fetko wasn't joking.

"He's very glad to see you," said Marilyn Levine, with a hard edge in her voice, prodding Fetko. "He's been worrying about it all week."

"Don't talk nonsense," said Fetko.

Marilyn gave Harris a furtive nod to let him know that

she had been telling the truth. She was standing with her arm still laced through Harris's, smelling pleasantly of talcum. Harris gave her hand a squeeze. He had spent the better part of his childhood waiting for Fetko to bring someone like Marilyn Levine home to raise him. Now he had a brief fantasy of yanking her out of the room by this warm hand, of hustling her and young Sid Luckman into the aubergine Chevy Impala and driving them thousands of miles through the night to a safe location. His own mother had fled Fetko when Harris was six, promising to send for him as soon as she landed on her feet. The summons never came. She had married again, and then again after that, and had moved two dozen times over the last fifteen years. Harris let go of his stepmother's hand. Probably there was no such safe place to hide her and the baby. Everywhere they went, she would find men like Fetko. For all Harris knew, he was a man like Fetko, too.

"Hello?"

Everyone turned. There was a wizened man standing behind Harris, three feet tall, a thousand years old, carrying a black leather pouch under his arm.

"I am Dr. Halbenzoller," he said regretfully. He had a large welt on his forehead and wore a bewildered, fearful expression, as if he had misplaced his eyeglasses and were feeling his way through the world. "Where are the parents?"

"I'm the boy's father," said Fetko, taking the old man's hand. "This is the mother—Marilyn. She's the observant one, here."

Dr. Halbenzoller turned his face toward Marilyn. He looked alarmed.

"The father is not Jewish?"

Marilyn shook her head. "No, but we spoke about it over the phone, Dr. Halbenzoller, don't you remember?"

"I don't remember anything," said Dr. Halbenzoller. He looked around the room, as if trying to remember how he had got to the outlandish place in which he now found himself. His gaze lingered a moment on Harris, wonderingly and with evident disapproval, as if he were looking at a Great Dane someone had dressed up in a madras jacket and taught to smile.

"I'm an existential humanist," Fetko told him. "That's always been my great asset as a coach. Over the long series, an atheistic coach will always beat a coach who believes in God." Fetko, whose own lifetime record was an existential 163–162, had been out of coaching for quite a while now, and Harris could see that he missed being interviewed. "Anyway, I don't feel I could really give the Jewish faith a fair shake—"

Dr. Halbenzoller turned to Marilyn.

"Tell them I'd like to begin," he said, as if she were his interpreter. He took the pouch from under his arm. "Where is the child?"

Marilyn led him over to the back of the room, where, beside the huddle of women, a card table had been set up and draped in a piece of purple velvet. Dr. Halbenzoller undid the buckles on his pouch and opened it, revealing a gleaming set of enigmatic tools.

"And the *sandek*," he said to Marilyn. "You have one?"

Marilyn looked at Fetko.

"Norm?"

Fetko looked down at his hands.

"Norm."

Fetko shrugged and looked up. He studied Harris's face and took a step toward him. Involuntarily, Harris took a step back. "It's like a godfather," Fetko said. "To the kid. Marilyn and I were wondering."

Harris was honored, and wildly touched, but he didn't want to let on. "If you want," he said. "What do I have to do?"

"Come stand next to me," said Dr. Halbenzoller slowly, as you would speak to a well-dressed and intelligent dog.

Harris went over to the velvet-covered table and stood

beside it, close enough to Dr. Halbenzoller to smell the
steam in his ironed suit.

"Do you have to be a doctor to do this?" he asked.

"I'm a dentist," said Dr. Halbenzoller. "Fifty years.
This is just a hobby of mine." He reached into the pocket
of his suit coat and took out a slim volume of cracked
black leather. "Bring the child."

Sidney Luckman Fetko was brought forward and placed
into Harris's arms. He was wide awake, motionless, his
lumpy little pinch-pot face peering out from the blue
swaddling cloth. He weighed nothing at all. Fetko's wife
left the room. Dr. Halbenzoller opened the little book and
began to chant. The language—Hebrew, Harris supposed—
sounded harsh and angular and complaining. Sid Luckman's
eyes widened, as if he were listening. His head hadn't
popped entirely back into place yet after his passage through
Marilyn Levine, and his features were twisted up a little on
one side, giving him a sardonic expression. This is my
brother, thought Harris. This is Fetko's other son.

He was so lost in the meaning of this that he didn't
notice when several seconds had gone by in silence.
Harris looked up. Dr. Halbenzoller was reaching out to
Harris. Harris just looked at his hands, callused and yellow
but unwrinkled, like a pair of old feet.

"It's all right, Harris," said Fetko. "Give him the baby."

"Excuse me," Harris said. He tucked Sid Luckman
under his arm and headed for the fire door.

HE SPRINTED across the back lot, past a long, rusting, red-
and-white trailer home with striped aluminum awnings in
which Harris's mother had once direly predicted that
Fetko would end his days, toward a swath of open land
that stretched away behind the dealership, a vast tangle of
blackberry brambles, dispirited fir trees, and renegade
pachysandra escaped from some distant garden. In his late
adolescence, Harris had often picked his way to a large

clearing at the center of the tangle, a circular sea of dead grass where for decades the mechanics who worked in the service bays had tossed their extinguished car batteries and pans of broken-down motor oil. At the center of this cursed spot, Harris would lie on his back, looking at the pigeon-colored Seattle sky, and expend his brain's marvelous capacity for speculation on topics such as women's breasts, the big money, and Italian two-seaters.

These days there was no need to pick one's way—a regular path had been cleared through the brush—and as they approached the clearing, Harris slowed. The woods were birdless, and the only sounds were the hum of traffic from Aurora Avenue, the snapping of twigs under his feet, and a low, hostile grunting from the baby. It had turned into a cold summer afternoon. The wind blew in from the north, smelling of brine and rust. As Harris approached the clearing, he found himself awash in regret, not for the thing he had just done or for shanked kicks or lost yardage or for the trust he had placed, so mistakenly, in others during his short, trusting, mistaken life, but for something more tenuous and faint, tied up in the memory of those endless afternoons spent lying on his back in that magical circle of poison, wasting his thoughts on things that now meant so little to him. Then he and Sid fell into the clearing.

Most of the trees around it, he saw, had been brought down, while those that remained had been stripped of their lower branches and painted, red or blue, with a white letter, wobbly and thin, running ten feet up the trunk. Exactly enough trees had been left, going around, to spell out the word POWERBALL. Harris had never seen a painted tree before, and the effect was startling. From a very tall pole at the center of the circle, each of nine striped rappelling cables extended, like the ribs of an umbrella, toward a wooden platform at the top of each of the painted trees. The ground had been patiently tilled and turned over, cleared of grass and rubbish, then patted down again, swept smooth and speckless as an infield. At the northern and southern poles of the arena stood a soccer-goal net, spray-painted gold. Someone had also painted a number of imitation billboards advertising Power Rub and the cigarettes, soft drinks, spark plugs, and malt liquors of fantasy sponsors, and nailed them up at key locations around the perimeter. The lettering was crude but the colors were right and if you squinted a little you might almost be persuaded. The care, the hard work, the childish attention to detail, and, above all, the years of misapplied love and erroneous hopefulness that had gone into its planning and construction seemed to Harris to guarantee the arena's inevitable destruction by wind, weather, and the creeping pachysandra of failure that ultimately entangled all his father's endeavors and overwhelmed the very people they were most intended to avail. Fetko was asking for it.

"Look what Coach did," Harris said to Sid, tilting the baby a little so that he might see. "Isn't that neat?"

Sid Luckman's face never lost its dour, sardonic air, but Harris found himself troubled by an unexpected spasm of forgiveness. The disaster of Powerball, when finally it unfolded, as small-scale disappointment or as massive financial collapse, would not really be Fetko's fault. Harris's entire life had been spent, for better or worse, in the struggling company of men, and he had seen enough by now to know that evergreen ruin wound its leaves and long tendrils around the habitations and plans of all fathers, everywhere, binding them by the ankles and wrists to their sons, whether the fathers asked for it or not.

"Get your ass back in there," said Fetko, coming up behind them, out of breath. "Asses."

Harris didn't say anything. He could feel his father's eyes on him, but he didn't turn to look. The baby snuffled and grunted in Harris's arms.

"I, uh, I did all this myself," Fetko said after a moment.

"I figured."

"Maybe later, if you wanted to, we could go over some of the fine points of the game."

"Maybe we could."

Fetko shook himself and slapped his palms together. "Fine, but now come on, goddammit. Before the little Jewish gentleman in there seizes up on us."

Harris nodded. "Okay," he said.

As he carried Sid past their father, Harris felt his guts contract in an ancient reflex, and he awaited the cuff, jab, karate chop, rabbit punch, head slap, or boot to the seat of his pants that in his youth he had interpreted as a strengthening exercise designed to prepare him for his career as an absorber of terrible impacts but that now, as Fetko popped him on the upper arm hard enough to make him wince, touching him for the first time in five years, he saw as the expression of a sentiment at once so complicated and inarticulate, neither love nor hatred but as elemental as either, that it could only be expressed by contusing the skin. Harris shifted Sid Luckman to his left arm and, for the first time ever, raised a fist to pop Fetko a good one in return. Then he changed his mind and lowered his hand and carried the baby through the woods to the dealership with Fetko following behind them, whistling a tuneless and impatient song through his teeth.

When they got back, Harris handed over Sid Luckman. Dr. Halbenzoller set the baby down on the velvet cloth. He reached into his pouch and took out a rectangular stainless-steel device that looked a little like a cigar trimmer. The baby shook his tiny fists. His legs, unswaddled, beat the air like butterfly wings. Dr. Halbenzoller brought the cigar trimmer closer to his tiny panatela. Then he glanced up at Harris.

"Please," he said, nodding to the fitful legs, and Harris understood that somebody was going to have to hold his brother down.

That Was Me

THE FOUR taverns of Chubb Island, Washington, were haunted almost exclusively by local drunks. The summer people did their drinking on the porches and decks of their summer houses or, when that paled, under the paper umbrellas at the bar of the Yang Palace. At the V.F.W., and at the Chubb Island Bow & Rifle Club, out on Cemetery Road, they poured gin and vodka, but to the summer people these places were to be avoided, being just a hair too laughable to be legendary. From time to time, particularly toward the end of August, when tedium, hot weather, and the dwindling promise of another summer agitated ancient Viking fibers in their brains, a party of adventurers from the pink and yellow houses along Probity Beach might attempt a foray into the Chubb Island Tavern, the Blue Heron, Peavey's, or the Patch. But they never stayed long. The local drunks—there must have been about sixty-five or seventy of them, many related by blood or sexual history—were a close-knit population, involved in an ongoing collective enterprise: the building, over several generations, of a basilica of failure, on whose

crowded friezes they figured in vivid depictions of bankruptcy, drug rehabilitation, softball, and arrest. There was
no role in this communal endeavor for the summer
islander, on leave, as it were, from work on the cathedral
of his or her own bad decisions.

It was unusual, therefore, to find not one but two
attractive strangers at the bar of the Patch on a Friday
night in early spring, studying the glints and gas bubbles in
their beers: a man and a woman, with an empty barstool
between them. It was not yet seven, and the Patch, a
dank, ill-lit, cramped cement structure that had once
served as the main building of a long-defunct strawberry-
processing plant, was almost empty. In the corner across
from the door, Lester Foley—elected by a plebiscite of
local drunks to the mayoralty of Berthannette, a minute
township made up of a general store and a post office, a
failed Shell station, and the Patch—was sleeping, curled
into a ball that did not seem large enough to be composed
of an entire man.

The man at the bar spun away on his stool from the
dispiriting sight of Lester, rolled up like a potato bug
with his hair matted down and a mysterious rime of
white feathers on his beard, and gave his attention to the
Patch's decor: promotional posters listing the locations
and dates of all the games the Seahawks had lost that
season; the threadbare baize of the pool table; a small
black-and-white photograph of a freak three-pound
strawberry that had turned up in the summer of 1948; and
the blinking, pink or blue names of several beers. The
stranger was a dark-eyed young man, thickset but small of
stature, better dressed than the usual Patch customer, even
for a Friday night, in a tweed blazer worn over a crew-
neck sweater that looked like lamb's wool but might even
have been cashmere. Only the fresh wad of black tape that
bound up his stylish bronze eyeglasses, and the day's
growth of stubble on his cheeks, argued at all in favor of

his admission, on a pro-tem basis, into the Chubb Island
losers' guild. There was something in the way his handsome jacket strained at the shoulders, in the gray shadow
on his jaw, that implied a deep reserve of resentment,
a list of grievances carried around in the billfold, on a
sheet of paper split and tattered with much refolding.
He looked like the kind of customer who drinks word-
lessly, and without apparent pleasure, all evening, like
a patient given control of his own morphine drip. He
looked like a man dangerously addicted to the correction
of mistaken people.

"I thought this was a happening place," he said now, to
nobody in particular, still gazing out into the neon gloom
of the barroom.

Mike Veal heard the remark but took advantage of
a continuing pressure problem with the Rainier tap to let
it pass. The customer was drinking a bottle of Pilsner
Urquell, which Mike had found only after much digging
around on his hands and knees, with his arm plunged
far into the icy recesses of the No. 2 cooler, behind the
box of microwavable Honey 'n' Jalapeño Cheesy Pork
Pockets. And of course Lester Foley had nothing to say on
the subject of the happeningness of the Patch.

"Why don't you put a buck in the jukebox?" said the
woman from her stool. "I bet they even have your
favorite song."

She was a long, bony woman, with an intelligent face a
little raw around the nostrils. In spite of her naturally
blond hair and a backside that projected with a certain
architectural audacity out over the rear edge of her stool,
the predominant impression she seemed likely to leave in
the mind of a man surveying a barroom on a Friday night
was one of elbows and knees. Although she was dressed
like a familiar type of weather-beaten, llama-raising, herb-
alistic island woman—denim overalls and duck boots, hair
pulled back from her forehead by a plain blue elastic

headband, face naked but for an uncertain streak of mauve on the lips—no one would ever have mistaken her for a native. She straddled her barstool with an equestrian aplomb that suggested both a genteel upbringing and an overeager attempt to look as though she belonged. A copy of *Un Sexe Qui N'est Pas Une,* in the original French, protruded from the right pocket of the big shearling coat she had draped over the seat of the stool between her and the man. Her fingers were devoid of rings.

" 'It's a Man's Man's Man's World,' " she continued, with a vague wave toward the jukebox.

"Is that my favorite song?" said the man. He reached into the inside pocket of his jacket and took out a fat wallet. "I didn't know."

"It's on there," said Mike Veal helpfully. "James Brown's greatest hits, on CD."

The woman nodded. She raised her bottle of light beer to the man. " 'This is a man's world,' " she sang, in a cracked little high-pitched James Brown wail. Then she turned away from him, folding back up into herself, as if she didn't want him to get the idea she was flirting. The man took a dollar from his wallet and walked over to the jukebox. He fed several more dollars into the slot. "Sex Machine" began to play, as irritating and irresistible as a ringing telephone. The woman took a swallow of her watery, pale beer, her eyes comically wide, as if amazed by her own thirst.

"This your first time in here?" Mike asked her.

She nodded. "It always looked so hopping. Cars in the parking lot."

"It's early yet," said Mike, looking at his watch. "They'll be showing up any time."

The tides of carousal on a Friday night on Chubb Island could be unpredictable. In general, the flow from Heron to Patch, Tavern to Peavey's, was even and steady through the evening, but sometimes a special event, a darts tournament or a personal milestone such as a divorce, a birthday, or an acquittal, could bottle things up for an hour or two. "Unless all of them died in, like, a car crash or whatever." He smiled with unconscious pleasure at this thought.

She nodded again and took another swallow.

"From the island?" said Mike.

"No," said the woman, "but I've been coming here my whole life."

"Family has a house?"

"On Probity Beach."

"Nice."

"I have a house of my own now. On Rhododendron Beach. I've been living here almost six years."

"You're a year-rounder, and you never been in here before?"

She shook her head. "I don't know. I guess I never had a reason before."

Leaving the question begged by this statement unasked, Mike went on tinkering with the Rainier tap. The woman lowered her eyes to the scuffed veneer of the bar, which was giving off its faint early-evening sting of ammonia. Originally, it had been the bar of Rudolph's, a dive in a Quonset hut out at the old Navy airfield, which burned down back in 1956. There were some senior members of the losers' guild who claimed they could still smell the fire on it.

The woman dabbed an indecipherable sketch with her fingertip in the mist on her glass. "Do you know a guy called Olivier?" she said, not looking up.

"Sure."

"He comes in here?"

"Does he?"

"I thought he did. I thought . . ."

"Are you looking for him?"

"No."

"Here," said the man, returning from the jukebox with his wallet clutched in one hand and a twenty-dollar bill in the other. He handed the bill to the woman. "From yesterday."

"Oh, yes," said the woman. "But it was only seventeen."

The man nodded. "I'll take the difference in beer." He held up his empty bottle to Mike Veal and gave it a shake. "Olivier?" he said.

"Olivier Berquet," said Mike, studying the two with fresh interest. "I guess he's, what, a Frenchman?"

"And I've heard an awful lot about that little French-man, let me tell you," the man said. "The Phantom Frog of Chubb Island." He turned to the woman. "How's that for a title? Can you get a poem out of that?"

"What's your name?" the woman said to Mike Veal.

"Mike."

"Mike, am I allowed to say 'fuck' in this bar?"

"I wouldn't try to stop you."

The woman turned to the man. "Fuck you, Jake," she said.

The door opened and, as always happened on a cold night when someone came in from outside, a low, mourn-ful moaning filled the bottommost levels of sound in the barroom, humming around the ankles of the customers like a roiling cloud. The Korg sisters, Ellen and Lisabeth, walked in, followed in short order by New Wave Dave Willard, Harley Dave Sackler, Debbie Browne, Ray Lindquist, Nice Dave Madsen, and a number of other employees of the Gearhead plant, just down the road from Berthannette. Gearhead made accessories and spe-cialty parts for sport-utility vehicles. It was the island's largest employer and the source of a small but steady cur-rent of the Patch's income. There had been an employees' meeting tonight, after work, which was why the bar had remained empty for so long. Now, with a great deal of sorrowful moaning and gusts of cold wind, it filled up quickly.

Lester Foley was awakened. This was done by Harley Dave's cracking open a can of beer next to his ear, which was followed by uproarious general laughter when he scrabbled awake like a dog at the sound of a can opener grinding away on its evening Alpo. Lester grinned his foolish feathered grin, took the beer that was his reward for making everyone laugh, and started in on one of his trademark mayoral disquisitions whose interminability was relieved only by their total lack of sense. The former handyman had been drinking steadily since 1975. In June of that year, Lester had got a job putting up a boathouse and dock for a summer family named Lichty, whose handsome young son, a boy of fifteen, took to tagging along with Lester and helping him with his work. In the evenings they hid in the driftwood piles down at the dark end of Probity Beach, smoking marijuana and drinking beer. On the first of July, they drove out to the Nisqually reservation and for twenty dollars filled the hatch of Lester's VW squareback with illegal fireworks. On the fifth of July, at two o'clock in the morning, at the end of the sturdy fir dock Lester had built, a Silver Salute with a defective fuse burst prematurely, before Lester and the boy could get clear of it. The explosion, which the investigator from the Chubb Island Fire Department had estimated as equal to the force of half a stick of industrial-grade dynamite, killed the Lichty boy and blew off Lester's right thumb and forefinger. Since then he had not worked much. It was rare that anything he said managed to be succinct or intelligible.

"You can't trust a woodpecker," he was insisting now to the Korg sisters, with that special undissuadableness of his. "They're just too goddam unreliable. I could have told you that from the get-go."

"Who said anything about a woodpecker?" said Lisabeth Korg.

BY EIGHT o'clock, there was not an empty stool at the bar,
quarters were lined up seven deep on the lip of the pool
table, and so many people were dancing around the
jukebox that Mrs. Magarac, the owner, who had come
straight from her twelve-step meeting, could barely navigate from the bar to the farthest booths with a sweating
tray full of beer.

"Well?" said the woman at the bar to the man she had
cursed. The crowding of the Patch had forced them onto
adjoining stools. She drew her bottle of beer across the air
before her, taking in the noise and laughter and smoke.
"Any likely prospects?"

"Oh, my God," said Jake. He closed his eyes. There
was a migraine translucence in the skin around his eyes.
He rolled his bottle of Pilsner Urquell, his fourth, across
his brow.

"What about her?" the woman said.

"Which one?"

"With the red hair. I know her. I think she works at
the Thriftway."

"Oh, yeah." He still had not opened his eyes. "I've
seen her. Curly."

"Cute, I think."

"I dislike this," said the man. "Can I just tell you that? I
never came to a bar like this before. Why should I start
now, just because——"

"You never came to this type of bar before, or you
never came to a bar in this manner?"

"Grace, I think I'd better—I think I'm going to
split."

"Don't be a wiener, Jake."

"No, I'm just——"

"Come on, weasel," she said, aiming at him with an

index finger. Looking at it, he went cross-eyed for a moment. "We made a deal. About tonight."

"Yeah, I know I made a deal," he said. "And I know what's going to happen. I'm going to go home alone, with a big goose egg in the romance department, while you zip off with Monsieur Olivier, on his little scooter, with his scarf tucked into his lapels—"

"He's here. That's him."

Jake's eyes snapped open and he checked out Olivier Berquet, just walking into the Patch. If he had really been expecting a natty little loafer-wearer, crest embroidered on the pocket of his blazer, sweater knotted cavalierly around his neck, he must have been disappointed. Olivier Berquet was not French at all, as it happened, but Québécois—a big-handed carpenter with a tall man's stoop, long blond hair, and a massively handsome face, craggy and pitted, a face that looked as if it had been carved with a pneumatic drill by a tiny workman dangling from the sheer granite cliff of Olivier's forehead. He wore a black motorcycle jacket, ripped blue jeans, and Roper's boots. He was well known on the island both for the quality of his work, which was high, and for the terrible treatment his wife received at his hands, which—though never definitively established in a court of law or through some famous public incident of the sort popular among the Patch's patrons—ranged, by local rumor, from the merely callous to the outright mean. At one time or another, he had troubled the evenings of all the island's bartenders. Now he had begun dancing, working his hips and bobbing his big Gutzon Borglum head. He was a good dancer, consciously so, leggy and languid, his movements not so much in time to the music as in illustration of it.

"He has a big butt," said Jake. "I've noticed that's something you like."

"Jake," said Grace, not responding. She pointed to

Jake's other side. He turned. The woman with the curly red hair, who was in fact a checker at the Thriftway in Probity Harbor, was standing beside him. He knew her after all: Brenda Petersen. She and some of her friends had washed Jake's car for him one Saturday morning almost six years earlier—his first summer on the island—to raise money for their senior-class trip. Since then their paths had crossed without issue or remark at least a couple of dozen times. Her bright red fusillade of skyrocket curls was her most striking feature, but her youth, her plumpness, and a startling lack of shyness all worked in her favor.

"Hi, there," she said. "Brenda."

She held out her hand, angled with a textbook display of confidence.

"Jake," he said.

"I was wondering if you wanted to dance with me—" She registered the way Jake's mouth hung open, the way Grace shifted a little on her stool. "But if you two are together I'll just go back over to my table there and shoot myself."

Jake turned to Grace, with a face that begged for mercy, his mouth forming inaudible words. Grace held out her hand to the girl and they shook.

"Grace."

"Hi. Brenda."

There was a wordless moment. "We're just friends," said Grace, with an embarrassed laugh. "Go on and dance, Jake."

The contrast between Olivier's and Jake's styles of dancing, had there been anyone in the bar sober or interested enough to notice it, was marked. Jake seemed somehow to wear not just his clothes but his entire body too tightly. He chopped at the air with his hands. He and Brenda didn't speak to each other—the crowd on the dance floor had forced them up against the jukebox, which was clanging loudly with Tom Petty's cover of

"Feel a Whole Lot Better." Brenda's best friend, Sharon Toole, shimmied up alongside her at one point, rolling a mocking but not unfriendly eye in the direction of Jake's dogged, cramped performance, and the two of them exchanged a smile.

Jake's departure from his place at the bar seemed to increase the male traffic around Grace. She remained folded carefully up into herself, legs crossed at the knee and then again at the ankle, fingers fitted carefully around the throat of her beer, but there was a perceptible rise in the volume and good humor along the adjacent barstools in Jake's absence.

Among those whom Grace found herself talking to was Lester Foley, who had come right toward her, in his off-kilter headlong style, head angled one way, shoulders another, listing to one side like Groucho Marx after a severe blow to the head. He had been drinking for an hour now and was at the nightly peak, such as it was, of his physical aplomb and his powers of concentration. At some point he had gone back into the men's room to run cold water through his hair and comb it back neatly with his pocket comb. There were still a number of feathers in his beard.

He reached out his right hand, with its three grimy fingers.

"Now you stepped in it," he said. He laughed a wicked little laugh.

"Pardon me?"

"I told you this would happen. I told everyone. Hell, I even told myself!"

"Leave her alone, Your Honor," said Mike Veal, looking a little uneasy. "Just ignore him," he said to Grace.

She had not let go of his hand.

"Lester," she said. "They used to call you Les."

"No more or less," he said, automatically.

"Do you remember me?"

"Sure I do," said Lester, without any great sincerity.

"My parents had the place next door. Next to the Lichtys."

He pulled his hand from hers. "The Lichtys." He scowled and squinted at her as if trying to read a surprising text printed in very small characters on her face. His wrinkles smoothed out, leaving a staff of clean pink lines on his forehead. The color left his cheeks. He was working harder than he had in quite some time.

"I used to hang around with Dane a lot," said Grace. "Their son. I braided your hair once, you probably don't remember. I used to give Dane these crazy things, with seaweed braided in, and little sand dollars and junk we found on the beach." She had started to braid the air on either side of her head, but now she put a hand to her mouth and laughed, as if she had embarrassed herself again.

"Grace Meadows," he said. "Blond girl?" He looked for confirmation of this recollected scrap of a summer fifteen years before. "Dane's girlfriend? Used to ride around on that motorbike of his. Go swimming with him in that cold, cold water. Always smoking my cigarettes. Grace Meadows, that you?"

"That was me," said Grace, too softly to be heard over the music.

"Uh-huh. Well." Lester stopped squinting, and left off trying to read her face. He rummaged around in the pocket of his filthy down coat and pulled out a surprisingly crisp one-dollar bill. "Well. You were crazy then, and I don't doubt that you are probably crazy today. Everyone is crazy nowadays, which looking around I'm sure you probably noticed by now." He laid the dollar bill on the bar. "A beer, please, Mr. Mike."

"Put that away," said Mike, flicking the dollar back toward Lester. He drew a pint and handed it to him. "But after this one you're cut off."

Lester opened his mouth to protest, but a big blond hand clapped him on the shoulder.

"Good evening, there, Mr. Mayor," said Olivier.

"Oh, no," said Lester. He peeled himself out from under Olivier's hand, and, with a last squint sidewise at Grace, ducked around to the farthest corner of the bar, where he stood for a time with his knobby fingers wrapped around the untouched pint of Rainier.

"I love that guy," said Olivier without apparent affection. He looked avidly at Grace, his eyes crinkling in a way that some uncharitable islanders might have described as patented, or even ominous.

"I thought I'd see you here," he said.

"I'm having a hard time believing it, myself," said Grace.

"Why didn't you come tomorrow, like I told you? We aren't playing tonight."

Olivier was the drummer for a local band known variously as the Tailchasers, the Chubb Island Four Piece, and Olivier and Bo and Johnny. They had a more or less permanent ongoing engagement at each of the four island taverns, which is to say that they played nearly every Saturday night at one of them, until the complaints mounted or Olivier got into a violent dispute with the proprietors, at which point, sufficient time having elapsed in the interval since their last appearance, they moved along to the next stop in the circuit.

"I know," said Grace. "You said you play country music."

"Most of the time."

"Well, I don't really like country music."

Olivier cocked his head and stared at her, his forehead crumpled in mock perplexity at her chilly tone. He was smarter than he looked—a condition as rare on Chubb Island as it is anywhere else. Mike Veal handed him the

beer he had ordered and Olivier drank down half of it in a
swallow.

"I'm not bothering you," he said. "I should go?"

She shook her head.

"How's the car?" he said, after a moment.

He saw that her gaze was focused on Brenda Petersen
and the dark little jerking man she was dancing with.
"Who is that guy?"

"That's my husband," she said. "His name is Jake."

"Your husband?" For a moment he looked puzzled.
"That's cool," he said, with the eye-crinkle on again.

"We're getting a divorce."

"Oh."

"We haven't had sex with each other in three and a
half years," she went on, with a sudden sweep of her arm.
"We stopped living together back in January. We haven't
had sex with anyone else, either."

"Huh."

"No sex. At all."

Her husband had stopped dancing. He was standing
in the middle of the dance floor, just standing there,
watching Grace, looking as if—over the stomping of
bootheels, over the labored whooping of off-duty sheriff's
deputy Royce T. Sturgeon, over the dog-kennel laughter
of a Friday night in the Patch, over the sounds of the
islanders all around him as they shook their hair, their
long key chains, the fringes on their vests—he had heard
or could guess every word that Grace had just said.

Grace saw Brenda Petersen pulling on his arm, asking
him if everything was all right. "I have no idea why I just
told you that," Grace said to Olivier. "I know I shouldn't
be saying it at all." She turned and took hold of both his
hands in hers. "I want you to forget what I said."

"Three and a half years," said Olivier. "Shit."

"Hard to believe, isn't it?" she said. She stood up, or

rather toppled in a more or less controlled manner off the stool, landing somehow on both feet. She still had not let go of his hands. "Come on."

"Tell you what," said Olivier. "My buddy John just came in the door, over there. I have to get with him for just a minute and then I'll take you up on that, all right?"

Grace watched him go.

She looked over at Jake again and saw that he was watching Olivier, too. He was rocking a little on the soles of his feet, and a weird, broken smile emerged. When Olivier came within a few feet of him, Jake held out his hand vaguely.

Over the ten years since his arrival on Chubb Island, Olivier Berquet had been involved in seventeen minor altercations in taverns, and four out-and-out brawls, in which teeth were scattered to the night air and men went to the urgent-care center to have bits of parking-lot gravel tweezed from their palms and cheeks. His name had appeared twice in the police log of the local weekly, the *Clam,* and when he was convicted of battery there had been an item on page 1. It took less provocation than a drunken, jealous, hard-up man out on a despairing date with his estranged wife to get Olivier swinging, as everyone in the room well knew.

On the jukebox, Jim Morrison shouted the last words of "Break On Through" and the song cut off. People stopped dancing. The cue ball slammed into the nine.

"Is there a problem?" Olivier said, calmly, rubbing his chin.

Jake reached out for Olivier's right hand, and grasped it.

"I just wanted to wish you all the luck in the world," he said.

There was no great sarcasm in Jake's tone, and in its absence Olivier seemed a little confused. He nodded warily, letting Jake work his hand up and down, the way he might have shaken with a man in an airport holding a Bible and a stack of brochures.

"Yeah," said Olivier. "Whatever, dude."

As the next song, "Born on the Bayou," came on, he pulled his hand from Jake's and jived his way heavily across the Patch and over to John Bekkedahl, a fat, bearded man wearing a Sturgis T-shirt. "Fuckin' yuppies," he muttered. Somebody laughed.

Grace went to Jake, who was standing by himself, still holding his hand out.

"What happened to Brenda?" she said.

"I don't know," said Jake. "She thinks we're screwed up."

"We are."

"What's the story with Olivier?"

"I think I scared him off with my evident madness."

"Do you want to dance?"

"No," she said. "Let's go home."

"Meaning what?" said Jake.

NOT QUITE sure of the answer, they didn't leave. They stayed past last call, keeping each other company at the bar, while the Patch, one by one or in twos and threes, exhaled its customers. Olivier went home with Carla Lacy, whose husband was on a boat in the Bering Sea, working fourteen-hour shifts feeding tuna carcasses to a rendering vat. Brenda Petersen left with a tall, good-looking kid named Al or Alf from Tacoma.

At last, Mike Veal threw on the overhead lights, driving the remaining patrons from the inky crevices of obscurity and glamour into which they had tucked themselves. For them it was like coming to in an emergency room, and they went out, sour and incoherently sad. A few diehards headed down the road to Peavey's, where the bar clock was known to be kept only seven minutes ahead of Pacific Standard. Still Jake and Grace remained on their stools, waiting out the ten-dollar bill that Jake had fed the jukebox. Mike Veal went around snuffing the neon signs, stacking chairs, and upending the other barstools. When he pulled the plug on the jukebox, they took the hint and settled their tab. Jake waited while Grace went to the toilet, and then they made cautious progress down the back hall and out into the chilly night.

As they came through the back door Jake stumbled over Lester Foley, who was sleeping under a pile of blankets beside the Dumpster. Grace stopped.

"Grace," Jake murmured.

"Sh-h-h." She knelt down beside Lester, and then, gently so as not to wake him, peeled a lank strand of hair from his hollow cheek.

"Grace, what are you doing?" said Jake. "Come on."

"Nothing," she said. "Be quiet."

She drew two more strands of hair from the oily mass under his stocking cap and wove them with the first into a stiff, skinny braid. She looked around in the gravel and mud at her feet and picked up the discarded cap from a bottle of Oly. Biting her lip, she squeezed the cap between her fingers until it curved inward on itself like a jagged whelk. She threaded the tip of the braid through it, and pinched it closed. Looking at her handiwork, she rocked back and forth on her toes, the leather of her duck shoes creaking.

"He's just sleeping it off, Grace," Jake said. He gave a tug on her collar, and she tipped back onto her heels. "He'll be fine."

"He knew Dane Lichty," Grace said.

"Not the way I do," said Jake.

Jake's car, a Honda station wagon, was parked at the far end of the lot. Jake started toward it, then stopped, and seemed to sag a little to one side. "Can't do it," he said. "I think I've had too much."

"Just get in," called Grace, running under the steadily increasing rain toward her car. "I'll take you."

They climbed into a raked, round-finned old Volvo P-1800 that looked gray in the halogen glow of the Patch's security flood but was really an elegant pale yellow, somewhere between the color of a manila folder and the back sheet of a parking citation. Grace had bought the car three days before from Olivier Berquet, for six hundred dollars. A few years back, Olivier had flipped it over on Cemetery Road, racing to make the ferry, but he had not mentioned this to Grace, although everyone else knew the story. Olivier had suggested to Grace that she have someone look it over, knowing somehow that she never would.

There was a flat, dishpan rattle as Jake closed the door on his side. Grace switched on the radio but did not start the engine. The only sound that emerged from the speakers was a fly-wing hum in the left channel.

"You always wanted one of these," said Jake.

She nodded.

"Hey," she said. "Now I finally get to see your place."

"It's small," said Jake.

"Is it too small?"

"I'm all right," he said. He rested his left hand on the knob of the gearshift. After a minute she laid hers on top of his.

"Nobody knows," she said.

"Nobody knows what?"

"Nobody knows the trouble we've seen."

"It's nice that we can share that," said Jake.

The rain dripped from the fir trees that overspread the Patch's back lot, and seeped slowly in through the windshield frame on Jake's side. The remaining unbroken panes in the greenhouse of the old strawberry plant, a gaunt ruin on the other side of the parking lot, chimed with rain.

"Well," Grace said. "I guess neither of us got lucky."

She twisted the key in the ignition, and turned out of the Patch's lot, onto the island highway. The last ferry of the night, of course, had pulled in at the Eastpoint dock eighteen minutes earlier. The cars in the opposite lane were strung like Christmas lights for a mile, coming out of Berthannette, and it must have been hard for Grace and Jake to be in her car as it filled up with the flash of other people's headlights, then went dark again, and to know that everyone who passed them was headed for home.

The first real writer I ever knew was a man who did all of his work under the name of August Van Zorn. He lived at the McClelland Hotel, which my grandmother owned, in the uppermost room of its turret, and taught English literature at Coxley, a small college on the other side of the minor Pennsylvania river that split our town in two. His real name was Albert Vetch, and his field, I believe, was Blake; I remember he kept a framed print of the Ancient of Days affixed to the faded flocked wallpaper of his room, above a stoop-shouldered wooden suit rack that once belonged to my father. Mr. Vetch's wife had been living in a sanatorium up near Erie since the deaths of their teenaged sons in a backyard explosion some years earlier, and it was always my impression that he wrote, in part, to earn the money to keep her there. He wrote horror stories, hundreds of them, many of which were eventually published in such periodicals of the day as Weird Tales, Strange Stories, Black Tower, *and the like. . . . He worked at night, using a fountain pen, in a bentwood rocking chair, with a Hudson Bay blanket draped across his lap and a bottle of bourbon on the table before him. When his work was going well, he could be heard in every corner of the sleeping hotel, rocking and madly rocking while he subjected his heroes to the gruesome rewards of their passions for unnameable things.*

—GRADY TRIPP,
Wonder Boys

In the Black Mill

BY AUGUST VAN ZORN

IN THE fall of 1948, when I arrived in Plunkettsburg to begin the fieldwork I hoped would lead to a doctorate in archaeology, there were still a good number of towns-people living there whose memories stretched back to the time, in the final decade of the previous century, when the soot-blackened hills that encircle the town fairly swarmed with savants and mad diggers. In 1892 the discovery, on a hilltop overlooking the Miskahannock River, of the burial complex of a hitherto-unknown tribe of Mound Builders had set off a frenzy of excavation and scholarly poking around that made several careers, among them that of the aged hero of my profession who was chairman of my dissertation committee. It was under his redoubtable influence that I had taken up the study of the awful, illustrious Miskahannocks, with their tombs and bone pits, a course that led me at last, one gray November afternoon, to turn my overladen fourthhand Nash off the highway from Pittsburgh to Morgantown, and to navigate, tightly gripping the wheel, the pitted ghost of a roadbed that winds up through the Yuggogheny Hills, then down into the broad and gloomy valley of the Miskahannock.

As I negotiated that endless series of hairpin and blind curves, I was afforded an equally endless series of dispiriting partial views of the place where I would spend the next ten months of my life. Like many of its neighbors in that iron-veined country, Plunkettsburg was at first glance unprepossessing—a low, rusting little city, with tarnished onion domes and huddled houses, drab as an armful of dead leaves strewn along the ground. But as I left the last hill behind me and got my first unobstructed look, I immediately noted the one structure that, while it did nothing to elevate my opinion of my new home, altered the humdrum aspect of Plunkettsburg sufficiently to make it remarkable, and also sinister. It stood off to the east of town, in a zone of weeds and rust-colored earth, a vast, black box, bristling with spiky chimneys, extending over some five acres or more, dwarfing everything around it. This was, I knew at once, the famous Plunkettsburg Mill. Evening was coming on, and in the half-light its windows winked and flickered with inner fire, and its towering stacks vomited smoke into the autumn twilight. I shuddered, and then cried out. So intent had I been on the ghastly black apparition of the mill that I had nearly run my car off the road.

" 'Here in this mighty fortress of industry,' " I quoted aloud in the tone of a newsreel narrator, reassuring myself with the ironic reverberation of my voice, " 'turn the great cogs and thrust the relentless pistons that forge the pins and trusses of the American dream.' " I was recalling the words of a chamber of commerce brochure I had received last week from my hosts, the antiquities department of Plunkettsburg College, along with particulars of my lodging and library privileges. They were anxious to have me; it had been many years since the publication of my chairman's *Miskahannock Surveys* had effectively settled all answerable questions—save, I hoped, one—about the vanished tribe and consigned Plunkettsburg once again to the mists of academic oblivion and the thick black effluvia of its satanic mill.

"SO, WHAT is there left to say about that pointy-toothed crowd?" said Carlotta Brown-Jenkin, draining her glass of brandy. The chancellor of Plunkettsburg College and chairwoman of the antiquities department had offered to stand me to dinner on my first night in town. We were sitting in the Hawaiian-style dining room of a Chinese restaurant downtown. Brown-Jenkin was herself appropriately antique, a gaunt old girl in her late seventies, her nearly hairless scalp worn and yellowed, the glint of her eyes, deep within their cavernous sockets, like that of ancient coins discovered by torchlight. "I quite thought that your distinguished mentor had revealed all their bloody mysteries."

"Only the women filed their teeth," I reminded her, taking another swallow of Indian Ring beer, the local brew, which I found to possess a dark, not entirely pleasant savor of autumn leaves or damp earth. I gazed around the low room with its ersatz palm thatching and garlands of wax orchids. The only other people in the place were a man on wooden crutches with a pinned-up trouser leg and a man with a wooden hand, both of them drinking Indian Ring, and the bartender, an extremely fat woman in a thematically correct but hideous red muumuu. My hostess had assured me, without a great deal of enthusiasm, that we were about to eat the best-cooked meal in town.

"Yes, yes," she recalled, smiling tolerantly. Her particular field of study was great Carthage, and no doubt, I thought, she looked down on my unlettered band of savages. "They considered pointed teeth to be the essence of female beauty."

"That is, of course, the theory of my distinguished mentor," I said, studying the label on my beer bottle, on which there was printed Thelder's 1894 engraving of the Plunkettsburg Ring, which was also reproduced on the cover of *Miskahannock Surveys*.

"You do not concur?" said Brown-Jenkin.

"I think that there may in fact be other possibilities."

"Such as?"

At this moment the waiter arrived, bearing a tray laden with plates of unidentifiable meats and vegetables that glistened in garish sauces the colors of women's lipstick. The steaming dishes emitted an overpowering blast of vinegar, as if to cover some underlying stench. Feeling ill, I averted my eyes from the food and saw that the waiter, a thickset, powerful man with bland Slavic features, was missing two of the fingers on his left hand. My stomach revolted. I excused myself from the table and ran directly to the bathroom.

"Nerves," I explained to Brown-Jenkin when I returned, blushing, to the table. "I'm excited about starting my research."

"Of course," she said, examining me critically. With her napkin she wiped a thin red dribble of sauce from her chin. "I quite understand."

"There seem to be an awful lot of missing limbs in this room," I said, trying to lighten my mood. "Hope none of them ended up in the food."

The chancellor stared at me, aghast.

"A very bad joke," I said. "My apologies. My sense of humor was not, I'm afraid, widely admired back in Boston, either."

"No," she agreed, with a small, unamused smile. "Well." She patted the long, thin strands of yellow hair atop her head. "It's the *mill,* of course."

"Of course," I said, feeling a bit dense for not having

puzzled this out myself. "Dangerous work they do there, I take it."

"The mill has taken a piece of half the men in Plunkettsburg," Brown-Jenkin said, sounding almost proud. "Yes, it's terribly dangerous work." There had crept into her voice a boosterish tone of admiration that could not fail to remind me of the chamber of commerce brochure. "*Important* work."

"Vitally important," I agreed, and to placate her I heaped my plate with colorful, luminous, indeterminate meat, a gesture for which I paid dearly through all the long night that followed.

I TOOK up residence in Murrough House, just off the campus of Plunkettsburg College. It was a large, rambling structure, filled with hidden passages, queerly shaped rooms, and staircases leading nowhere, built by the notorious lady magnate, "the Robber Baroness," Philippa Howard Murrough, founder of the college, noted spiritualist and author and dark genius of the Plunkettsburg Mill. She had spent the last four decades of her life, and a considerable part of her manufacturing fortune, adding to, demolishing, and rebuilding her home. On her death the resultant warren, a chimera of brooding Second Empire gables, peaked Victorian turrets, and baroque porticoes with a coat of glossy black ivy, passed into the hands of the private girls' college she had endowed, which converted it to a faculty club and lodgings for visiting scholars. I had a round turret room on the fourth and uppermost floor. There were no other visiting scholars in the house and, according to the porter, this had been the case for several years.

Old Halicek, the porter, was a bent, slow-moving fellow who lived with his daughter and grandson in a suite of rooms somewhere in the unreachable lower regions of the house. He too had lost a part of his body to the great mill in his youth—his left ear. It had been reduced, by a device that Halicek called a Dodson line extractor, to a small pink ridge nestled in the lee of his bushy white sideburns. His daughter, Mrs. Eibonas, oversaw a small staff of two maids and a waiter and did the cooking for the dozen or so faculty members who took their lunches at Murrough House every day. The waiter was Halicek's grandson, Dexter Eibonas, an earnest, good-looking, affable redhead of seventeen who was a favorite among the college faculty. He was intelligent, curious, widely if erratically read. He was always pestering me to take him out to dig in the mounds, and while I would not have been averse to his pleasant company, the terms of my agreement with the board of the college, who were the trustees of the site, expressly forbade the recruiting of local workmen. Nevertheless I gave him books on archaeology and kept him abreast of my discoveries, such as they were. Several of the Plunkettsburg professors, I learned, had also taken an interest in the development of his mind.

"They sent me up to Pittsburgh last winter," he told me one evening about a month into my sojourn, as he brought me a bottle of Ring and a plate of Mrs. Eibonas's famous kielbasa with sauerkraut. Professor Brown-Jenkin had been much mistaken, in my opinion, about the best-laid table in town. During the most tedious, chilly, and profitless stretches of my scratchings-about in the bleak, flinty Yuggoghenies, I was often sustained solely by thoughts of Mrs. Eibonas's homemade sausages and cakes. "I had an interview with the dean of engineering at Tech. Professor Collier even paid for a hotel for Mother and me."

"And how did it go?"

"Oh, it went fine, I guess," said Dexter. "I was accepted."

"Oh," I said, confused. The autumn semester at Carnegie Tech, I imagined, would have been ending that very week.

"Have you—have you deferred your admission?"

"Deferred it indefinitely, I guess. I told them no thanks." Dexter had, in an excess of nervous energy, been snapping a tea towel back and forth. He stopped. His normally bright eyes took on a glazed, I would almost have said a dreamy, expression. "I'm going to work in the mill."

"The *mill*?" I said, incredulous. I looked at him to see if he was teasing me, but at that moment he seemed to be entertaining only the pleasantest imaginings of his labors in that fiery black castle. I had a sudden vision of his pleasant face rendered earless, and looked away. "Forgive my asking, but why would you want to do that?"

"My father did it," said Dexter, his voice dull. "His father, too. I'm on the hiring list." The light came back into his eyes, and he resumed snapping the towel. "Soon as a place opens up, I'm going in."

He left me and went back into the kitchen, and I sat there shuddering. *I'm going in.* The phrase had a heroic, doomed ring to it, like the pronouncement of a fireman about to enter his last burning house. Over the course of the previous month I'd had ample opportunity to observe the mill and its effect on the male population of Plunkettsburg. Casual observation, in local markets and bars, in the lobby of the Orpheum on State Street, on the sidewalks, in Birch's general store out on Gray Road where I stopped for coffee and cigarettes every morning on my way up to the mound complex, had led me to estimate that in truth, fully half of the townsmen had lost some visible portion of their anatomies to Murrough Manufacturing, Inc. And yet all my attempts to ascertain how these often horribly grave accidents had befallen their bent, maimed, or limping victims were met, invariably, with an explanation at once so detailed and so vague, so

rich in mechanical jargon and yet so free of actual information, that I had never yet succeeded in producing in
my mind an adequate picture of the incident in question,
or, for that matter, of what kind of deadly labor was performed in the black mill.

What, precisely, was manufactured in that bastion of
industrial democracy and fount of the Murrough millions?
I heard the trains come sighing and moaning into town in
the middle of the night, clanging as they were shunted
into the mill sidings. I saw the black diesel trucks, emblazoned with the crimson initial *M,* lumbering through
the streets of Plunkettsburg on their way to and from the
loading docks. I had two dozen conversations, over endless mugs of Indian Ring, about shift schedules and union
activities (invariably quashed) and company picnics, about
ore and furnaces, metallurgy and turbines. I heard the
resigned, good-natured explanations of men sliced open by
Rawlings divagators, ground up by spline presses, mangled
by steam sorters, half-decapitated by rolling Hurley plates.
And yet after four months in Plunkettsburg I was no closer
to understanding the terrible work to which the people of
that town sacrificed, with such apparent goodwill, the
bodies of their men.

I TOOK to haunting the precincts of the mill in the early
morning as the six o'clock shift was coming on and late at
night as the graveyard men streamed through the iron gates,
carrying their black lunch pails. The fence, an elaborate
Victorian confection of wickedly tipped, thick iron pikes
trailed with iron ivy, enclosed the mill yard at such a distance from the mountainous factory itself that it was impossible for me to get near enough to see anything but the
glow of huge fires through the begrimed mesh windows. I
applied at the company offices in town for admission, as a
visitor, to the plant but was told by the receptionist, rather
rudely, that the Plunkettsburg Mill was not a tourist facility.

My fascination with the place grew so intense and distracting that I neglected my work; my wanderings through the abandoned purlieus of the savage Miskahannocks grew desultory and ruminative, my discoveries of artifacts, never frequent, dwindled to almost nothing, and I made fewer and fewer entries in my journal. Finally, one exhausted morning, after an entire night spent lying in my bed at Murrough House staring out the leaded window at a sky that was bright orange with the reflected fire of the mill, I decided I had had enough.

I dressed quickly, in plain tan trousers and a flannel work shirt. I went down to the closet in the front hall, where I found a drab old woolen coat and a watch cap that I pulled down over my head. Then I stepped outside. The terrible orange flashes had subsided and the sky was filled with stars. I hurried across town to the east side, to Stan's Diner on Mill Street, where I knew I would find the day shift wolfing down ham and eggs and pancakes. I slipped between two large men at the long counter and ordered coffee. When one of my neighbors got up to go to the toilet, I grabbed his lunch pail, threw down a handful of coins, and hurried over to the gates of the mill, where I joined the crowd of men. They looked at me oddly, not recognizing me, and I could see them murmuring to one another in puzzlement. But the earliness of the morning or an inherent reserve kept them from saying anything. They figured, I suppose, that whoever I was, I was somebody else's problem. Only one man, tall, with thinning yellow hair, kept his gaze on me for more than a moment. His eyes, I was surprised to see, looked very sad.

"You shouldn't be here, buddy," he said, not unkindly.

I felt myself go numb. I had been caught.

"What? Oh, no, I—I—"

The whistle blew. The crowd of men, swelled now to more than a hundred, jerked to life and waited, nervous, on the balls of their feet, for the gates to open. The man with the yellow hair seemed to forget me. In the distance an equally large crowd of men emerged from the belly of the mill and headed toward us. There was a grinding of old machinery, the creak of stressed iron, and then the ornamental gates rolled away. The next instant I was caught up in the tide of men streaming toward the mill, borne along like a cork. Halfway there our group intersected with the graveyard shift and in the ensuing chaos of bodies and hellos I was sure my plan was going to work. I was going to see, at last, the inside of the mill.

I felt something, someone's fingers, brush the back of my neck, and then I was yanked backward by the collar of my coat. I lost my footing and fell to the ground. As the changing shifts of workers flowed around me I looked up and saw a huge man standing over me, his arms folded across his chest. He was wearing a black jacket emblazoned on the breast with a large *M*. I tried to stand, but he pushed me back down.

"You can just stay right there until the police come," he said.

"Listen," I said. My research, clearly, was at an end. My scholarly privileges would be revoked. I would creep back to Boston, where, of course, my committee and, above all, my chair would recommend that I quit the department. "You don't have to do that."

Once more I tried to stand, and this time the company guard threw me back to the ground so hard and so quickly that I couldn't break my fall with my hands. The back of my head slammed against the pavement. A passing worker stepped on my outstretched hand. I cried out.

"Hey," said a voice. "Come on, Moe. You don't need to treat him that way."

It was the sad-eyed man with the yellow hair. He interposed himself between me and my attacker.

"Don't do this, Ed," said the guard. "I'll have to write you up."

I rose shakily to my feet and started to stumble away, back toward the gates. The guard tried to reach around Ed, to grab hold of me. As he lunged forward, Ed stuck out his foot, and the guard went sprawling.

"Come on, professor," said Ed, putting his arm around me. "You better get out of here."

"Do I know you?" I said, leaning gratefully on him.

"No, but you know my nephew, Dexter. He pointed you out to me at the pictures one night."

"Thank you," I said, when we reached the gate. He brushed some dust from the back of my coat, handed me the knit stocking cap, then took a black bandanna from the pocket of his dungarees. He touched a corner of it to my mouth, and it came away marked with a dark stain.

"Only a little blood," he said. "You'll be all right. You just make sure to stay clear of this place from now on." He brought his face close to mine, filling my nostrils with the sharp medicinal tang of his aftershave. He lowered his voice to a whisper. "And stay off the beer."

"What?"

"Just stay off it." He stood up straight and returned the bandanna to his back pocket. "I haven't taken a sip in two weeks." I nodded, confused. I had been drinking two, three, sometimes four bottles of Indian Ring every night, finding that it carried me effortlessly into profound and dreamless sleep.

"Just tell me one thing," I said.

"I can't say nothing else, professor."

"It's just—what is it you do, in there?"

"Me?" he said, pointing to his chest. "I operate a sprue extruder."

"Yes, yes," I said, "but what does a sprue extruder *do*? What is it *for*?"

He looked at me patiently but a little remotely, a distracted parent with an inquisitive child.

"It's for extruding sprues," he said. "What else?"

. . .

THUS REPULSED, humiliated, and given good reason to fear that my research was in imminent jeopardy of being brought to an end, I resolved to put the mystery of the mill out of my mind once and for all and get on with my real business in Plunkettsburg. I went out to the site of the mound complex and worked with my brush and little hand spade all through that day, until the light failed. When I got home, exhausted, Mrs. Eibonas brought me a bottle of Indian Ring and I gratefully drained it before I remembered Ed's strange warning. I handed the sweating bottle back to Mrs. Eibonas. She smiled.

"Can I bring you another, professor?" she said.

"No, thank you," I said. Her smile collapsed. She looked very disappointed. "All right," she said. For some reason the thought of disappointing her bothered me greatly, so I told her, "Maybe one more."

I retired early and dreamed dreams that were troubled by the scratching of iron on earth and by a clamoring tumult of men. The next morning I got up and went straight out to the site again.

For it was going to take work, a lot of work, if my theory was ever going to bear fruit. During much of my first several months in Plunkettsburg I had been hampered by snow and by the degree to which the site of the Plunkettsburg Mounds—a broad plateau on the eastern slope of Mount Orrert, on which there had been excavated, in the 1890s, thirty-six huge molars of packed earth, each the size of a two-story house—had been picked over and disturbed by that early generation of archaeologists. Their methods had not in every case been as fastidious as one could have hoped. There were numerous areas of old digging where the historical record had, through carelessness, been rendered illegible. Then again, I considered, as I gazed up at the ivy-covered flank of the ancient, artificial hillock my mentor had designated B-3, there was always the possibility that my theory was wrong.

Like all the productions of academe, I suppose, my theory was composed of equal parts of indebtedness and spite. I had formulated it in a kind of rebellion against that grand old man of the field, my chairman, the very person who had inculcated in me a respect for the deep, subtle savagery of the Miskahannock Indians. His view—the standard one—was that the culture of the builders of the Plunkettsburg Mounds, at its zenith, had expressed, to a degree unequaled in the Western Hemisphere up to that time, the aestheticizing of the nihilist impulse. They had evolved all the elaborate social structures—texts, rituals, decorative arts, architecture—of any of the world's great religions: dazzling feats of abstract design represented by the thousands of baskets, jars, bowls, spears, tablets, knives, flails, axes, codices, robes, and so on that were housed and displayed with such pride in the museum of my university, back in Boston. But the Miskahannocks, insofar as anyone had ever been able to determine (and many had tried), worshiped nothing, or, as my teacher would have it, Nothing. They acknowledged neither gods nor goddesses, conversed with no spirits or familiars. Their only purpose, the focus and the pinnacle of their artistic genius, was the killing of men. Nobody knew how many of the unfortunate males of the neighboring tribes had fallen victim to the Miskahannocks' delicate artistry of torture and dismemberment. In 1903 Professor William Waterman of Yale discovered fourteen separate ossuary pits along the banks of the river, not far from the present site of the mill. These had contained enough bones to frame the bodies of seven thousand men and boys. And nobody knew why they had died. The few tattered, fragmentary blood-on-tanbark texts so far discovered concerned themselves chiefly with the recurring famines that plagued Miskahannock civilization and, it was generally theorized, had been responsible for its ultimate collapse. The texts said nothing about the sacred arts of killing and torture. There was, my teacher had persuasively argued, one reason for this. The deaths had been purposeless; their justification, the cosmic purposelessness of life itself.

Now, once I had settled myself on spiteful rebellion, as every good pupil eventually must, there were two possible paths available to me. The first would have been to attempt to prove beyond a doubt that the Miskahannocks had, in fact, worshiped some kind of god, some positive, purposive entity, however bloodthirsty. I chose the second path. I accepted the godlessness of the Miskahannocks. I rejected the refined, reasoning nihilism my mentor had postulated (and to which, as I among very few others knew, he himself privately subscribed). The Miskahannocks, I hoped to prove, had had another motive for their killing: They were hungry; according to the tattered scraps of the Plunkettsburg Codex, very hungry indeed. The filed teeth my professor subsumed to the larger aesthetic principles he elucidated thus had, in my view, a far simpler and more utilitarian purpose. Unfortunately, the widespread incidence of cannibalism among the women of a people vanished four thousand years since was proving rather difficult to establish. So far, in fact, I had found no evidence of it at all.

I knelt to untie the canvas tarp I had stretched across my digging of the previous day. I was endeavoring to take an inclined section of B-3, cutting a passage five feet high and two feet wide at a 30-degree angle to the horizontal. This endeavor in itself was a kind of admission of defeat, since B-3 was one of two mounds, the other being its neighbor B-5, designated a "null mound" by those who had studied the site. It had been thoroughly pierced and penetrated and found to be utterly empty; reserved, it was felt, for the mortal remains of a dynasty that failed. But I had already made careful searches of the thirty-four other tombs of the Miskahannock queens. The null mounds were the only ones remaining. If, as I anticipated, I found no evidence of anthropophagy, I would have to give up on the mounds entirely and start looking elsewhere. There were persistent stories of other bone pits in the pleats and hollows of the Yuggoghenies. Perhaps I could find one, a fresh one, one not trampled and corrupted by the primitive methods of my professional forebears.

I peeled back the sheet of oiled canvas I had spread across my handiwork and received a shock. The passage, which over the course of the previous day I had managed to extend a full four feet into the side of the mound, had been completely filled in. Not merely filled in; the thick black soil had been tamped down and a makeshift screen of ivy had been drawn across it. I took a step back and looked around the site, certain all at once that I was being observed. There were only the crows in the treetops. In the distance I could hear the Murrough trucks on the tortuous highway, grinding gears as they climbed up out of the valley. I looked down at the ground by my feet and saw the faint imprint of a foot smaller than my own. A few feet from this, I found another. That was all.

I ought to have been afraid, I suppose, or at the least concerned, but at this point, I confess, I was only angry. The site was heavily fenced and posted with NO TRES-PASSING signs, but apparently some local hoodlums had come up in the night and wasted all of the previous day's hard work. The motive for this vandalism eluded me, but I supposed that a lack of any discernible motive was in the nature of vandalism itself. I picked up my hand shovel and started in again on my doorway into the mound. The fifth bite I took with the little iron tooth brought out something strange. It was a black bandanna, twisted and soiled. I spread it out across my thigh and found the small, round trace of my own blood on one corner. I was bewildered, and again I looked around to see if someone was watching me. There were only the laughter and ragged fingers of the crows. What was Ed up to? Why would my rescuer want to come up onto the mountain and ruin my work? Did he think he was protecting me? I shrugged, stuffed the bandanna into a pocket, and went back to my careful digging. I worked steadily throughout the day, extending the tunnel six inches nearer than I had come yesterday to the heart of the mound, then drove home to Murrough House, my shoulders aching, my fingers stiff. I had a long, hot soak in the big bathtub down the hall from my room, smoked a pipe, and read, for the fifteenth time at least, the section in *Miskahannock Surveys* dealing with B-3. Then at 6:30 I went downstairs to find Dexter Eibonas waiting to serve my dinner, his expression blank, his eyes bloodshot. I remember being surprised that he didn't immediately demand details of my day on the dig. He just nodded, retreated into the kitchen, and returned with a heated can of soup, half a loaf of white bread, and a bottle of Ring. Naturally after my hard day I was disappointed by this fare, and I inquired as to the whereabouts of Mrs. Eibonas.

"She had some family business, professor," Dexter said, rolling up his hands in his tea towel, then unrolling them again. "Sad business."

"Did somebody—die?"

"My uncle Ed," said the boy, collapsing in a chair beside me and covering his twisted features with his hands. "He had an accident down at the mill, I guess. Fell headfirst into the impact mold."

"What?" I said, feeling my throat constrict. "My God, Dexter! Something has to be done! That mill ought to be shut down!"

Dexter took a step back, startled by my vehemence. I had thought at once, of course, of the black bandanna, and now I wondered if I was not somehow responsible for Ed Eibonas's death. Perhaps the incident in the mill yard the day before, his late-night digging in the dirt of B-3 in some kind of misguided effort to help me, had left him rattled, unable to concentrate on his work, prey to accidents.

"You just don't understand," said Dexter. "It's our way of life here. There isn't anything for us but the mill." He pushed the bottle of Indian Ring toward me. "Drink your beer, professor."

I reached for the glass and brought it to my lips but was swept by a sudden wave of revulsion like that which had overtaken me at the Chinese restaurant on my first night in town. I pushed back from the table and stood up, my violent start upsetting a pewter candelabra in which four tapers burned. Dexter lunged to keep it from falling over, then looked at me, surprised. I stared back, chest heaving, feeling defiant without being sure of what exactly I was defying.

"I am not going to touch another drop of that beer!" I said, the words sounding petulant and absurd as they emerged from my mouth.

Dexter nodded. He looked worried.

"All right, professor," he said, obligingly, as if he thought I might have become unbalanced. "You just go on up to your room and lie down. I'll bring you your food a little later. How about that?"

THE NEXT day I lay in bed, aching, sore, and suffering from that peculiar brand of spiritual depression born largely of suppressed fear. On the following morning I roused myself, shaved, dressed in my best clothes, and went to the Church of St. Stephen, on Nolt Street, the heart of Plunkettsburg's Estonian neighborhood, for the funeral of Ed Eibonas. There was a sizable turnout, as was always the case, I was told, when there had been a death at the mill. Such deaths were reportedly uncommon; the mill was a cruel and dangerous but rarely fatal place. At Dexter's invitation I went to the dead man's house to pay my respects to the widow, and two hours later I found myself, along with most of the other male mourners, roaring drunk on some kind of fruit brandy brought out on special occasions. It may have been that the brandy burned away the jitters and anxiety of the past two days; in any case the next morning I went out to the mounds again, with a tent and a cookstove and several bags of groceries. I didn't leave for the next five days.

My hole had been filled in again, and this time there was no clue to the identity of the filler, but I was determined not to let this spook me, as the saying goes. I simply dug. Ordinarily I would have proceeded cautiously, carrying the dirt out by thimblefuls and sifting each one, but I felt my time on the site growing short. I often saw cars on the access road by day, and headlight beams by night, slowing down as if to observe me. Twice a day a couple of sheriff's deputies would pull up to the Ring and sit in their car, watching. At first whenever they appeared, I stopped working, lit a cigarette, and waited for them to arrest me. But when after the first few times nothing of the sort occurred, I relaxed a little and kept on with my digging for the duration of their visit. I was resigned to being prevented from completing my research, but before this happened I wanted to get to the heart of B-3.

On the fourth day, when I was halfway to my goal, George Birch drove out from his general store, as I had requested, with cans of stew, bottles of soda pop, and cigarettes. He was normally a dour man, but on this morning his face seemed longer than ever. I inquired if there was anything bothering him.

"Carlotta Brown-Jenkin died last night," he said. "Friend of my mother's. Tough old lady." He shook his head. "Influenza. Shame."

I remembered that awful, Technicolored meal so many

months before, the steely glint of her eyes in their cavernous sockets. I did my best to look properly sympathetic.

"That is a shame," I said.

He set down the box of food and looked past me at
the entrance to my tunnel. The sight of it seemed to dis-
turb him.

"You sure you know what you're doing?" he said.

I assured him that I did, but he continued to look
skeptical.

"I remember the last time you archaeologist fellows
came to town, you know," he said. As a matter of fact I did
know this, since he told me almost every time I saw him. "I
was a boy. We had just got electricity in our house."

"Things must have changed a great deal since then,"
I said.

"Things haven't changed at all," he snapped. He was
never a cheerful man, George Birch. He turned, hitching
up his trousers, and limped on his wooden foot back to
his truck.

That night I lay in my bedroll under the canvas roof of
my tent, watching the tormented sky. The lantern hissed
softly beside my head; I kept it burning low, all night
long, advertising my presence to any who might seek to
come and undo my work. It had been a warm, springlike
afternoon, but now a cool breeze was blowing in from
the north, stirring the branches of the trees over my head.
After a while I drowsed a little; I fancied I could hear the
distant fluting of the Miskahannock flowing over its rocky
bed and, still more distant, the low, insistent drumming of
the machine heart in the black mill. Suddenly I sat up:
The music I had been hearing, of breeze and river and far-
off machinery, seemed at once very close and not at all
metaphoric. I scrambled out of my bedroll and tent and
stood, taut, listening, at the edge of Plunkettsburg Ring.
It *was* music I heard, strange music, and it seemed to be
issuing, impossibly, from the other end of the tunnel I had

been digging and redigging over the past two weeks—
from within mound B-3, the null mound!

I have never, generally, been plagued by bouts of great
courage, but I do suffer from another vice whose outward
appearance is often indistinguishable from that of bravery:
I am pathologically curious. I was not brave enough, in
that eldritch moment, actually to approach B-3, to inves-
tigate the source of the music I was hearing; but though
every primitive impulse urged me to flee, I stood there,
listening, until the music stopped, an hour before dawn. I
heard sorrow in the music, and mourning, and the beating
of many small drums. And then in the full light of the
last day of April, emboldened by bright sunshine and a
cup of instant coffee, I made my way gingerly toward the
mound. I picked up my shovel, lowered my foolish head
into the tunnel, and crept carefully into the bowels of
the now-silent mound. Seven hours later I felt the shovel
strike something hard, like stone or brick. Then the hard-
ness gave way, and the shovel flew abruptly out of my
hands. I had reached, at last, the heart of mound B-3.

And it was not empty; oh no, not at all. There were
seven sealed tombs lining the domed walls, carved stone
chambers of the usual Miskahannock type, and another
ten that were empty, and one, as yet unsealed, that held
the unmistakable, though withered, yellow, naked, and
eternally slumbering form of Carlotta Brown-Jenkin. And
crouched on her motionless chest, as though prepared to
devour her throat, sat a tiny stone idol, hideous, black,
brandishing a set of wicked ivory fangs.

Now I gave in to those primitive impulses; I panicked.
I tore out of the burial chamber as quickly as I could and
ran for my car, not bothering to collect my gear. In
twenty minutes I was back at Murrough House. I hurried
up the front steps, intending only to go to my room,
retrieve my clothes and books and papers, and leave behind
Plunkettsburg forever. But when I came into the foyer I

found Dexter, carrying a tray of eaten lunches back from the dining room to the kitchen. He was whistling light-heartedly and when he saw me he grinned. Then his expression changed.

"What is it?" he said, reaching out to me. "Has something happened?"

"Nothing," I said, stepping around him, avoiding his grasp. The streets of Plunkettsburg had been built on evil ground, and now I could only assume that every one of its citizens, even cheerful Dexter, had been altered by the years and centuries of habitation. "Everything's fine. I just have to leave town."

I started up the wide, carpeted steps as quickly as I could, mentally packing my bags and boxes with essentials, loading the car, twisting and backtracking up the steep road out of this cursed valley.

"My name came up," Dexter said. "I start tomorrow at the mill."

Why did I turn? Why did I not keep going down the long, crooked hallway and carry out my sensible, cowardly plan?

"You can't do that," I said. He started to smile, but there must have been something in my face. The smile fizzed out. "You'll be killed. You'll be mangled. That good-looking mug of yours will be hideously deformed."

"Maybe," he said, trying to sound calm, but I could see that my own agitation was infecting him. "Maybe not."

"It's the women. The queens. They're alive."

"The queens are alive? What are you talking about, professor? I think you've been out on the mountain too long."

"I have to go, Dexter," I said. "I'm sorry. I can't stay here anymore. But if you have any sense at all, you'll come with me. I'll drive you to Pittsburgh. You can start at Tech. They'll help you. They'll give you a job. . . ." I could feel myself starting to babble.

Dexter shook his head. "Can't," he said. "My name came up! Shoot, I've been waiting for this all my life."

"Look," I said. "All right. Just come with me, out to the Ring." I looked at my watch. "We've got an hour until dark. Just let me show you something I found out there, and then if you still want to go to work in that infernal factory, I'll shake your hand and bid you farewell."

"You'll really take me out to the site?"

I nodded. He set the tray on a deal table and untied his apron.

"Let me get my jacket," he said.

I PACKED my things and we drove in silence to the necropolis. I was filled with regret for this course of action, with intimations of disaster. But I felt I couldn't simply leave town and let Dexter Eibonas walk willingly into that fiery eructation of the evil genius, the immemorial accursedness, of his drab Pennsylvania hometown. I couldn't leave that young, unmarked body to be broken and split on the horrid machines of the mill. As for why Dexter wasn't talking, I don't know; perhaps he sensed my mounting despair, or perhaps he was simply lost in youthful speculation on the unknown vistas that lay before him, subterranean sights forbidden and half-legendary to him since he had first come to consciousness of the world. As we turned off Gray Road onto the access road that led up to the site, he sat up straight and looked at me, his face grave with the consummate adolescent pleasure of violating rules.

"There," I said. I pointed out the window as we crested the rise. The Plunkettsburg Ring lay spread out before us, filled with jagged shadows, in the slanting, rust red light of the setting sun. From this angle the dual circular plan of the site was not apparent, and the thirty-six mounds appeared to stretch from one end of the plateau to the other, like a line of uneven teeth studding an immense, devouring jawbone.

"Let's make this quick," I said, shuddering. I handed him a spare lantern from the trunk of the Nash, and then we walked to the edge of the aboriginal forest that ran upslope from the plateau to the wind-shattered precincts of Mount Orrert's sharp peak. It was here, in the lee of a large maple tree, that I had set up my makeshift camp. At the time the shelter of that homely tree had seemed quite inviting, but now it appeared to me that the forest was the source of all the lean shadows reaching their ravening fingers across the plateau. I ducked quickly into my tent to retrieve my lantern and then hurried back to rejoin Dexter. I thought he was looking a little uneasy now. His gait slowed as we approached B-3. When we trudged around to confront the raw earthen mouth of the passage I had dug, he came to a complete stop.

"We're not going inside there," he said in a monotone. I saw come into his eyes the dull, dreamy look that was there whenever he talked about going to work in the mill. "It isn't allowed."

"It's just for a minute, Dexter. That's all you'll need."

I put my hands on his shoulders and gave him a push, and we stumbled through the dank, close passage, the light from our lanterns veering wildly around us. Then we were in the crypt.

"No," Dexter said. The effect on him of the sight of the time-ravaged naked body of Carlotta Brown-Jenkin, of the empty tombs, the hideous idol, the outlandish ideograms that covered the walls, was everything I could have hoped for. His jaw dropped, his hands clenched and unclenched, he took a step backward. "She just died!"

"Yesterday," I agreed, trying to allay my own anxiety with a show of ironic detachment.

"But what . . . what's she doing out here?" He shook

his head quickly, as though trying to clear it of smoke or spiderwebs.

"Don't you know?" I asked him, for I still was not completely certain of his or any townsman's uninvolvement in the evil, at once ancient and machine-age, that was evidently the chief business of Plunkettsburg.

"No! God, no!" He pointed to the queer, fanged idol that crouched with a hungry leer on the late chancellor's hollow bosom. "God, what is that thing?"

I went over to the tomb and cautiously, as if the figure with its enormous, obscene tusks might come to life and rip off a mouthful of my hand, picked up the idol. It was as black and cold as space, and so heavy that it bent my hand back at the wrist as I hefted it. With both hands I got a firm grip on it and turned it over. On its pedestal were incised three symbols in the spiky, complex script of the Miskahannocks, unrelated to any other known human language or alphabet. As with all of the tribe's inscriptions, the characters had both a phonetic and a symbolic sense. Often these were quite independent of one another.

"Yu . . . yug . . . gog," I read, sounding it out carefully. "Yuggog."

"What does that mean?"

"It doesn't mean anything, as far as I know. But it can be read another way. It's trickier. Here's tooth . . . gut— that's hunger—and this one—" I held up the idol toward him. He shied away. His face had gone completely pale, and there was a look of fear in his eyes, of awareness of evil, that I found, God forgive me, strangely gratifying. "This is a kind of general intensive, I believe. Making this read, loosely rendered, hunger . . . itself. How odd."

"Yuggog," Dexter said softly, a thin strand of spittle joining his lips.

"Here," I said cruelly, tossing the heavy thing toward him. Let him go into the black mill now, I thought, after he's seen *this*. Dexter batted at the thing, knocking it to the ground. There was a sharp, tearing sound like matchwood splitting. For an instant Dexter looked utterly, cosmically startled. Then he, and the idol of Yuggog, disappeared. There was a loud thud, and a clatter, and I heard him groan. I picked up the splintered halves of the carved wooden trapdoor Dexter had fallen through and gazed down into a fairly deep, smooth-sided hole. He lay crumpled at the bottom, about eight feet beneath me, in the light of his overturned lantern.

"My God! I'm sorry! Are you all right?"

"I think I sprained my ankle," he said. He sat up and raised his lantern. His eyes got very wide. "Professor, you have to see this."

I lowered myself carefully into the hole and stared with Dexter into a great round tunnel, taller than either of us, paved with crazed human bones, stretching far beyond the pale of our lanterns.

"A tunnel," he said. "I wonder where it goes."

"I can only guess," I said. "And that's never good enough for me."

"Professor! You aren't—"

But I had already started into the tunnel, a decision that I attributed not to courage, of course, but to my far greater vice. I did not see that as I took those first steps into the tunnel I was in fact being bitten off, chewed, and swallowed, as it were, by the very mouth of the Plunkettsburg evil. I took small, queasy steps along the horrible floor, avoiding insofar as I could stepping on the outraged miens of human skulls, searching the smoothed, plastered walls of the tunnel for ideograms or other hints of the builders of this amazing structure. The tunnel, or at least this version of it, was well built, buttressed regularly by sturdy iron piers and lintels, and of chillingly recent vintage. Only great wealth, I thought, could have managed such a feat of engineering. A few minutes later I heard a tread behind me and saw the faint glow of a lantern. Dexter joined me, favoring his right ankle, his lantern swinging as he walked.

"We're headed northwest," I said. "We must be under the river by now."

"Under the river?" he said. "Could Indians have built a tunnel like this?"

"No, Dexter, they could not."

He didn't say anything for a moment as he took this information in.

"Professor, we're headed for the mill, aren't we?"

"I'm afraid we must be," I said.

We walked for three quarters of an hour, until the sound of pounding machinery became audible, grew gradually unbearable, and finally exploded directly over our heads. The tunnel had run out. I looked up at the trapdoor above us. Then I heard a muffled scream. To this day I don't know if the screamer was one of the men up on the floor of the factory or Dexter Eibonas, a massive hand clapped brutally over his mouth, because the next instant, at the back of my head, a supernova bloomed and flared brightly.

I WAKE in an immense room, to the idiot pounding of a machine. The walls are sheets of fire flowing upward like inverted cataracts; the ceiling is lost in shadow from which, when the flames flare brightly, there emerges the vague impression of a steely web of girders among which dark things ceaselessly creep. Thick coils of rope bind my arms to my sides, and my legs are lashed at the ankles to those of the plain pine chair in which I have been propped.

It is one of two dozen chairs in a row that is one of a hundred, in a room filled with men, the slumped, crew-cut, big-shouldered ordinary men of Plunkettsburg and its neighboring towns. We are all waiting, and watching, as the women of Plunkettsburg, the servants of Yuggog, pass noiselessly among us in their soft, horrible cloaks stitched from the hides of dead men, tapping on the shoulder of now one fellow, now another. None of my neighbors, however, appears to have required the use of strong rope to conjoin him to his fate. Without a word the designated men, their blood thick with the dark earthen brew of the Ring witches, rise and follow the skins of miscreant fathers and grandfathers down to the ceremonial altar at the heart of the mill, where the priestesses of Yuggog throw oracular bones and, given the result, take hold of the man's ear, his foot, his fingers. A yellow snake, its venom presumably anesthetic, is applied to the fated extremity. Then the long knife is brought to bear, and the vast, immemorial hunger of the god of the Miskahannocks is assuaged for another brief instant. In the past three hours on this Walpurgis Night, nine men have been so treated; tomorrow, people in this bewitched town that, in a reasonable age, has learned to eat its men a little at a time, will speak, I am sure, of a series of horrible accidents at the mill. The women came to take Dexter Eibonas an hour ago. I looked away as he went under the knife, but I believe he lost the better part of his left arm to the god. I can only assume that very soon now I will feel the tap on my left shoulder of the fingers of the town librarian, the grocer's wife, of Mrs. Eibonas herself. I am guiltier by far of trespass than Ed Eibonas and do not suppose I will survive the procedure.

Strange how calm I feel in the face of all this; perhaps there remain traces of the beer in my veins, or perhaps in this hellish place there are other enchantments at work. In any case, I will at least have the satisfaction of seeing my theory confirmed, or partly confirmed, before I die, and the concomitant satisfaction, so integral to my profession, of seeing my teacher's theory cast in the dustbin. For, as I held, the Miskahannocks hungered; and hunger, black, primordial, unstanchable hunger itself, was their god. It was indeed the misguided scrambling and digging of my teacher and his colleagues, I imagine, that awakened great Yuggog from its four-thousand-year slumber. As for the black mill that fascinated me for so many months, it is a sham. The single great machine to my left takes in no raw materials and emits no ingots or sheets. It is simply an immense piston, endlessly screaming and pounding like the skin of an immense drum the ground that since the days of the Miskahannocks has been the sacred precinct of the god. The flames that flash through the windows and the smoke that proceeds from the chimneys are bits of trickery, mechanical contrivances devised, I suppose, by Philippa Howard Murrough herself, in the days when the revived spirit of Yuggog first whispered to her of its awful, eternal appetite for the flesh of men. The sole industry of Plunkettsburg is carnage, scarred and mangled bodies the only product.

One thought disturbs the perfect, poison calm with which I am suffused—the trucks that grind their way in and out of the valley, the freight trains that come clanging in the night. What cargo, I wonder, is unloaded every morning at the docks of the Plunkettsburg Mill? What burden do those trains bear away?

Dracula Doesn't Rock and Roll

by Debbie Dadey
and
Marcia Thornton Jones

illustrated by John Steven Gurney

A
LITTLE APPLE
PAPERBACK

SCHOLASTIC INC.
New York   Toronto   London   Auckland   Sydney
Mexico City   New Delhi   Hong Kong

ISBN 0-439-04399-9

Text copyright © 1999 by Marcia Thornton Jones and Debra S. Dadey.
Illustrations copyright © 1999 by Scholastic Inc.
SCHOLASTIC, LITTLE APPLE PAPERBACKS, THE ADVENTURES OF THE BAILEY
SCHOOL KIDS, and associated logos are trademarks and/or registered
trademarks of Scholastic Inc.

12 11 10 9 8 7 6 5 4 3 2 1   9/9 0 1 2 3 4/0

Printed in the U.S.A.   40

First Scholastic printing, November 1999

To Amanda and Steve Carson, two great kids — DD

To Steve Jones, Greer Streetman, Wayne Baker,
and Harvey Johnson — four rock-and-roll
basement monsters! — MTJ

Contents

Dracula Doesn't Rock and Roll

1

Coffin

"What a great day!" Melody sang and danced down the snow-covered sidewalk. She was walking down Delaware Boulevard after school with her friends Howie, Liza, and Eddie.

"Are you crazy?" Howie asked, looking up at the gray sky. "It's freezing out here."

Melody nodded, her black pigtails swinging beside her ears. "I know, isn't it great? I love winter."

Liza shivered and hugged her coat tighter as they neared the Clancy Estate. "Since when do you love winter?"

Eddie tried to scoop up a snowball but only got a few flakes in his glove. "What good is winter if you can't have a snowball fight?"

1

Liza giggled when she heard a rumbling sound. "Is your stomach growling again?" she asked Eddie.

Eddie pulled his baseball cap down to try to cover his red ears. "No, but I am hungry."

"You're always hungry lately," Howie told his friend.

Eddie shrugged. "My grandmother says I must be growing."

Liza's eyes got wide. "That noise is growing, too," she said. "And it sounds like it's coming from the Clancy Estate."

The kids stared at their teacher's home. It was a big, old house with broken shutters and cracked windows. The iron fence surrounding the yard was rusty and the open gate squeaked when the wind blew. Most kids at Bailey Elementary thought the Clancy Estate was haunted and that their teacher, Mrs. Jeepers, must be a vampire to live there.

Grrrm! Grrrm! "There it is again,"

Howie said, covering his ears. "That sound gives me the creeps."

"I think it's coming from the basement," Eddie told them.

"It sounds like someone is in terrible pain," Melody said with a gulp.

"Someone or something," Eddie said.

Liza stared at the dark windows of the house. "Maybe we should try to help."

"Are you kidding?" Eddie snapped. "Don't you remember what's in Mrs. Jeepers' basement?"

"I remember," Melody whispered, thinking back to the long wooden box that looked just like a coffin. The long box was locked from the inside and they were sure they had heard something moving inside it.

"Oh my gosh," Liza squealed. "What if that noise is someone trying to get out of the coffin?"

2

Burglar

"Let's go home and get a snack," Eddie suggested. "I bet my grandmother made cookies."

"But what about the noise?" Liza asked.

"Who cares?" Eddie said.

Liza put her hands on her hips. "Are you scared?"

Eddie shook his head. "I'm not scared of anything," he bragged.

"That proves you're crazy," Melody said. "There are some things you should be scared of, and creepy noises coming from basements are one of them."

Liza rubbed her mittens together to stay warm. "Do you think Mrs. Jeepers could be hurt in there?" she asked.

Howie shook his head. "No, Mrs. Jeepers always stays late at school to grade papers. It can't be her."

"Maybe it's a burglar caught in a trap," Melody suggested.

"Serves them right," Eddie said. "They shouldn't be stealing from Mrs. Jeepers."

Liza nodded. "Stealing is wrong," she agreed, "but nobody should have to suffer. Maybe we should look in the window and check it out. Then we could go back to school and tell Mrs. Jeepers about it."

Melody groaned. "I don't think this is such a good idea, but I guess it wouldn't hurt to look." The four kids pushed past the squeaky iron gate and over the frozen grass. They edged closer and closer to the basement window.

Argggghhh! Errrrrkkkkk! The noise got louder and louder. Liza put her hands over her ears. "What a horrible sound," she said.

"It sounds like a monster," Howie whispered.

The kids were almost close enough to

touch the basement window. One of the glass panes in the window was cracked and the other was completely missing. A piece of cardboard covered the empty spot.

Melody gulped and looked at Eddie. "You look first," she said.

"Me?" Eddie squeaked. "Why me?"

"Because you said you weren't afraid of anything," Howie whispered.

Eddie pulled his baseball cap down tighter over his head and wished he wasn't such a bragger. He stepped closer to the window.

EEEEEEEEKKKKKKK! A screech blasted out of the basement window. It was so loud the kids thought their ears were going to explode. Liza screamed, "RUN!"

3

Winterfest

Melody, Howie, and Eddie watched Liza sprint down Delaware Boulevard and dodge behind a clump of bushes.

"Liza's imagination is getting the best of her," Melody said, but she didn't sound like she believed it.

Just then a steady pounding like the sound of a monster's heartbeat started. It began slowly and then picked up speed until Howie's teeth rattled. Suddenly a high-pitched squawk erupted from the basement, sending goose bumps racing up Eddie's arms.

"Maybe Liza isn't so silly," Melody said with a shaking voice.

Howie nodded. "Let's get out of here!" he screamed.

Melody didn't wait for him to say it

twice. She raced down the street with Howie. Eddie took one last look at the basement door and hurried after his friends. They jumped over the bushes and landed right next to Liza.

"Smooth move," Eddie told his friends once he caught his breath. "If it was burglars, they know we're out here now."

Liza whimpered and looked up into the darkening sky. "What if it isn't burglars?" she asked. "What if it's vampires

beating their wings, getting ready to swoop over Bailey City?"

"Maybe the noise was a puppy dog trying to find some doggy bones," Eddie argued.

"Then the puppy must be the size of a dragon, and the only bones it'll be looking for are the kind that belong to kids," Melody told him. She poked Eddie's arm to prove her point.

"We have to run back to school and tell Mrs. Jeepers before whatever is down there destroys her basement," Liza said.

"We could go home and call the police," Howie suggested.

Eddie shook his head. "We don't have to go anywhere because there's Mrs. Jeepers now."

Mrs. Jeepers was bundled up in a long black cape with shiny black polka dots. Her cape kept getting swept back by the cold winter wind, like huge bat wings. Her black pointy-toed boots kicked up

the snow as she walked down Delaware Boulevard. The only thing that wasn't black was her red hair tied back with a black-and-yellow polka-dotted ribbon.

Liza waited until Mrs. Jeepers was almost to their hiding place before jumping from behind the bush. "We have to warn you," Liza blurted. "You can't go home!"

Melody, Howie, and Eddie pushed their way through the bushes and nodded. "There's something terribly wrong," Melody added.

Mrs. Jeepers remained calm as the kids explained the strange goings-on in her basement. When they got to the part about the noises, Eddie did his best to make the sounds himself, but Mrs. Jeepers gently rubbed her brooch and Eddie got quiet immediately. The kids were pretty sure that the mysterious green pin Mrs. Jeepers always wore had some kind of magic that made kids behave.

Finally, the kids finished telling their teacher about the strange noises, but Mrs. Jeepers didn't seem upset at all.

"I am so glad you enjoyed the BATs," she said in her strange Transylvanian accent. "They are using my basement to practice for the Winterfest."

She smiled her odd little half smile and added, "You are just going to die when they perform!"

4

BATs

"I don't want to die," Liza moaned the next day before school.

Howie, Melody, and Eddie had met her under the oak tree on the school's playground. At least three inches of snow layered all the branches, and icicles hung from the nearby swing set. Eddie was busy stomping a path in the snow around the giant tree. He acted like he wasn't listening to a single word anyone was saying.

"Nobody's going to die," Howie said, patting Liza on the shoulder.

"But Mrs. Jeepers said we would die when the BATs performed at the Winterfest," Liza whimpered.

Every winter the city had a big celebration in the gymnasium of Bailey

School. This year's Winterfest was just two days away.

"Don't worry," Howie told her. "We don't even know what BATs means."

"If it's a secret only Mrs. Jeepers knows about, then it must be bad," Liza said with a shiver.

"We don't know that for sure," Howie said. "Once we find out what BATs stands for I'm sure everything will be fine."

"I know all about bats," Eddie said. "They're what you use to slam baseballs out of the field."

"I don't think that's the kind of bats Mrs. Jeepers is hiding in her basement," Liza said.

"There is only one kind of bat our vampire teacher would protect," Melody said, "and that's the kind with wings! We only have two days left until Winterfest, and for all we know Mrs. Jeepers just brought her vampire buddies to a two-thousand-year reunion."

"Do vampires have reunions?" Eddie asked.

Melody jabbed him on the arm. Eddie stumbled and fell back against the tree. When he did, a pile of snow fell from the branches above and landed right on his head.

"How would I know?" Melody asked. "Do I look like a vampire?"

"No," Howie whispered, "but *he* does."

Melody, Liza, and Eddie looked where Howie pointed. A man dressed in black floated from shadow to shadow, being careful not to walk on the sidewalk where the winter sun shone brightly on the ground. He wore a long black coat that dragged through the snow. Its collar was pulled up high, and a big black cowboy hat cast his face in deep shadows.

The man acted like he didn't want to be seen. He looked up and down the street before hurrying across the school's parking lot. Then he pulled open the door to

Bailey Elementary School and slipped inside.

"Who was that?" Eddie asked.

Melody scratched her head with a gloved hand. "He reminded me of someone," she said.

Howie nodded. "Me too," he said. "And it's someone straight out of a horror movie!"

5

Mr. Drake

Liza shivered as the bell rang and the kids walked toward the school. "I just hope that guy doesn't go near the third grade. He gave me the creeps."

But Liza wasn't so lucky. When they entered their classroom the tall stranger in black stood in front of the blackboard, whispering to their teacher, Mrs. Jeepers. Melody gulped. "Maybe they're planning a vampire reunion right now."

"Don't you know who that is?" Howie whispered as he sat down at his desk.

Melody shook her head, but Liza spoke up. "That's Mr. Drake, our old school counselor."

"You mean Count Dracula," Eddie said.

The four kids remembered when Mr. Drake had been Bailey School's counselor. His office was as dark as a cave and he was always drinking pink lemonade. Some kids were sure he was the most famous vampire of all — Dracula.

Liza took out a pencil and sheet of paper to copy the spelling words from the board. "Eddie," she said softly, "we shouldn't call Mr. Drake names. He's probably just a very nice school counselor."

"Counselor, my eyeball," Eddie snapped. "His office looked more like a cave, and I bet he's from Transylvania, just like Mrs. Jeepers. You know what that means."

"Just because someone is from Transylvania, it doesn't mean he or she is a vampire," Melody said.

"No," Howie admitted, "but just look at him. You have to admit he doesn't look like an ordinary school counselor."

The four kids stared at Mr. Drake. He held a huge black case in one hand and a glass of pink lemonade in the other.

Mrs. Jeepers smiled and pointed to the case several times. Mr. Drake smiled, showing his pointy eyeteeth, and Mrs. Jeepers clapped her hands. "Class," Mrs. Jeepers said in her Transylvanian accent. "We have a special treat today."

Eddie groaned. "I hope my neck isn't the treat."

Mrs. Jeepers flashed her green eyes at Eddie and continued talking. "I am sure you remember Mr. Drake, our former school counselor. He is a member of the rock band that'll be making a special performance at this year's Winterfest."

"Performance?" Eddie whispered. "Is that what vampires call it when they suck your blood?"

Melody gulped as Mr. Drake sat the long black case on Mrs. Jeepers' desk. "Maybe he has his bat friends in that case," Melody said softly.

Liza sniffed. "I think my nose is going

to bleed." Sometimes Liza got a nose-
bleed when she was upset.

"Don't bleed," Howie warned her.
"Vampires go nuts at the sight of blood."

"Oh my gosh," Liza squealed. "He's
opening the case."

6

Rock and Roll

Melody giggled. "It's only a guitar," she said with relief.

"I knew it all along," Eddie bragged.

"That's not just any guitar," Howie said. "It's an electric guitar."

Eddie's eyes got big. "Cool!"

Liza slumped down into her seat. "I'm just glad it's not a box of bats."

Mr. Drake's eyes swept around the room, looking at every student. Liza sunk even lower in her seat, but Melody sat up straight and raised her hand. "Mr. Drake," Melody said, "I thought Bailey City made you sick."

"Melody!" Mrs. Jeepers said, her hand touching her brooch.

Melody quickly continued. "I mean, I

27

thought you quit being a counselor here because of your allergies."

Mr. Drake licked his lips and smiled again. "You have a wonderful memory," Mr. Drake said in a hoarse accent. "My doctor has given me allergy medicine that allows me to live anywhere. Now I have a new career." When Mr. Drake smiled his eyeteeth flashed white.

Liza whimpered when she saw Mr. Drake's eyeteeth. "Modern medicine is just wonderful," Liza said.

Mr. Drake held up his electric guitar. It was bright red except for a black bat stenciled on one end. Mr. Drake strapped the guitar around his neck and plugged it into a big black box sitting on the floor.

BLAMMM! TWANG! TING! Liza held her hands over her ears. "He's not going to suck our blood," Liza whispered. "He's going to drive us insane with the noise."

"All tuned up," Mr. Drake said with a smile. "Who is ready to rock and roll?"

A few kids raised their hands uncertainly as Mr. Drake took a sip of pink lemonade and then continued. "This is a song I wrote. It is called 'Bailey City Rock.'"

Mr. Drake strummed his guitar and started singing. Melody couldn't believe it — it actually sounded good. Mr. Drake strummed and plucked and bent the strings on his guitar. His voice was deep and rough, and the beat of the song was fast. Melody looked around the classroom. Carey, Jake, and Huey stood in the aisle, clapping their hands. Liza tapped her toes. Even Howie sang along.

"Rock on, Bailey City, rock on!
When the sun goes down,
Have a rock-and-roll marathon!
Shake, rattle, and roll your bones,
Our beat warms your blood,
'Til the dark meets dawn!
Rock on, Bailey City, rock on!"

Melody turned around to see if Eddie was enjoying the song. Melody gasped. Eddie must have liked the music. He was hitting two pencils against his desk as if he were playing the drums. But that's not what worried Melody.

Eddie was staring straight ahead as if he were in a trance.

7

King of Rock and Roll

Eddie couldn't wait for school to be over. He never could. But after hearing Mr. Drake play his electric guitar Eddie was even more excited than usual to get out of class. All during math, he tapped his pencil to the beat of "Bailey City Rock." During science, he couldn't stop humming. Mrs. Jeepers flashed her green eyes at Eddie, but he didn't seem to notice.

"You better be quiet," Liza warned, "before Mrs. Jeepers gets really mad." Once Eddie had pushed his teacher too far by shooting spitballs. Mrs. Jeepers had taken Eddie out into the hall. None of the other kids knew what had happened but it must have been bad because Eddie refused to tell them. He never

wanted to make her that mad again, so he tried to be good until the bell finally rang.

"Mr. Drake's guitar is the coolest thing I've ever seen," Eddie told his friends when they got outside. As usual, Eddie, Howie, Melody, and Liza had met under the oak tree on the playground. The sun was shining and the snow sparkled like a field of diamonds. But Eddie didn't even notice.

"I want to start my own rock band," he said.

"Are you crazy?" Melody asked. "Your grandmother would never let you have a rock band."

Howie nodded. "Grandmothers usually like old-fashioned music like Elvis and the Beatles."

"The Beatles sound like some kind of bug," Liza said.

Eddie rolled his eyes. "A beetle is a bug, but the Beatles were only the most famous rock-and-roll band ever."

Liza shrugged. "Who knows, maybe Eddie could become famous, too."

"Yeah," Melody giggled. "Eddie has so many rocks in his head, he could be the next king of rock and roll."

"Very funny," Eddie said with a sneer. "But you wait and see. I'm going to be in a rock band so I can play an electric guitar just like Mr. Drake!" To prove his point, Eddie danced around the tree, pretending to play a guitar. He sang "Bailey City Rock" at the top of his lungs. It sounded more like he was screaming.

"Do you have to be so loud?" Liza asked, holding her fingers in her ears.

Eddie still pretended to play the guitar. "Everybody knows rock and roll is loud, loud, LOUD!" he screamed.

"I just don't understand why Mr. Drake would want to start a band," Howie said. "After all, he had a perfectly good job as a school counselor. It's a known fact that teachers, counselors, and principals can't stand loud noises. That's why

they're always trying to make Eddie be quiet."

"Are you kidding?" Eddie asked. "Just think how exciting being in a rock band could be. I bet Mr. Drake got tired of all that quiet boring stuff that happens in schools."

Liza sniffed. "Working in a school is exciting, too. After all, no two days are ever the same."

Eddie rolled his eyes. "I'll give you three good reasons why being in a band is better than working in a school," he said. Eddie held up one finger. "First of all, if the band makes it big Mr. Drake will be rich, rich, rich."

"That's a big *if*," Melody interrupted. "Most bands never earn a dime."

Eddie ignored her and held up another finger. "Second of all, he could get famous. Girls will love him."

"Is that why you want to start a rock band?" Liza teased. She batted her eyelashes at Eddie. Melody made kissy noises.

Eddie shook his head and raised another finger. "The third reason is that it would be *fun* and that's why I would want to do it."

"Don't you realize it takes hours and hours of practice for a band to be good?" Howie asked.

"Practice shmactice," Eddie blurted. "All I have to do is turn on the stage lights and start playing. Entire cities will be hypnotized by how good I am."

"That's it," Howie gasped. "I know why Mr. Drake came to Bailey City. And if I'm right, I know exactly what BATs stands for. Trouble!"

8

Vampire Feast

Howie slumped against the tree and slid to the ground. His face was as pale as the snow that covered the playground.

"What's wrong?" Melody asked Howie.

"Are you going to faint?" Liza asked.

Eddie picked up a handful of snow. "A little snow in his face should perk him up."

Liza grabbed Eddie's hand before he could rub the snow in Howie's face. "Maybe you should go for help instead," she suggested.

Howie shook his head sadly. "There's nobody who can help," he moaned. "We're doomed. All of us."

"What are you talking about?" Liza asked.

"Mr. Drake doesn't want to have a Win-

terfest," Howie explained. "He's planning a Vampire Feast."

"What does playing a guitar have to do with a vampire banquet?" Eddie wanted to know.

"I figured it all out," Howie said. "The BATs plan to lure everybody to the Winterfest. Once we're there, everyone will be seated in the gym. The lights will be turned down so low we won't be able to see our hands in front of our faces. That's when it will happen."

Liza nodded. "That's exactly how the Winterfest always happens," she said. "As soon as the lights are turned down the band starts playing music."

Howie dropped his voice to a whisper. His friends had to kneel in the snow just to hear him. "I'm not talking about music," Howie told them. "I'm talking about a trap. A trap set by vampires."

Melody gasped. "I think I understand. You think that when the lights are turned off Mr. Drake and his band of Dracula buddies will swoop down and slurp up all the blood in the city!"

"Exactly," Howie said.

"That's disgusting," Liza said.

"Besides," Melody said, "you never even proved Mr. Drake was Dracula."

"After all," Liza added, "Dracula doesn't rock and roll."

"Or does he?" Howie said. "We have to find out — and stop those rocking vampires!"

A cloud passed over the sun, casting the entire playground in shadows. Liza shivered and Melody zipped her coat all the way up to her chin. "You better not let Mr. Drake hear you talking about him," Liza warned. "You might hurt his feelings."

"I don't want to hurt his feelings," Howie agreed. "I don't want anybody to get hurt. That's why we have to do something."

9

Bloodmobile

"I want to rock and roll all night!" Eddie screeched the next morning as Liza, Melody, and Howie walked up to him on the playground. It was cold and the snow on the ground crunched under their feet, but it wasn't loud enough to drown out Eddie's singing.

Eddie grinned at his friends. "I have a plan," he said. "If I save my allowance for the rest of this year, I'll probably have enough money to buy a used guitar."

"Why don't you just ask for one for Christmas?" Liza asked.

Eddie slapped Liza on the back. "You're a genius," he told her. "My grandmother is always trying to get me to play an instrument. I bet she'd love to buy me a guitar."

44

"I have a plan, too," Melody told her friends.

"Great," Eddie said. "You get the drums and we can start jamming."

Melody shook her head. "I'm not talking about drums and guitars. I'm talking about saving us from Mr. Drake."

"Oh, brother," Eddie groaned. "Not that again."

Melody gave Eddie a look that would break guitar strings. "This is important."

"Okay," Howie said. "Just tell us your plan."

"We'll give Mr. Drake exactly what he wants," Melody explained.

Liza shrieked. "He can't have any of my blood! I'm too young for the bloodmobile."

"This isn't a bloodmobile," Eddie said with a snicker. "This is more like a batmobile."

"Let's just stay calm," Howie said, "and listen to what Melody has to say."

Melody looked at her friends seriously.

"The first thing we have to do is to make the BATs famous. Then they'll forget about us. They'll be too busy playing at concerts and signing autographs to think about draining all the blood from Bailey City."

Liza put her hands on her hips. "How are we going to do that?"

"Just think about the most famous person you know," Melody said. "How did they get famous?"

"He played basketball better than anyone in the entire world," Eddie said.

"Does Mr. Drake play basketball?" Liza asked.

Howie slapped his forehead and groaned. "Basketball is not the point."

"It is to me," Eddie snapped.

Melody stomped her foot on the frosty grass. "People get famous by advertising and that's what we have to do for Mr. Drake."

Howie snapped his fingers. "Good idea," he said. "If we let enough people

know about Mr. Drake's band he'll become so famous he'll leave Bailey City
alone."

"And our necks," Liza said, rubbing
her neck.

"Then we all agree," Howie said. "Let's
do it!"

10

IT'S COMING!

Eddie stuck out his tongue as he finished painting the last letter of his sign. He held it up to show Liza and Howie. A little of the green paint dripped off the edge onto the kitchen floor, but the kids didn't notice.

Liza read the sign out loud. "'IT'S COMING!'" she read. "What does that mean?"

"Nobody will know what IT is," Howie added.

Eddie nodded. "That's right, so they'll all wonder. We have to get people interested and curious."

"Eddie makes sense," Liza said, picking up a paintbrush. She made neat letters on a piece of white poster board. IT'S COMING TO WINTERFEST.

"But we have to get everyone talking

about the band," Howie said, "and we can't do that if they don't know their name."

Liza nodded. "I've got it," she said. She dipped her brush in the red paint. She added BATS to the top of each sign. The dripping paint looked like blood.

Soon Howie, Liza, and Eddie had a pile of BATS . . . IT'S COMING signs stacked on Melody's kitchen table. "Why are we doing all this work?" Eddie complained. "This is all Melody's idea and she's not even helping."

"Where is she anyway?" Liza asked.

Howie pointed toward the hall. "She's in the family room making phone calls to tell people about Mr. Drake's band."

"Who is she calling?" Eddie asked.

Howie shrugged. "She wouldn't tell."

"Whoever it is, I hope she asked her mother first," Liza said. "She could get in big trouble."

Melody rushed into the kitchen full of smiles. "Okay, I'm done. Let's go hang up the posters."

The four friends taped posters up all around the library, Burger Doodle, and Bailey School. Kids stopped playing on the playground to read the signs.

"What's BATs?" a kid named Nick asked.

A boy named Jake shrugged. "BATs must be a new store in town."

A girl named Carey shook her head, making her blond curls swing. "You guys don't know anything. My dad told me that there's a new restaurant opening that's going to put Bailey City on the map."

"You're both wrong," Eddie told them.

"Then what is BATs?" Nick asked again.

Eddie grinned. "You'll have to wait until Winterfest. Tell all your friends and parents about BATs."

Melody, Liza, Howie, and Eddie walked home from the playground. "I hope this works," Liza said.

"It better work. The Winterfest is tomorrow," Melody said. "This is our only chance."

11

Vampire Dropouts

"Look," Melody squealed in the school gym at the Winterfest. "There's that WMTJ reporter. She is so good-looking."

Liza nodded. "And smart, too. If she likes the BATs, everybody will like them."

The reporter stood beside Mr. Drake. The kids listened as the cameras recorded her. "We're reporting live from the Bailey School gym. We've just found out the meaning of the mysterious signs popping up all over the city." The reporter held up one of the IT'S COMING signs. "IT is a sensational new rock band called the BATs. What exactly does BATs stand for?" the reporter asked and held the microphone in front of Mr. Drake.

Howie, Melody, Liza, and Eddie held

their breaths. Mr. Drake sucked pink lemonade through a straw before answering. Then he smiled so big the kids saw his pointy eyeteeth from their seats across the room. "BATs," Mr. Drake said in his Transylvanian accent, "means we're the BEST ACT in TOWN!"

The reporter laughed. "We'll see if that's true. We're going to give the tristate area a taste of your music right after these messages from our sponsors."

The cameras went dead and Liza jumped up and down. "We did it! We did it!" she shouted. "The BATs are going to be famous."

Several parents stared at Liza. Melody put her finger to her lips. "Be quiet," Melody said. "We haven't done anything yet."

"But the gym is full," Eddie told her. "I've never seen so many people at the Winterfest."

"Oh, no," Howie said. "Once Bailey City gets a look at this band we can for-

56

get about them being famous." Howie pointed to the band.

The kids stared at Mr. Drake's band. They were definitely not dressed like most of the people in Bailey City. Two of the men had long hair that stuck out as if they'd been electrocuted. One man had shaved his head and had a tattoo on his arm. A woman in the band had bright red hair with black lips. All of the BATs were dressed completely in black. Every band member had a glass of pink lemonade sitting beside them.

"They look more like a band of vampire school dropouts than a rock band," Eddie admitted.

Liza clapped her hands. "I know what we could do," she said. "We could run home and get them nice cheerful clothes to wear."

"It's too late," Melody said. "They're already tuning up."

Liza covered her ears and took a seat. The gym was full of folding chairs facing

the BATs' stage. Eddie, Melody, and Howie took seats beside Liza, but not before noticing that lots of other people in the gym had their hands over their ears, too. "It doesn't look good for the BATs," Howie said sadly.

"And that's bad news for us," Melody added. "We're sitting ducks in a vampire arcade."

The lights in the gym went dim and Liza whimpered. Without even thinking about it Liza, Melody, Howie, and Eddie all put their hands over their necks as the band started playing.

The parents in front of Melody stared in silence. So did the people beside Eddie. "I don't think they like it," Eddie told his friends.

"They hate it. We're doomed. We'll never get rid of Mr. Drake now," Liza moaned as the band finished their first song. Then Mr. Drake hit a loud chord on his guitar. The rest of the band joined in as Mr. Drake sang, "Rock on, Bailey City, rock on!"

"Now look," Howie whispered. The kids looked around. The other students and even their parents smiled. Two fourth graders banged their hands on the seats in front of them and Eddie pretended to play the guitar. All around them people clapped to the beat.

Melody saw the cameras from WMTJ recording the people dancing in the aisles. Pretty soon, everyone was up and

dancing. Even Liza, Melody, and Howie clapped their hands. Howie saw Mrs. Jeepers dancing with Principal Davis. The camera got them all on television.

Eddie was having a great time. He twirled around in his chair. He sang every line as loud as he could but he still couldn't drown out the BATs. They were so loud the floor shook.

When the BATs finished "Bailey City Rock" everyone cheered for more. The BATs played song after song. The crowd

loved them all. When the band ended the concert the crowd yelled for them to keep playing, but a woman in a green bodysuit and purple hair whisked the BATs off the stage.

"I wonder who that is?" Melody asked.

Liza breathed a sigh of relief. "I don't care if she's the president of Timbuktu. I'm just glad she took them away before they bit my neck."

"We're safe," Howie agreed. "At least until we find out if our plan worked."

"It has to work," Melody said softly, "or we're in big trouble. Vampire trouble!"

12

Bailey City Monster

Liza and Melody watched Eddie swinging from the branch of the oak tree the next morning. Eddie was singing "Bailey City Rock" at the top of his lungs when Howie rushed up.

Howie shook the newspaper in his hands to get his friends' attention. "Look what I found in the paper!" Howie shouted over Eddie's singing. "It made the front page!"

Eddie jumped down from the tree's branch. "I have news, too," Eddie said. "I want to be the first to tell."

Melody, Liza, and Howie crowded around Eddie. "Did your grandmother buy you an electric guitar?" Melody asked.

Eddie shook his head. "She said I had

to learn to play piano before I could get a guitar. But I came up with another plan!"

"What is it?" Liza asked.

Eddie stood up tall and puffed out his chest. "I decided to join the BATs!" he told them.

"No. You can't," Howie said.

"Howie's right," Melody told Eddie. "Mr. Drake and his batty musicians would never let a kid join their band."

"You don't know that for sure," Eddie snapped. "I'm going to ask Mr. Drake this afternoon and I bet he'll say yes."

Howie shook his head. "You're wrong," he told Eddie. "Because Mr. Drake isn't even in Bailey City!"

"What do you mean?" Eddie asked.

"It's all in here," Howie said, pointing to the newspaper. "Right on the front page."

"Let me see that," Eddie said and snatched the paper from Howie's hand. He held it up so all the kids could see the headlines. "'BATs GO ON TOUR,'" Eddie read out loud. "BATs proved their name was true last night at the Bailey City Winterfest. They really were the BEST ACT in TOWN!"

Howie nodded. "The rest of the article explains everything. That lady with the purple hair was the manager for the Dead Beats. They want the BATs to open for them."

"Wow!" Eddie said. "The Dead Beats are the hottest band around."

"Then we did it," Melody said with a grin. "We helped make the BATs famous."

"And we got them to leave town before they drained us dry," Liza said. "We're safe from Dracula!"

"All that vampire talk went to your heads," Eddie told her. "Mr. Drake isn't Dracula, he's a famous rock-and-roll guitar player, and I'm going to be just like him!"

To prove his point, Eddie started

singing at the top of his lungs. He
jumped and hopped and wiggled his hips
in time to his song.

Howie laughed. "Dracula might not
rock and roll, but there is one Bailey City
monster left who has rocks in his head,"
he said. "And his name is Eddie!"

Debbie Dadey and Marcia Thornton Jones have fun writing stories together. When they both worked at an elementary school in Lexington, Kentucky, Debbie was the school librarian and Marcia was a teacher. During their lunch break in the school cafeteria, they came up with the idea of the Bailey School kids.

Recently Debbie and her family moved to Aurora, Illinois. Marcia and her husband still live in Kentucky where she continues to teach. How do these authors still write together? They talk on the phone and use computers and fax machines!

Creepy, weird, wacky, and
funny things happen to
the Bailey School Kids!™
Collect and read them all!

The *Adventures* of

THE BAILEY SCHOOL KIDS®

The Adventures of
THE BAILEY SCHOOL KIDS®

❏ BAS0-590-25783-8 #28 **Unicorns Don't Give Sleigh Rides** $3.50

❏ BAS0-590-25804-4 #29 **Knights Don't Teach Piano** $3.99

❏ BAS0-590-25809-5 #30 **Hercules Doesn't Pull Teeth** $3.50

❏ BAS0-590-25819-2 #31 **Ghouls Don't Scoop Ice Cream** $3.50

❏ BAS0-590-18982-4 #32 **Phantoms Don't Drive Sports Cars** $3.50

❏ BAS0-590-18983-2 #33 **Giants Don't Go Snowboarding** $3.99

❏ BAS0-590-18984-0 #34 **Frankenstein Doesn't Slam Hockey Pucks** .$3.99

❏ BAS0-590-18985-9 #35 **Trolls Don't Ride Roller Coasters** $3.99

❏ BAS0-590-18986-7 #36 **Wolfmen Don't Hula Dance** $3.99

❏ BAS0-590-99552-9 **Bailey School Kids Joke Book** $3.50

❏ BAS0-590-88134-5 **Bailey School Kids Super Special #1:**
Mrs. Jeepers Is Missing! $4.99

❏ BAS0-590-21243-5 **Bailey School Kids Super Special #2:**
Mrs. Jeepers' Batty Vacation $4.99

❏ BAS0-590-11712-2 **Bailey School Kids Super Special #3:**
Mrs. Jeepers' Secret Cave $4.99

❏ BAS0-439-04396-4 **Bailey School Kids Super Special #4:**
Mrs. Jeepers in Outer Space $4.99

Available wherever you buy books, or use this order form

Scholastic Inc., P.O. Box 7502, Jefferson City, MO 65102

Please send me the books I have checked above. I am enclosing $_____ (please add $2.00 to cover shipping and handling). Send check or money order — no cash or C.O.D.s please.

Name _____

Address _____

City_____ State/Zip _____

Please allow four to six weeks for delivery. Offer good in the U.S. only. Sorry, mail orders are not available to residents of Canada. Prices subject to change.
BSK399